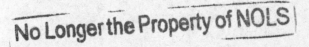

ABOUT THE AUTHOR

FRED VENTURINI's short fiction has been published in *The Booked. Anthology*, *Noir at the Bar, Vol. 2*, and *Surreal South '13*. In 2014, his story "Gasoline" will be featured in Chuck Palahniuk's *Burnt Tongues* collection. He lives in Southern Illinois with his wife and daughter.

THE
HEART
DOES
NOT
GROW
BACK

FRED VENTURINI

PICADOR

NEW YORK

THE HEART DOES NOT GROW BACK. Copyright © 2011, 2014 by Fred Venturini. All rights reserved. Printed in the United States of America. For information, address Picador, 175 Fifth Avenue, New York, N.Y. 10010.

www.picadorusa.com

www.twitter.com/picadorusa • www.facebook.com/picadorusa

picadorbookroom.tumblr.com

Picador® is a U.S. registered trademark and is used by St. Martin's Press under license from Pan Books Limited.

For book club information, please visit www.facebook.com/picadorbookclub or e-mail marketing@picadorusa.com.

Library of Congress Cataloging-in-Publication Data

Venturini, Fred.
    The heart does not grow back : a novel / Fred Venturini. — First Picador edition.
        pages cm
    ISBN 978-1-250-05221-6 (trade paperback)
    ISBN 978-1-250-05222-3 (e-book)
    1. Life change events—Fiction.   2. Regeneration (Biology)—Fiction.   I. Title.
    PS3622.E63H43 2014
    813'.6—dc23
                        2014015670

Design by Jonathan Bennett

Anatomical illustrations courtesy of the Florida Center for Instructional Technology

Picador books may be purchased for educational, business, or promotional use. For information on bulk purchases, please contact Macmillan Corporate and Premium Sales Department at 1-800-221-7945, extension 5442, or write specialmarkets@macmillan.com.

First published under the title *The Samaritan*

First Picador Edition: November 2014

10 9 8 7 6 5 4 3 2 1

For Tom Pigg, 1982–2009

THE
HEART
DOES
NOT
GROW
BACK

PROLOGUE

GRADUATION WAS SUPPOSED TO GO LIKE THIS:

Mack and me on the stage, waiting our turn to snag diplomas. The gym is packed and I look into the corners of the bleachers, into the drawn curtains of the stage we're on, into the faces of the crowd, some of them staring back through the glass eyes of camcorders and cameras, and I remember all the little things that brought us here. I find my mother, who's sitting in one of the reserved seats with Regina. Regina's already graduated, playing volleyball for the local community college, waiting on me to graduate so that she can get into a four-year school near Boston, because I'm headed to Harvard. We're in love, and experimenting with all the ways love can be expressed. I have a promise ring in my pocket—that awkward high school trinket that's supposed to be the cheap precursor to an engagement ring. She already has my class ring, which I've never worn, purchased just for her, wrapped in yarn so that it will fit her finger, my mark upon her in pewter and emerald.

Mack's dad is there. Sure, he slugged Mack a few times with those calloused lineman's hands, scarring his knuckles on Mack's orbital bones, but he's at the graduation and for one night, they'll hug and cry and Mack will go away to his division-one baseball program, already drafted by the Cincinnati Reds or some other Midwest team who caught wind of his skills and potential.

Principal Turnbull will announce Mack's full scholarship to a place like Northwestern or Southern Illinois, something close to home but Division I all the way. He'll announce that he's a late-round draft pick, and his rights belong to a bona fide actual Major fucking League Baseball team.

The principal will announce my full scholarship to Harvard, where I will study law so that I can best negotiate Mack's contracts when he really needs a big-time agent. Everyone who used to call me nerd or fuckwad now wishes they had a premium scholarship to a prestige school. They wish they had Regina Carpenter following them to Boston. They will cling to their moderate high school accomplishments in the classroom and in sports, and they'll go to the community college for two years, which is just a glorified high school with ashtrays and a bigger parking lot, and then they'll never finish and go crawling back to the family farm, or the family gravel business, or the family truck business.

That night, Mack and I will drink until we're half-blind and fuck our hot girlfriends and people will congratulate us time and time again, and the compliments will never get old. The sun will come up and we'll have to leave the women behind for our summer vacation, which we've been saving for. Why not spend our savings? We won't have to spend a dime at college out of pocket, so we'll rent that Ford Mustang convertible we talked about all the time and leave in the midafternoon, just after lunchtime, headed west for California, and the days and miles will uncurl before us, melting together until no day and no mile matters; there's just possibility and the certainty we can bend moments until they're congruent with our will.

We'd imagined this. We'd talked about this, and wanted this and there it would be, better than we could have hoped for, just absolutely fucking perfect.

When you get to a moment you've waited so long for, sometimes you can't enjoy it. Sometimes you realize you wasted so much valuable time waiting, wishing away hunks of your life, imagining the goals and moments and successes and dreams. After a while, life shifts from this big thing in front of you to this hazy, distant thing behind you, but in that moment, we wouldn't care because the wait was worth it.

We'd waited through grade school to become junior high-schoolers. We'd waited to become freshmen. We'd waited to become seniors. We'd waited for our graduation, for college, for a life we had figured out. We'd waited not knowing that waiting was the same as dying.

Sometimes dreams come true. Other times, you end up counting backward from ten with a mask on your face, drifting away under anesthesia thinking, *I can't believe I fell for this.*

PART ONE
THE BLIND MAN

ONE

WHEN I WAS IN SIXTH GRADE I HATED RECESS. I DIDN'T play sports, which left me alone, choosing to pass the time on a swing or just walking around with my head down and my hands jammed in my pockets. Not that I hated being alone—I actually preferred it, but during recess, everyone could see that you were alone and judged you accordingly.

I was swinging one day when they came to me with a blindfold. There were three of them—Lynn, Amy, and Kara—that cluster of grade-school girls that could never be broken apart, a clique tougher to split than atoms. They explained the rules of the blind-man game.

I can't say I wasn't paralyzed by tits and legs, hair and smiles. I could mention specifics, but really, it doesn't matter what those parts looked like, only that they had them.

"Do you trust me, Dale?" one of them said. I don't remember which one, but it doesn't matter; they were one person back then, one voice meant to draw you into trouble, hypnotic as strippers and capable of the same broken promises.

Of course I didn't trust them, but of course I couldn't turn them down. They put the blindfold on me, touching my neck and face, their fingernails clicking as they tied the knot.

They led me through the playground with a scrap of T-shirt

serving as the blindfold, the material so thin I could see every-thing through a milky-white screen. School was almost out and even in May, the Illinois heat felt strong enough to make stones burst. I soaked the blindfold with sweat fueled by heat and nerves.

We neared the metal post of the jungle gym. I knew they were going to lead me right into it, face-first. And I saw it coming, a metal pole I'd climbed dozens of times, making my hands smell like pennies for the rest of the school day.

Of course I knew that entertainment was the sole purpose of the blind-man game, so what was I supposed to do? Ruin their game and risk them never speaking to me again? I'd waited years for this encounter, and I wasn't going to fuck it up. I took my medicine—hard. I made it more real than they expected, going forehead first, dazing myself, falling down on purpose so I could have their hands upon me again. They bent over, laughing, their hot breath on my face smelling like cafeteria sloppy joes and potato chips and heaven, their long hair dangling against my skin, a wilderness of girls surround-ing me as I got to my feet.

With vision limited, my ears were greedy for sound—basketballs dribbling as tennis shoes clopped against blacktop, the skid of gravel and the occasional hollow thud of a kickball game, the voices of squealing kids melded together into a mess of noise, like a chorus of crickets screeching at night, or what God hears when he listens to all the prayers at once.

The swing-set post came next, and I took it on forehead-first. Then the chain-link fence. They tripped me over a teeter-totter with one of the saddles missing. I thought I was entertaining them, that we could do this forever, every recess, maybe even do it before senior graduation, or in the backyard of our house, where I would live with three wives who smiled every time I tripped over the coffee table or ran face-first into the patio door.

After pinballing around long enough, I sensed other kids following us around, enjoying the festivities. Having so many eyes on me gave me a sick comfort, like sitting down on a toilet seat that was delightfully warmed by someone else's dirty ass. They kept leading me along and I loved having their attention, even if it was centered on my torture. Then, the screen of white began to reveal a moving shadow, not a pole. The dribble of a basketball became increasingly louder, along with the cries of sports jargon, such as "Screen!" or "Help!" and hands clapping, hoping to receive a pass. Other shadows joined. We were nearing the main basketball court, where the boys played serious, competitive pickup games during recess periods.

The girls were going to lead me into a squadron of distracted players to interrupt the game and see what would happen. Seeing a pole coming and embracing the blow is one thing, but this would have different consequences. I didn't think having the attention of the elite boys of sixth grade in this fashion was good for my long-term health—but I especially feared Mack Tucker.

Mack "Truck" Tucker was the superstar basketball and baseball player. He had no noticeable intelligence that I could detect from my dark and silent corner of the classroom, but he was the epicenter of the sixth grade because his rugged looks belied his age and his athletic prowess was unmatched, allowing him to meet the two most important criteria in life—the girls fawned over him, and the guys wanted to be him. Guys would practice their asses off with the intention of dethroning him on the court or striking him out in playground games of stickball. These brave souls were perpetually left in his wake on his way to a smooth jumper, or with their hands on their hips, watching Mack trot around makeshift bases, winking at girls, the ball not landing until he was almost to second base. Girls were like a Greek chorus perpetuating his myth, scribbling about him on the cardboard backs of loose-leaf notebooks, enclosing his name in hearts and arrows, putting their own names under his with a plus sign in the middle.

From my silent and insignificant perch, I always thought the guy was a dick. He ignored the glorious affection of girls, and treated the guys as his assistants, aloof from them. He often came to school with bruises on his arms, neck, or cheeks, and he would tell the story of a fight won but never witnessed. I never understood how looking beat-up on a daily basis could win you the reputation of toughness and strength. If he were so fucking strong and tough, wouldn't he avoid the black eyes, the fingerprints on his neck, the band of yellow and black circling his upper arms? Once in a while, sure, a lucky shot would land, but all the time? When it came down to it, I was probably the only one who thought his father hit him. A lot. Probably because my own father whipped my ass a time or two before he disappeared. The lasting memory of my father centers on pancakes. I complained about the pancakes he made one morning, so he grabbed me by the shirt, dragged me into my bedroom, and threw me into the wall, leaving a Dale-sized hole in the sheetrock I spent a whole weekend helping him fix.

If I let those girls throw me into the fray, I was about to shake the beehive of Mack Tucker, who loved an audience and was tempered by his daddy's fists. He often spent time relegated to "The Wall," watching recess with his back against the brick facade of the school, supervised by a teacher who did not allow him to break contact with said Wall, the punishment of choice for students back then. Most kids would eventually sink to their asses, curled up against the base of the Wall, ashamed and disappointed at the sight of other kids at play, prevented by grade-school law to join them. Mack would stand the whole time, his shoulders back and chest out, not caring that the other kids were playing—hell, they were playing *without him,* so it was a punishment to the whole school, if his body language were to be believed. And he spent plenty of time on the Wall because if you crossed him, if you beat him, if you got his attention, chances were, he was going to take his shirt off and beat the shit out of you. Taking off his shirt was a warning shot, for sure—a habit that he never broke, as if to give his opponents a chance for flight before the fight.

The guys were so engrossed in the game of hoops I don't think they even noticed three of the cutest girls in our class with dork-ass Dale Sampson, blindfolded, in tow. I saw Mack Tucker and knew that the girls were just test-driving me for this, the big one. They were going to use me to get his attention. The strategy was actually kind of brilliant—they couldn't really get into the middle of the game without pissing Mack and the other boys off, but they could toss me in there and see what happened.

I wasn't going to let those girls get me involved with Mack Tucker. And what a bunch of brutal bitches they were—the moment my body hesitated against their guidance, the moment any sort of tightness began to bind my muscles, they shoved me right into the game. I careened forward just as Mack got an entry pass and took a power dribble, knocking his defender aside with a simple turn of his hips. He turned right into me and his shoulder found the center of my chest, drilling me backward with such force that I fell on my shoulder blades and almost kneed myself in the face, folding in half as I crashed onto the pavement. He made me wish for the days of simple poles and fences as dots formed against the white haze of the blindfold. I scrambled to take it off, aware of the laughter all around me despite being stunned by the fall. I figured I would take it off to find Mack standing over me, fuming, perhaps geared up for a punch or kick.

I flicked off the blindfold and Mack wasn't there. The fine dust of the blacktop ground into my palms as I got to my feet. Mack had the basketball pinned against his hip, talking casually to the three girls, who were smiling. I couldn't hear what they were saying through the laughter, chatter, and throbbing in my head—a lump was already forming.

I ignored the catcalls of idiot and dumbass, unable to believe that their ploy had worked—Mack had always resisted them. Sure, I overheard girls gnashing on rumors of steamy overnight tent stays or a make-out session here and there, but no girl could boast that they were going steady with Mack. As long as he kept them in play, I figured I would always have a chance by default, and here I was, manipulated in a game where my anguish entertained them, their inherent viciousness cloaked by silky hair and perfectly applied makeup.

I touched behind my ear and my fingers came away with a light, sticky coating of blood, and I thought to myself, Where the hell is the recess monitor?

Then, a miracle—the smiles of all three girls fell away. They hurried away from Mack, their huddle broken, and he turned around, smiling, looking at me as a whistle blared in the air, signaling the end of recess. Kids scurried to form the line, but Mack and I didn't move. Some of the basketball boys lingered, but he waved them off.

"Get in line, you shitheads," he said, and they obeyed.

"You let those bitches fuckin' blindfold you, man?" he asked.

I thought the answer was fairly obvious, so I didn't say anything.

"They're the Axis of Evil," he added. "Amy is Germany. She is in charge. It was mostly her idea. She also stuffs her bra. Did you know that shit?"

I shook my head.

"Anyway, whenever one of these chicks tells you what to do, always do the opposite."

That sounded rather strange, considering I'd seen my father do the exact opposite of my mother's requests for years before he left—*Don't hit Dale, don't hit me, don't get drunk, please get a job.*

"They never talk to me. I didn't know what to do."

"Now they're gonna."

"Why's that?"

"I told them you were my buddy and to quit fucking with you."

To my knowledge, Mack had no friends, just subjects.

"Why did you say that? I don't know you."

"I didn't like what they did, that was all." Mack was a showman and a fighter, but it turned out he wasn't a bully. He wasn't like his father. When he came up with all those bullshit stories explaining away his bruises, I think he sensed that I saw right through them, just in the incredulous look I gave him when he had the rest of our grade enraptured in his tales. In a weird way, I think saving me that day was Mack's first act of rebellion against his father's violence, a rehearsal for the stand he'd have to make someday. I was someone quiet and scared, someone he recognized a little too intimately, someone he might have been if he didn't feed that weak part of himself to the Mack "Truck" Tucker furnace that burned hotter every passing day.

"It's not like we're going to be butt buddies or anything," he continued. "Just go back to being your weird, quiet self and shit will be normal. Or you can grow a pair of balls and pick up a basketball once in a while instead of playing on the swing set like a little bitch. You're thirteen, for chrissakes, you still got He-Man toys at home?"

The fact that he was right about my He-Man toys gave me a chill.

"Anyway, you're the smart one, man. Everyone knows that. That's why they don't talk to you. You read me?"

"I guess," I said as we got into line. The Axis of Evil kept looking back at me, and I found myself petrified by the eye contact. But the few glimpses I got were different now, as if Mack had sprinkled fairy dust on me and I suddenly existed.

Mack Tucker was my best friend because he saved me from the desolate silence of sixth grade with his unique brand of chaos. And even though our friendship was a rough ride over the years, and our plans would get smashed and dented at every turn, Mack, chaos, and I got along for a long, long time.

TWO

I GOT READY FOR SCHOOL ONE MORNING WHILE MOM slept, which wasn't anything new. I don't resent her for not being up early, her apron stained from a home-cooked breakfast, buzzing around the kitchen like some caffeine-fueled hummingbird. She worked a lot and needed the rest, and fuck it, I was a big boy perfectly capable of pouring milk over a bowl of Captain Crunch.

She wasn't a TV mom with kisses and baby talk—she was more like a rumor, a phantom, someone there but never quite there because of her work schedule, but whatever she was, I always had things to eat, the lights stayed on, we got air-conditioning in the summer and I had clothes without holes. All of these amenities made me upper class in Verner, Illinois, population 650.

Not to say our house was worth a shit. The ceiling had brown rings from water damage, discolored bull's-eyes so you knew where to put the water buckets when clouds started gathering. For some reason I can't explain, turning on the air conditioner while the water was running would send an electric current through all the water pipes. The paint on the siding was gray and bubbling, the concrete steps were split down the middle, with one side sinking. Ants and mice could not be denied entry. Mom and I often wore shoes in the house and I feared falling asleep on the floor while watching television.

Now that he could drive, Mack picked me up most mornings in his dad's old Chevy. We nicknamed it "Old Gray." He carried two gallons of water in the bed in case we overheated, which was roughly once a month, depending on the weather. I was nearing the end of my freshman year of high school, still without a girlfriend despite Mack's pleas to be more confident and social.

First period was PE, but Mack and I never participated in the regular PE functions. The teacher, Mr. Gunther, was the baseball coach, and he allowed Mack to work out instead of playing dodge ball or floor hockey or whatever weird sport was lined up for the week. Even though I didn't play on the baseball team, thanks to my Mack affiliation, I had the same permission to skip PE. We would go into the basement near the coach's office and lift weights.

Well, I wouldn't technically lift weights—I would spot Mack as he tried to bench press as much as possible. Benching was about the only exercise he ever did in the weight area, which wasn't so much a weight area as it was a cold room with a concrete floor adorned by spiderwebs and murky, dust-slathered windows.

He'd bench-press a few sets and then we'd head upstairs onto the school stage, set up tees, and hit Wiffle balls into the curtain. He would whack them as hard as he could, pick them up, and hit them again. He never adjusted the tee or worked on hitting specific kinds of pitches.

I hit the Wiffle balls with him. We would hit in the near darkness, the only light a floor lamp behind us, making small talk between the *tink-thump* of an aluminum bat driving a plastic ball into a heavy curtain.

That morning, we didn't talk for about ten swings, but I could tell he had something brewing in that devious brain.

"I talked to Jolynn about you last night," he said. Jolynn was his flavor of the week, a lithe and freckled girl with black hair and an easy smile. Mack was rife with stories of her flexibility and wanton behavior in her parents' camper.

"Not during the sex, I hope," I said.

"I mentioned she should try to hook you up or something."

I stopped hitting. I had no impression of my looks or reputation. I certainly didn't trust my own perception; I had to rely on the opinions of others, and I never got those opinions, not even from Mack—he mostly talked about himself, but that was just the way he was.

I kept waiting. I didn't know Jolynn aside from her smile and the sex stories. The comments he was about to share would be the unbiased verdict of my social status. He hit, picked up the ball, and hit again.

"Well?"

"Oh," he said, stopping for a moment. "No dice, pretty much." He set up the ball with a steady hand, ignoring me.

"What the hell, man?" I said. "Did she say anything specific?"

"No, dude. I mean, she called you 'okay.' That's a nice way of saying she thinks you're not ugly, but what does she or any other girl have to work with? You don't talk to them. You basically hardwire your jaw shut around chicks. Seriously. Speak the fuck up and maybe they'll know something about you other than your grade point average."

"What's that supposed to mean?" My bat felt like a weapon, lighter than normal, the grip soft in my palms as the barrel rested on my shoulder.

"It means you make good grades so you're a fuckin' dork.

A nerd. You're quiet, so that's the way it's gonna be until you break that shit up."

"So I should fail classes to—"

"Fuck no, man. Hell no! I'm saying take a chance and speak up. Crack one of those sick-ass jokes you crack around me. You think I've been friends with you these last few years for you to help me with my homework? Well, you're right. Kidding—no, you're funny as fuck when you let loose, but you never let loose."

I stood there, bat on shoulder, with nothing else to say. He picked up my ball from the tee and held it in his fingers, held it up to my face.

"You see this thing? I fucking dominate it because I swing hard. If I hit it, it's gone. Fuckin' gone."

He put the ball on my tee. I didn't like what he was saying, but the slivers of truth prickled me, pissing me off. For once, I swung hard, my teeth and hands cinched tight. I missed, striking the neck of the tee underneath. The tee toppled, rolling into the curtain. A hard vibration rattled through the aluminum bat, stinging my hands, and I flung it into the curtain. The ball landed in front of me, at my feet, going nowhere while Mack laughed his ass off.

"You never miss," I said.

"I only batted .650 last year, so—"

"No, with girls. You've always got your pick of the litter. You never miss."

He smiled and picked up my bat. "You never swing."

After eating lunch, students gathered in the gymnasium. Clusters of like-minded and like-dressed students stood in circles or sat on the bleachers in groups that faced each other, their voices mixing in with the sound of basketballs thumping against the gym floor as pickup games spontaneously erupted.

Mack and I never subjected ourselves to the cliquish dynamics of lunch hour. Basketball was a distraction, according to Mack, so we gave it up to concentrate on baseball. So during lunch, we hit more Wiffle balls. Each thump would cause a wave in the curtain seen by a couple hundred high school kids, since the stage was the visual centerpiece of the gymnasium. For plays and graduations, the janitors just cranked up the basketball hoops and opened the curtain. I'm sure Mack enjoyed a public forum for something as mundane as practice, but no one could make fun of his obsessive hitting habits because they paid off in the form of massive home runs when most guys couldn't two-hop the fence.

That day, we didn't hit during lunchtime. Mack complained about sore pecs, so he pulled out a dollar bill and bought us a pair of strawberry Crush sodas, then we wandered into the gym, where he soaked up the female stares trained on his every move.

"I'm thinking I'm done with Jolynn," he said. "And now I'm thinking about the twins."

The Carpenters—twin girls, cheerleaders, with blue eyes that could wilt any adolescent boy. Perhaps the dust of memory makes me overstate them, but when I think of those eyes, I think of polished stones in a creek bed, the water cold and clear. Identical twins with no discernible difference, but it seemed to me that one of them, Regina, was more social than the other, always laughing and chatting it up with her girlfriends while Raeanna was always on the bleachers reading a paperback while her purse rested between her feet.

He guzzled his Crush and squeezed the can into an hourglass shape before I was half-done with mine. He belched. "I'm going to let you pick."

"Pick what?" I asked.

"Whichever one you want."

"I've never talked to either one of them." I paused, considering just what he was saying. "Why are you asking me this? You're the one who should be picking."

"I heard one of them likes you," he said. "Just want to see if you can pick the one. See if it's destiny."

"I know you're bullshitting. They don't even know me."

"It's not about knowing you, man, you gotta learn this shit by now. You hang out with me, so you got this mysterious shit going on, don't you get it? Use it!"

"What did you hear?"

He sat down on the empty bleachers at the end of the gym, shoulders slack, eased back, as if the school could burn down right that second and he'd just brush the ashes off his shoulder and ask who turned up the thermostat.

"One of them said you're cute. You think they're cute?"

"They're beautiful," I said.

"Fuckin' pick one!"

"Regina," I said, not knowing why, sealing my fate. She was the social one, but again, it didn't matter. They may as well have been unicorns.

"Bingo."

"You're lying," I said, not looking at him but looking at Regina. She was in an animated conversation among that huddled circle of gossiping girls that has always existed, from the playground to high school and then into the adult world somewhere, a lunch table or water cooler or beauty salon.

I could see those damn eyes from across the gym. She had rosy cheeks without the bumps and crags of teenage skin, chestnut hair that was shoulder length, teased up, curving into her ears and neck. She wore a wide-collared sweater, revealing naked handles of collarbone. Sometimes during lunch hour, she would practice with her cheerleading friends. She could jump and backflip, handstand and toss, her legs and calves hard with corded muscle. She was beautiful in that perfect way a girl is beautiful when you can't ever imagine talking to her.

"So if you want to make this happen, first, you let me—" Mack began, but I walked away from him midsentence and headed for Regina. *Let me,* he said, as usual, but something like this, I couldn't let him. I couldn't stop him either. I had one chance to take this one for myself, before he railroaded me into something embarrassing. I was still suspicious that the girl even knew who the hell I was. Mack could have picked a name from a hat at random, manufacturing a story to get me into the mix, a grand experiment to see if his machismo would turn me into a desirable commodity, like some testosterone-laced pixie dust.

Mack grabbed my shoulder. "Don't get all macho and blow this, you gotta be a surgeon to get her away from those other girls. It's like she's a tumor and you're a doctor, and she's surrounded by all this delicate tissue that fuckin' hates that you're trying to talk to her. I don't even screw with the girl herds, man, so think about this. If you want to swing for the fences, at least wait for a fat pitch."

"I have to say something," I said. "Otherwise, today's just another day of hitting Wiffle balls and making good grades."

He looked at me for a moment and I gave him a sly smile. He nodded and took his hand off my shoulder. "Make a joke, man," he said. "Give her some of that funny Sampsonite shit."

I walked up to the girls and saw that they had eager smiles on their faces. They didn't look at me—instead, they giggled or looked down at their feet or pretended to dig in their purses.

All except Raeanna. I didn't notice her until then. She sat on the highest bleacher, behind all of them. No girls were next to her. She looked at me with the same startling eyes as her sister, peering over her romance novel, *A Rose at Sunset,* complete with a sun-bronzed cowboy, shirtless, on a horse. I couldn't hold her gaze, tucking my hands in my pockets, glancing down and saying, "Regina," as if to start a sentence. I don't remember what I meant to say, but the minute I said her name, every other face deflated. Maybe she really did think I was cute. Maybe they all did.

That misconception was warm while it lasted, but it didn't last long.

"I hope this is good news," she said.

"I guess it depends," I said, stalling, not knowing what she was talking about.

"Well? Did he send you over?" she said, stressing the *he* in such a way that meant Mack. Hence the busted smiles from the rest of them. But screw it, I was all in.

"No, but we were talking about you because I think you're absolutely beautiful, and even though I don't say much to many girls around here, it's not because I'm shy or nerdy or anything like that, it's just that you're the first girl I've ever thought was really worth saying something to."

The rest of the girls giggled at this, and I couldn't stop the red from flooding my face, the hot pinpricks of embarrassment swelling in my cheeks, but I kept looking at her and only her because I knew she liked what I said. But Mack was right. Her friends were there.

"Sorry, but you're wasting your time."

I stood there and took the full brunt of it. The other girls kept laughing—except Raeanna. She bent a sympathetic wince into a half smile and I almost cried. I just shrugged and told

Regina, "Well, I still mean it. It would just be nice to talk to you more, but I understand what you all must think of me."

With that, I walked away, enduring the catcalls of "Crash and burn!" and "Return to sender!" but I kept my head up, battling the urge to sob that built in the upper parts of my lungs, rising up through me and knocking at my eyes. I saw the curtain ripple as a ball struck it from behind the stage, and knew where Mack was, but instead of going to join him, I slipped into the empty boys' locker room. I cranked the plastic lever on the towel dispenser, plucking two fistfuls of rough, brown paper, then sat in a stall and cried them wet.

THREE

AS A FRESHMAN, MACK WAS BY FAR THE BEST PLAYER ON the team and the upperclassmen hated him for it, at least at first. He could crack eighty miles an hour with his fastball and he also had a wicked slider and knuckleball that I'd seen in my backyard hundreds of times. I always hit him rather well, figuring he was taking it easy on me, but for everyone else in the conference, the task was about as impossible as it was to keep him off base. The first game of his career was against the conference champions, a powerhouse team, the Brownstown Bombers. They had a senior-stacked lineup that was poised to repeat their domination. Then Mack happened. He allowed one hit, struck out a dozen, and went five-for-five with two jacks in a blowout win.

Once it was clear that Mack was the key to getting that elusive trophy, the hazing and jealousy started to soften. He was the only freshman invited to parties I didn't want to attend in the first place, and I regularly turned them down even though he tried like hell to get me to go. The one time I did tag along, it was me, Mack, Guy Cain, and Kevin Braddy piled into the back of Clint Phillips's truck. I had no idea what we were headed out to do that night. We sailed along black country roads. We drank beers on an abandoned bridge. Guy and Kevin were seniors, and I could tell that they were cool with Mack, and suffered his alpha-male bravado with the same casual distance I'd achieved over the years. Clint though, was something else. He was a cold, leering hombre, and while the others had come to terms with the talent gap between Mack and themselves, Clint was conceding nothing. He only chimed in to minimize Mack's accomplishments—if Mack recounted how he approached an at-bat that resulted in a homer, Clint would quickly counter with "Wind was blowing out, though." I didn't think Mack had it in him to brush it off, but he always did—probably because fighting meant missing baseball games.

When we were done with the beers, I was told that the loose baseball bats in the back of the truck were for that grand backwoods tradition of bashing mailboxes. I'd like to say that I was mature enough to not enjoy the fuck out of it, but it was fun as hell. I found something therapeutic and hilarious about watching a mailbox crinkle and dent in the floodlights of Clint's pickup.

Mack, of course, took it a step too far. He urged us all to "watch this shit." He took the gas can out of Clint's trunk and doused a sturdy-looking Rubbermaid mailbox with a few splashes. Then, he lit it on fire. He had a lighter on him but didn't smoke—I guess he'd planned this ahead of time to impress the seniors. He started whaling on the mailbox, but not with the full brunt of his strength. I could tell he was waiting for something—and that thing turned out to be the owner of the house. L. Lewis, according to the letters on the box.

The screen door opened and the laughter stopped. A deep voice hollered, "What the fuck you sons of bitches doing out there!"

"Your mailbox is on fire!" Mack screamed. "I'm trying to put the motherfucker out!"

With his obviously rehearsed line out of the way, he jumped into the bed of the truck. Clint didn't hit the gas. "Come on, man!" Kevin yelled, smashing his palm into the rear-window glass. L. Lewis got closer. He had a shotgun in his hands. Everyone was pleading with Clint to drive. The dome light was ticked on, and I saw him in the rearview mirror. I saw the glee in his face, letting the situation unravel to the point of desperation. Lewis fired the shotgun, and I'm still not sure if it was rock salt or the pellets from a shell that hit the side of the truck, but the sound was thunderous and everyone sank into the gritty bed of the truck, the swill of beer and rainwater flowing in the little channels of the plastic bed liner. I was down there with everyone. I heard Kevin crying. Guy screamed until his voice was hoarse. Mack grabbed me by the arm. "We gotta run for it," he said, and we both scrambled to jump out of the truck when Clint mercifully slammed the accelerator. The tires sprayed gravel and the back of the truck fishtailed, but once the tread bit down on the street, we blasted off, the engine screaming.

We stopped in the grain-elevator parking lot where we originally met. Clint got out, his eyes watering from wicked, ugly laughter. He could barely seem to catch his breath. Mack pinned him by the neck against the side of the truck, his right fist coiled, his knuckles trembling.

"Let him go," I said. I knew what the price was if he hit him.

"Fuck you," Mack said. "I ever get the chance, you're done, you little shit."

"Do you always do what your boyfriend asks you to do?" Clint said.

I got between them. Guy and Kevin were already getting into their own trucks, pissed and shaken. "He's not worth it," I said.

Clint was still laughing. Always laughing. The door closed. He dropped his truck into gear. The giggling wasn't for show. Bashing mailboxes wasn't perilous enough for him, it wasn't enough of a high. It took more for him to get a rush. I wondered what he was like when he was alone, the things he did for those kinds of kicks, and decided I didn't want to know.

A few weeks later, the baseball team was opening up the spring portion of the season against Carsonville. I wanted nothing more than to marinate in my Regina-related failure by zoning out in my bedroom, but Mack insisted I come watch him pitch.

He struck out the side on a pale spring day. The infield was black with moisture, with soggy patches of Diamond Dry surrounding all the bases. The wind was blowing in from left. The American flag mounted high above the center-field fence rippled loud enough to hear from home plate. I remember these details because I was sitting in the front bleacher behind home plate when Regina sat down next to me wearing a Gap sweatshirt and a smile.

I looked up at her and couldn't muster a word.

"Why did you say that the other day?" she asked.

"I don't know," I said.

"Do you really like me?"

Did I? Mack had put me on her scent and suddenly I was in love. I had no legitimate reason to give her.

"Mack said you—"

"I don't care what he said," she said.

"You looked disappointed when you realized he didn't send me over, though. Like you were hoping that I was carrying a message from him."

"You'll just have to figure that part out for yourself."

"Yeah. Sorry."

"Here." She handed me a piece of notebook paper, with little bits loose from where she took it off the spiral, folded three times, and I brushed up against fingers smooth with lotion.

"Sometimes you just like someone," she said. "I can't fault you for that. Rae's the same way."

"What's this?" I asked.

"You never had a girl slip you her phone number before?"

"No. I thought this stuff was done with cell phones, anyway. Not that I have one."

"My mom won't get me one until this crapola town gets a cell phone tower. Besides, notes are a little more meaningful, don't you think?" I nodded. "Well, there you go," she said.

"You want me to call you?"

The question was stupid, but she looked like she expected it, perhaps even feared it. She waited for a long while and said, "For the record, you seem like a sweet guy." She got up and left without even staying for the game.

She had come specifically to give me a piece of paper that had her phone number, just seven digits, forgoing the formality of an area code. She hadn't written anything but numbers, yet it was still that perfect handwriting reserved for only girls, with each number's shape nearing geometric perfection.

In the bottom of the first, Mack turned on the first fastball he saw, cutting a low line drive through the wind and into the Pepsi-sponsored scoreboard in left field, breaking two bulbs in the "o" lit up under the visitor's score. He trotted around the bases, touching home plate as he looked up at me and said, "The Natural, motherfucker!" with a double-bicep pose. The ump warned him about swearing as he high-fived his jealous teammates on his way into the dugout. It was one of those rare moments when things were perfect for both of us at the same time.

When I called Regina, it felt like my public speaking class, the knots building in the middle of me, every word I intended on saying sounding lame. Crumbs on the linoleum stuck to my socks as I paced the kitchen, holding the phone, suffering from a paralysis each time I considered dialing—a sure sign I liked her even more than I let myself admit—all this without ever really talking to her, a crush sparked by her looks, her lotion, and the chemicals of teenage lust that poisoned logic.

She picked up the phone, sparing me the awkward, traditional Asking of the Father, something Mack had mentioned before, and absolutely hated.

Regina and I shared a weird kind of small talk, the language of avoiding the true issues at hand. I mentioned the weather when I really wanted her to know that I was a decent guy, that I liked her and wanted to go on a date with her sometime. She mentioned her registration for cheerleading camp, which was coming up this summer, when I sensed what she really wanted me to know was that her friends would make fun of her if we went on a date, so it wasn't happening, but she was decent enough to offer a spoonful of hope.

Just when I sensed she was getting around to saying something substantial, maybe about us, another phone call came in. She was polite enough to not click over immediately, asking if I could call her back after the weekend, during which she'd presumably be out having a good time while I was putting some miles on my Nintendo.

Mack had assured me she'd play hard to get, but that she'd eventually say yes. He insisted that my bold move on her had changed my social standing. He maintained that I would clear the fence and be "hitting the skins" in no time, his favorite Mackism. I didn't care about the skins. I just wanted the nervous pressure of planning a date.

I saw her on Monday at school. The sun was vibrating off the glass doors behind her, sending thick strands of light over her shoulders, into her hair. I asked her if she wanted to maybe talk over lunch. She countered by asking me to call her at seven. I sensed a little bit of annoyance, but Mack knew his shit, always had, so I had to trust him and make the call.

I was careful about my plan that night—her house was four miles away, in an adjacent small town called Meeker. The sun wasn't quite down, but it was dark enough for me to move undiscovered. She had willow trees in her yard and I could see the glowing, moving silhouette of a television through the thin curtains of the living room. When I got closer, I could hear the murmur of the evening news. I kept my back to the siding of the house, the ridges digging into me, scooting along as if I were steadying myself on a ledge.

At the back of the house, I found her window. I crept through a partial alley, the ground moist, the siding in the back spotty with growing moss.

From my angle through the glass I saw a pink comforter on the bed. The walls were plastered with posters—boy bands, cheerleading, a movie poster for *Bring It On*. Enough evidence for me—I didn't want to risk getting caught taking a direct view. Staying low to the ground, I reached up and put a single rose on her windowsill. The flower was an eight-dollar job from the Wal-Mart florist, complete with baby's breath and a green cellophane sheath.

Once I got home, I dialed with greedy fingers. I was proud of the rose, and grateful for the much-needed shot of confidence.

Even though the girl who answered sounded like Regina, since she and Raeanna were twins, I couldn't be sure, so I asked for her.

I heard a long, disappointed sigh and knew it was Raeanna on the phone. She didn't tell me that Regina wasn't there, she just said, "She wanted me to tell you sorry, but she can't."

"Can't what?" Clarity was important to me.

"She's not going to talk to you, not because she wants to be mean, she just doesn't want to go out with you," Rae said, sounding upset. "I don't think she was going to this whole time. But you're a super nice guy, and cute, and all that."

"Can I talk to her?" I asked.

"I'm sorry," she said. "Really. I think you're a nice guy, Dale. She can be like that. I hope you're not upset."

"It's hard to get pissed about being rejected when I didn't even get as far as asking her anything to be rejected about. I mean, that's got to be a first, right?"

Rae laughed a little. "I guess. Maybe you should call the Guinness Book of World Records."

"Famous for failure," I said, and offered up a fake chuckle, as if I didn't really believe it.

"Don't say that," she said. "You're the guy silly girls like Regina will wish they had when they grow up."

"Thanks," I said, and meant it. "Look outside her window, on the windowsill. That's for you. For doing your sister's dirty work."

I think Raeanna wanted to talk more, but I was hurting, faking my way through the humor, so I hung up and stared at the television. When I couldn't muster any real tears, I knew that I'd expected a "no" all along.

FOUR

WHEN I STARTED MY JUNIOR YEAR, REGINA WAS DATING Clint Phillips. I had no explanation for it. I didn't know how he operated in his social circles, or class. He must have been exceptionally gifted at hiding whatever it was I'd glimpsed on our night out bashing mailboxes. As for him reaching down into the junior class for a girlfriend, my crash-and-burn story with Regina was something that I couldn't live down, a story that had a long life in the halls of a small school. I truly think that Clint went after Regina as a way to fuck with Mack by magnifying my heartache, getting the girl who'd said no to me so publicly, but I kept that little theory to myself. Even if it was true, it didn't work. It barely registered with Mack. The baseball season was approaching and he was on my ass to try out for the team.

He insisted that if I could hit him, I could hit anyone. He told me I had a great arm and that by working out with him, I had the potential to be one of the best players on the team. I was just hitting my growth spurt, right at six feet tall with a build thicker than seniors two years older than me. Mack was still clocking in at five-foot-eight and holding, but he was built like the trunk of an old oak tree.

I couldn't commit. I couldn't imagine the awesome threat of failing in front of people who expected me to fail. Unlike

33

Mack, the adoration of others as a group never mattered to me. He enjoyed rumors and confrontation and having a trove of girlfriends. He liked newspaper clippings and keeping track of his batting average at home in a loose-leaf notebook, just to make sure the junior-high kids who kept the scorebooks weren't fucking him out of a few precious points in his quest for another six-hundred batting average. I had zero ambitions when it came to sports, or anything for that matter. I only made grades because it was easy, not because I cared.

The first practice was that afternoon and Mack offered me my last chance as the bell rang—I could head out to the diamond where wannabes would show up with gloves and sweatpants, ready to make a mark during tryouts. And they really weren't tryouts—with a school so small, everyone who wanted a spot pretty much got to dress up and sit on the bench. They got to take batting practice and they got to ride the bus to road games. They got out of school a little early sometimes, and girls would make glittery posters with their jersey numbers to hang in the hallway.

I told Mack no for a final time and headed for the parking lot, where a fleet of buses growled, idling, waiting to suck up kids and spit them out on corners and driveways. This was usually my chance to steal a look at Regina as she walked across the parking lot to where Clint's mud-spattered truck was parked. She always had books under her arm, a purse slung over her shoulder, and she was always playing with her long brown hair. Since she'd made it clear she didn't want me, of course that magnified my delirious and inexplicable desire for her. I spent my junior year in a trance of juvenile rejection, that special depression reserved for first loves. I never pursued another girl and I didn't care that no adoration, not even a rumor of a crush, floated my way. Mack was always pointing out other girls to go after, but it always came back to Regina. I was Regina's if she wanted me, and I could wait as long as it took.

But that day, I didn't see her walking across the parking lot. Behind the lot was the baseball diamond, and I noticed Regina and Raeanna sitting on the bleachers.

I saw Mack pacing the outside of the dugout, aggressively stretching his shoulder while all the other players were standing around with their gloves tucked into their armpits. I never got on the bus. While Coach Gunther was addressing the players, telling them about expectations and responsibility, I walked up, glove in hand, wearing gym shoes and jeans, and took a knee with the rest of the players. A murmur drifted from up front as players whispered and nudged that yes, Dale Sampson was trying out for the team.

"Giving this a go, Dale?" Gunther said.

The players were silent, waiting for me to answer.

"You got it, Coach. Figure if I can hit Mack, I can hit anyone in the conference." Mack turned around and gave me the thumbs-up while the rest of the team stifled laughter.

Clint, much to my disappointment, had developed into a hell of a baseball player, so naturally, he and Mack were the captains for the intrasquad game, and picked the teams. Mack picked me first. The game was going to be three innings of live baseball. Coach Gunther wanted to gauge players in game situations on day one to see what he was working with.

Mack took the mound and struck out the first two hitters. Clint got aboard with a bloop single that had him clapping with excitement as he rounded first. He stole second on the next pitch but ended up being stranded when the next hitter popped out.

Mack pumped his fist and pointed at me in a "let's go" gesture. Jogging in from the outfield, I realized that this game, played with no crowd, meant everything. Just a bunch of boys in mismatched sweatpants with flecks of mud kicked up the backs of the legs hoping to crack the everyday batting order. The alternative was becoming a bench monument, shivering in the cold of spring while Mack and the defending conference champions ran around the field with steam coming off their sweating necks.

Clint took the mound and retired the side in order, throwing nothing but his fastball-changeup combo. He had a lively fastball, not with the sheer velocity of Mack's, but he threw across the seams in a way that cut it, making it move a little in the strike zone. From the dugout, I watched Clint's eyes—he knew his roster spot was locked, but he was intent on impressing Regina. She was his girlfriend of at least three months, but he carried himself like a man trying to win her over for the first time.

"He gets a hot piece of ass, and suddenly, he thinks his shit smells like roses," Mack said, sitting next to me in the dugout. He stood up and began twisting the handle of a bat, in case a runner got on and he would get a shot at Clint. "He's normally a cocksucker, but he sure has a bounce in his step now that makes me want to slug the fucker even more."

I watched Clint's exaggerated windup. He whipped a ball down the center of the plate—Matt Nelton, our catcher, was calling balls and strikes. "Sorry, Jerry," Matt said to one of the wannabe players. "That was strike three, man."

Inning over. I snagged my glove and headed into the outfield. Mack grabbed my shoulder. "Hey, you're hitting after me next inning, all right? So don't freeze up like a bitch. Let's jack this fucker."

Mack retired the side in order, the only contact being a weak pop-up from Todd Lake, a fat, short kid who had no business on the ball diamond. He acted like the out was a World Series grand slam, his body language heightened as he snapped the Velcro off his gloves in mock frustration.

As Clint took his warm-up tosses, I stood in the on-deck circle with a bat in my hands and a helmet at my feet, waiting for Mack's at-bat. He never took warm-up swings, he just flexed against the handle of the bat, twisting it, gazing not at Clint, but through him.

Mack's athletic successes were usually rooted in what I called his hate gland. Those invisible secretions were often pumping through his blood whenever he started with the gazing and flexing. He convinced himself of his opponent's transgressions. He played and fought and broke up with girls in an angry fashion, and he worked at the anger. Tried for it, even. Standing there, I knew he was assigning all kinds of blame to Clint—Clint was the reason his father hit him. Clint made his mother leave. Clint thought he was better than him. Clint was laughing at him. Clint didn't respect him.

Mack turned to Regina. "You shouldn't have come to practice," he said.

"And why is that?" She looked cold, her arms crossed, her cheeks red against the spring air. Rae looked decidedly more comfortable in the cool weather, her chin resting on her palm.

"You're about to see what a talentless bitch your boyfriend is."

She shook her head at him with a sly smile, but he didn't see it, digging into the plate for his at-bat. The first pitch was a one-hopper in the dirt. Mack pointed the bat at Clint. "I'm not fuckin' walking," he bellowed. "Throw a strike or I'll climb that fence and bang her myself."

"You're so mature," Regina said as Clint wound up. The next pitch buzzed Mack's chin. He jerked back in time to evade it.

"Enough of that crap!" Gunther hollered, sitting on a bucket down the third baseline, jotting his notes. "Play ball or I'll send you both to the locker room."

Mack dug in. Clint looked pissed, his windup bigger and longer than ever, tipping off a fastball. Not that Mack needed the tipoff. He drilled a line drive that screamed through the infield. Clint turned his head and flailed with his glove as the ball whizzed by his ear. Mack rounded first without slowing down, stretching it into a double without a throw.

I was up. I walked by Regina and said, "Mack's an asshole, isn't he?" She didn't respond. The chain-link fence between us may as well have been a brick wall.

"Fresh meat," Clint yelled as I dug in. Only he and I knew the real stakes. He knew I was jealous of his girlfriend, and I knew he was with her mostly to give me and Mack the finger. I wasn't afraid of his fastball, and knowing he didn't have many other pitches in his arsenal, I was expecting one. What I wasn't expecting was the view of his motion—I'd never seen another pitcher wind up other than Mack. This guy's herky-jerky motion was not only distracting, it hid the ball quite well. The fastball was on top of me before I could trigger my swing, knocking off my timing. I missed.

I took a step out of the batter's box to breathe. "Get in the box, Sampson. Unless you're scared," Clint yelled, throwing the ball into the heel of his glove, impatient.

"Get him, baby!" Regina said, clapping her sleeve-muffled hands together. Not a peep until he was pitching against me. Nice.

I dug into the box and heard her again, softer, saying, "Don't be nervous, Dale. You can do it."

Embarrassment ran through me like a loose fire—did she know I tried out only because she was on those bleachers?

That I was nervous only because of her sitting behind me, with her boyfriend on the mound?

I was in the box, but I wasn't ready to hit. His long windup started. The ball exploded out of his hand. I barely saw it until, once again, it was almost to the plate.

My grip slid up the barrel. I didn't jab at the ball. Instead, I "caught" it with the barrel, just like the TV analysts described during Cubs broadcasts. I lofted a soft bunt down the third-base line. Since he threw the fastball with all his gumption, the momentum carried him off the mound toward the first-base line. I ran, kicking up chunks of infield. I made the mistake of slowing down and looking back—Clint had the ball, but he had zero chance of throwing me out. Mack rounded third, a stupid base-running play on his part born of his arrogant need to impress. Being a good ballplayer wasn't enough for Mack—he had to go beyond the bar he set for himself each and every time. If he hit four homers in a game in five at-bats, he would lament the homer he didn't hit. If someone fast could score from second on a hit into the outfield, he wanted to score from second on a bunt. Clint, naturally, caught him in a rundown. I rounded first and headed for second, figuring it was too early in the season for rusty players to execute a successful rundown on Mack Tucker.

As I hit the second-base bag, Clint threw the ball away, scattering Coach Gunther from his ball bucket. Mack scored easily. I headed for third myself, watching the left-fielder sprint to the ball. As he was picking it up, I realized I was going too fast and the infield was too muddy to properly decelerate. I felt too close to slide into third. In fact, I never slid into a base before, it was never part of my practices with Mack, so I just rounded the bag, my own need to score picking up momentum.

The catcher was gone. He was near first base to back up a possible throw on the bunt, and now he was caught as a spectator. Clint was the pitcher and his job was to cover home plate. What he lacked in athleticism he made up for in execution. He was the kind of player who knew exactly where he was supposed to be in all situations, so even though the attempted rundown had him out of position, he got there in plenty of time, waiting for the ball to beat me home.

His face gave away the quality of the outfielder's throw—I saw his eyes get wide, then glide along the sockets, tracking the incoming baseball. I was close, but not close enough. I was toast. A high throw and I could slide under it, but he was already dropping to a knee to block the plate, tipping off a low or one-hop throw.

Mack wasn't waving his hands to slide—he was smacking his hand on his shoulder, as if I would consider anything other than a full-speed collision.

I bashed into Clint, shoulder to shoulder, my higher position driving him into the ground. He crumbled, falling onto his back as the ball skipped to the backstop. I was on top of him, his legs and arms fumbling and thrashing like pissed-off snakes. I took my right hand and smacked the plate with an open palm, like a ref giving a final, definitive count in a wrestling match.

After scoring, I rolled off and stood up to relish the play. I didn't get to celebrate—Clint punched me in the base of the neck, sending hot currents of tingle into my fingers and feet. I fell to my knees and collapsed to the ground. He kicked me in the rib cage with the tip of his shoe, the molded pitcher's toe darting into the soft tissue between my ribs.

I rolled over and through the blur of my vision, I saw his elbow cocked, fist raised, as if to deliver the deathblow. The sky was cloudless, the color of wet chalk. Coach Gunther was screaming for us to stop. Clint's face was tight flesh and shadows. The kick burned inside of me and I couldn't find the breath or strength to stop him. The fist began its descent and in that split second I had come to terms with the fact he was going to punch me and hurt me, and I would just have to keep taking the blows until someone could pull him off. There would be no heroic defeat of Clint Phillips in the presence of Regina Carpenter today.

He never finished the punch. Mack crashed into him with twice the impact and speed I could've mustered on the base paths, leaving me free. I turned over, and Mack already had one hand clenched in the center of Clint's shirt, the other hand unleashing rapid-fire punches, bashing Clint in the cheeks, lips, temples, and hands as he tried to shield himself from the barrage.

Now dismounted from Clint, Mack stood, his breath coming in short bursts—running base paths couldn't wind him, but this did. He turned and walked away, heading toward the school, leaving his glove behind.

I tried to sit up but couldn't, a band of crippling pain tightening around my lungs and midsection. But I could still let my head lean over, looking back, seeing that the twins were gone.

I knew I was busted up worse than bumps and bruises, but I wasn't bleeding like Clint was—his face was ballooning, blowfish-style, with dots of blood leaking from contusions on his cheeks and jaw. His nose bled, spilling red ribbons across his lips.

I hobbled toward the locker room. Mack was my ride home and he had already stormed inside. The two hundred or so yards to the side door looked like an eternal distance—I couldn't take a full breath and wheezed with each step, my damaged ribs poking against my lungs. My entire spine was a hot sword, pulsing with each beat of my heart, the base of my neck knotted and hard, making my head feel like it weighed a thousand pounds.

"Hey, Sampson, you okay over there?" Coach Gunther hollered. He was busy with the blood and bruises of Clint, and I just looked sore. I couldn't gather the breath to scream back at him, so I just gave him a thumbs-up and kept hobbling toward the school.

"He shouldn't have done that." Regina's voice. My neck stiff, I turned my shoulders in order to turn my head, and she was walking beside me. "You look hurt," she added.

"My ribs," was all I could muster. At least this time, I had an excuse to not be clever since I could barely talk. A dizziness washed up on me, probably because my blood couldn't handle the lack of fresh oxygen combined with her sudden appearance.

"Stop. Let me see." Just like that, she was pulling up my shirt, the hands of a woman grazing my skin for the first time since the blind-man game, and nothing good or electric came from the touch, just a blazing agony as she found a blue splotch forming around a dent in my rib cage. "I think you've got broken ribs," she said. "You need to go to the hospital."

She looked back at the ball diamond. I wish I knew what she was thinking, looking over there. Concern for Clint? Hoping that Gunther would take over the responsibility of helping me?

"Mack was my ride," I said with effort. More silence. She looked around, diamond, school, me, the parking lot.

Finally: "I'll take you. You can call your mom from the hospital."

I shambled the short distance to her Chevy Cavalier. A shitty car—purple, with rashes of rust—but a car all the same. The twins shared a car, which meant Rae was around somewhere, but I wasn't in a mood to ask who might give her a ride home. Probably Clint, the doting boyfriend, when he finally got his shit together. It was twelve miles to civilization, Grayson, a place with a hospital, gas stations, and two McDonald's—one on each side of town. A town with a Wal-Mart florist who once made a rose meant for her, picked up by my mother, a difficult feat to afford and coordinate. A rose that failed.

We spent a long silence in the car. Knowing I had broken ribs, feeling the pins of bone against my lungs, I concentrated on breathing. I had seen in movies where broken ribs could plunge into the lungs themselves and bleed a person out internally. I monitored my breath for any rasping or fluid but found no bubbles, which calmed me. Regina looked straight ahead, both hands on the wheel.

I considered what to say for almost the entire ride, hoping she would speak first. I knew I had to say something, but what? *I meant what I said on the phone freshman year, Regina. I wish I could call you again sometime, Regina. I love you, Regina, any other girl would be settling for less. I'm sorry I'm a dork, Regina, but it looks like I can play baseball, so there's that.*

"Thank you" is what I said, the town blooming in size as we got closer.

"No, it's fine."

"It was . . . nice . . . to have you there," I said, pausing for short gasps of breath.

"I was surprised to see you," she said. "Why did you decide to come out for baseball this year?"

Maybe I was playing up my injury a little too much when I just pointed at her and smiled.

She smiled too, and then looked straight ahead again. We stayed quiet until we got to the hospital. I tried to soak up those final moments in the front seat of her car, the CD cases neatly lined up in her console, Wallflowers, Jewel, Pearl Jam. The scent of clean and cinnamon, a dust-free dash, a hairbrush stuffed into the side pocket of the door. The pain in my neck and back turned to ice, freezing my hunched posture.

She bypassed the ER doors, gliding into the parking lot.

"You could have just dropped me off," I said.

"Someone should stay until the doctor takes you or your mom gets here. We'll have to call her."

"Clint's hurt too," I said, testing the waters.

She looked at me with haughty disappointment, as if I'd underestimated her—that cheerful, scolding look reserved for boyfriends or spouses, a look I never truly forgot.

"It's a silly nosebleed, and he had it coming for what he did."

"I know," I said, opening the door. "He's an asshole, and you deserve more than that."

She didn't answer, and helped me through the sliding doors. The triage nurse asked me a bunch of questions and called my mother at work. Regina sat in a chair and waited, not even picking up a magazine.

"My mom's coming," I said. "I'll see a doctor soon, I think. You can go if you want to."

"Do you want me to?" she asked, the tilt of her head and hair in such a way to make her celestial, the kind of pose you see in a shampoo commercial when the girl's looking casual with her fantastic new hair. What was she fishing for? She knew I liked her. She knew I didn't want her to go. Why did she want to hear it?

"I've never hurt worse, but I've never felt better," I said.

She patted me twice on the thigh. "I'll see you at school. Get well soon." If only I saw who was really sitting next to me in that moment, all of her, not just her face, everything twisting me into a mistake that cost so many of us everything. She left through the automatic double doors and the sun died all around her as she looked back to wave one more time.

I got fitted with a torso belt for my broken ribs and a hard collar for the neck sprain, a collar I was to wear for eight weeks, except for in the shower. The doctor's hands were tough and he told me that broken ribs hurt and heal slow, urging me to keep the belt on for support and protection. I got a prescription for pain medicine we couldn't afford to fill, and before we left, I filled out paperwork to get free medical care because we were poor and had no health insurance.

Mom was quiet during the drive home. Parts of me felt good and high, and parts of me hurt, and looking at Mom during that car ride, well, that punched me in places I didn't know existed. She looked nothing like the mother I pictured in my mind when I thought of her. I figured age had done the fading—slivers of her hair had gone white, stark against the slick, black strands I was accustomed to. Her makeup looked brighter, but not on purpose—her skin was somehow bleaching, looking like candle wax, revealing blush and mascara in greater relief. Her eyes looked closer to her brain than her eyelids, like something about her had shrunk.

"Are you all right?" I asked, a strange reversal of that particular question, considering her near-hysterical concern when she arrived at the hospital.

Her eyes turned glassy and she tried to act surprised by the question. "A son always knows, I guess. I'm just not feeling good."

If I had pushed her, if I had listened to her, if all the dominos fell just so, maybe I could have saved her. It's one of those things where you blame yourself no matter what anyone says, because not blaming yourself would just hurt worse.

We got home and she heated up two cans of chicken-noodle

soup, then put me to bed. We were both in bad shape, but here she was, bringing my covers to my chin like I was a little boy again, kissing my forehead with a tenderness I had long forgotten. Any self-respecting teenager would wave her off with a "Jeez, Mom," but she looked so happy to be taking care of me, I just told her I loved her and asked her to turn off the light.

I lay in the dark, the hard collar digging into the back of my head, making sleep feel impossible. The slow onset of sleep gave me a satisfactory warmth, a distance between my body and mind.

I promised myself I would try out next year, which made me feel a little better. So with that settled, I let myself fantasize about Regina, about the ways our ride to the hospital could have gone differently. In my mind, it ended with me leaning in to kiss her. Strangely, she wouldn't let me kiss her in the fantasy, not without seducing her a bit first. She insisted on hearing me recite all the reasons I cared for her and wanted to kiss her and only her. My reasons were terrible. Everyone called her pretty or smart, fantasy-Regina said. She wanted to know why she first caught my eye. But she didn't—Mack had pointed her out to me, and I just gravitated to the hope of someone liking me.

I couldn't come up with any reasons fantasy-Regina wanted, not even without the pressure of her being there, not even with all the time in the world to dream them up. So in my fantasy, we didn't kiss, skipping straight to the hot sex as a clumsy virgin might imagine it, the ghost of her enjoying my first time more than any real Regina ever would, and me beating off to it, feeling like I was cheating on the girl who drove me to the hospital.

I fell asleep in my collar and rib belt and salty-wet underpants, dreaming of baseball fields and blood while Mom died a little bit more in the other room.

FIVE

LATER THAT YEAR, THE BASEBALL TEAM LOST IN THE conference championship game and Mack didn't come to school for three days. Clint loved asking, "Where's the great Mack Tucker? He still trying to get out of the fourth inning?" He said it in the hallways, the gymnasium, the parking lot. A few times he tried to get my attention in the hallway with his catcalls, but I would just turn away and bury my nose in my locker.

We might have won that game—and probably a few more during that 11–5 season—if Clint had been eligible to play. He was a damn good left-handed hitter, but he didn't play thanks to my injuries, which were serious enough to compel Principal Turnbull to wipe out his season via suspension. The broken ribs were my first broken bones. Up to that point, I had the usual cuts and scrapes—a skinned knee here and there, a constellation of bruises from falling out of a tree that looked ripe for climbing—but never anything serious, nothing that tipped me off to the full breadth of my healing prowess. The doctor told me the ribs would heal in one to two months, with a dull ache that might last even longer than that. I felt one hundred percent in three days and chalked it up to good fortune.

After the suspension was handed down to Clint, the hallways and locker rooms weren't easy. I endured Clint's lingering glares and tried to keep my distance.

On the third day of Mack's absence, Clint must have figured his chance to isolate me from Mack's defense was an opportunity he couldn't pass up. I stuffed a geometry book into my locker, closed the door, and a hand shoved me face-first into the metal. The ridges of the locker's vent dug into my forehead. Before I hit the ground, I knew it was Clint. He must have been waiting behind me, coiled and ready to strike. I wonder how many students watched and waited without warning me so they could see a good old-fashioned ass whipping. The kicks came again, aiming for my just-recovered ribs. I balled up to protect myself, but one kick caught me in the temple, twisting my neck. My hard collar had been gone for weeks now and my neck felt perfect, but the kick pushed fresh numbness through me, flushing my nervous system with acidic heat, ending with an icy tingle in my toes.

The chatter of students was blunted in my ears. I could see sneakers gathered around me, shins covered with jeans as a circle of people formed to watch the beating.

I fought back, trying to time his kicks so that I could catch his leg and drop him, like I'd seen in the movies. Turns out kicks are much faster in real life—I opened up to welcome his leg and catch it, and his toe hit me right in the chest. I smelled the rubber of his shoe as the blow gonged through me. Looking straight up, I saw the haze of fluorescent lights, random faces, and Clint, his arms now held by Principal Turnbull and Mr. Gilbert, the agriculture teacher. They were about to drag him away when I saw the shadow of Clint's rising foot and the black outline of his heel coming down like a falling eclipse, stomping into my face, crushing my nose and smashing the back of my head against the floor.

The darkness didn't leave me until much later, when I woke in a hospital bed. Mack was asleep in the corner chair. The clock above him said it was seven at night. My nostrils were gritty with blood, and my head and neck were pounding, a percussion section with chaotic rhythm.

"Yo," I whispered loudly. "Mack, hey."

He bolted upright.

He got up and stretched. "We gotta call your mom. She wanted us—"

"What the fuck did you do?" I asked before he could finish. He looked worse off than me, both eyes blackened, a rash-bruise around his forearm. He walked toward the hospital bed with a limp, then smiled through blood-crusted lips.

"Pop tenderized me over the title game," he said. He pulled up a chair next to the bed. "You should see that old fucker though. I got him back this time. Got him good."

"Damn, man, I'm sorry."

"I got him good," he said again, then picked up the phone and started dialing. I heard the tones rattle as he pushed the buttons, and then he got a freaked-out look and hung up the phone, his eyes fixated on the doorway.

"What?" I asked.

He just pointed, and there was Regina with a balloon that said GET WELL SOON.

"I can come back if you have a visitor," she said.

"I was just going on a hospital Jell-O run," Mack said, hobbling away. "You want anything?"

"No, thanks," she said.

"I wasn't talking to you," he said, giving her a cold look.

She returned it, and won the staring contest when he finally left the room.

"Hey," I said.

She tied the balloon to the rail of my bed.

"How you doing?"

"Better now," I said. She pulled up a chair and sat next to me.

"I'm that much of a morale boost, huh?" she said. "Well, I can't stay long."

"Just showing up means a lot," I said.

She looked sad, started to say something, then stopped.

"What?"

"Nothing."

"Clint's a fucking nut job," I said, a thought I wouldn't have parted with if the painkillers hadn't tamped down my nerves.

"I know," she said.

"Why are you with him? Why stay?"

She took a long time to answer, clearly indecisive. I took that as a small win, but looking back, there was so much more to see. I was still blindfolded, letting pretty girls bounce me off of playground equipment. "At least we have that much in common," she said finally.

"I'm not sure what you mean."

"Asking that question. All the time. Trying to make sense of it."

"He's not holding you hostage," I said, knowing immediately I might have overstepped a boundary. Stupid drugs.

She shook her head, leaned in, and kissed me on the cheek. "Now, don't you go and suck the helium out of that balloon."

She left, and Mack actually came back with Jell-O. My mother arrived after her shift was over. She slept in a chair next to my bed, both of us hoping a night of sleep would bring about a much-needed slice of healing. I slipped in and out of sleep every couple of hours, and in those black hours that are neither night nor morning, I felt my mother holding my hand, her palm clammy. She was smoothing my hair with her other hand, just being next to me. I could feel the edges of her knuckles, the thin glide of her fingers, and I heard the unsteady breath of her crying. I kept my eyes shut and tried not to cry because I knew her sorrow was not for me alone. I should have known then it was cancer. I'd never observed cancer personally, but it claimed so many fictional characters in TV shows and movies, the symptoms should have been evident. Her hand was skeletal, the flesh and tissue fed to the furnace of malignant cells torching her entire body.

The initial prognosis of a broken nose seemed like a reach to me. I never had a problem breathing after the injury. The scrape on my head was gone almost overnight. My ribs had no lingering soreness and my neck felt fantastic, as if Clint kicked something back into place instead of out of whack. I felt prime and complete, all cylinders firing. I had no choice but to call it more luck, maybe good genes. What else could I have done? Was I supposed to rebreak my bones to test the process? Some people were fast healers. I didn't think anything of it, I was just thankful to be ahead of the healing curve. The heat-death of spring held the promise of summer, when I wouldn't be forced into the clumsy glove of hallways and classrooms. And because Clint's latest assault had resulted in expulsion, the rest of the school year flew by, smooth and conflict-free.

On the last day of school, rumor spread of a party at Ted

Painter's house. I hadn't officially been invited, but Mack insisted that I go. I refused, the thought of awkward mingling outweighing Mack's obvious disappointment. This wasn't my first party refusal, but this one pissed him off something terrible.

"Sometimes I'm afraid you're going to be you forever," Mack said, and didn't talk to me the rest of the day.

A piece of loose-leaf paper was in my locker. Someone had folded it up and stuffed it through the vent. The note was on its side, halfway open, with ruffled bits frilling the edge like lace.

I've been thinking about things. I hope you will be at the party. We should talk. I need to tell you something. Signed with a single letter: *R.*

Thanks to the loose curriculum of the final day of class, Mack was in the weight room instead of biology when I got the note. I trotted down to see him and he greeted me with a grunt, grinding out a few bench-press reps.

"What now?" he said. "You decide to quit school or something? Become a nun?"

"I'm going tonight," I said. "I need a ride." I tossed him the note. He unfolded it, read it, then flicked it away.

"I'll give you a ride, but don't be all focused on one chick. She's bad karma, man, don't you get it?"

"It's getting me into the scene," I said, picking the note up from the concrete floor. "I figured you'd be happy."

"I'll be straight-up God-damned happy when you can go out for the baseball team or go to a party because you want to, not because you're trying to impress some moody whore whose boyfriend stomped your ass twice."

"She can't stay with him. She just can't."

"Doesn't matter," he said. "She's a fucking ho."

"Don't say that," I said.

"She is, man. She cheated on him."

"You didn't tell me you heard that."

"That's because it was with me."

He dropped back onto the bench and started repping out his next set. I could only wait for him to finish before speaking again.

"Did you have sex with her?"

He slapped at his own back, hugging himself with ballistic stretches. I wanted to kill him, but knew any move down here, alone, would end up with me getting another no-expenses paid trip to the hospital.

"No. She sucked my dick."

"What?"

"You don't want to know, dude, seriously. She's bad news, that's all you need to know."

"Why did you do it?"

"It was like"—he snapped his fingers—"and she was blowing me in Justin Wilson's bedroom. And in case you're wondering, she was sober as a priest. Clint was drunk off Natty Light, hugging the cat's litter box in the laundry room."

"But you knew how much I liked her."

"Shit, it could have been you, if you ever went to parties. Yet another Dale no-show, so I figured it would prove she's a fucking slut so you could get on with things. The next thing you know I'm done and I felt bad about it, so I figured I'd just not tell you and let you grow out of it, you know, out of respect for your feelings. But that ain't happenin', so I'm telling you here and now, she's a whore. And dude, even if you could get past it, she's not even a good whore. She used too much tooth and spit my load into a pair of penny loafers."

He dropped into another set and started pumping away. By the time he was done, I was gone, intent on getting to the party myself, hoping that the delicate, handwritten loops on my note could trump the harshness of Mack's revelation.

SIX

THE PARTY WAS AT A FARMHOUSE FLANKED BY A SILO
and barn with a lengthy vein of gravel for a driveway. The at-
tendance looked to be epic, with dozens of cars lined up along
the blacktop country road, half hanging in ditches overgrown
with wild grass.

The porch light was on, and some students I recognized
sat on the rails with red plastic cups in their hands. All eyes
were on me as I shuffled up the steps.

"Good old Silent Sampson," Billy Stannely said, a thick and
zitty kid, a year younger than me. He leaned by the door, his
glassy, drunk eyes glimmering in the ugly light. "Can't believe you're here. Cups are five bucks, or did you bring choco-
late milk?"

I ignored him and went inside.

The house was lit with dusty bulbs stuffed in chandeliers.
The place was old, with high ceilings and hardwood floors already splattered with beer, tacky against my shoes. Plastic cups
were in most hands, people broken off into splinter groups, talking and drinking.

In the kitchen, Dirk Gaston, a senior and the basketball
team's star point guard, was pumping the keg, flirting with
the girls in line. Mack once told me pumping the keg was "the

first step to pumping a chick's ass," so it didn't surprise me to see Dirk, another high school lady killer, manning the post. Ted sat on his kitchen counter with a big sleeve of cups stacked next to him.

I took a deep breath and wandered into the spotlight of the kitchen, a five-dollar bill, my only money, folded in my hand.

"Hey, Ted, can I get a cup?" It was early, but he already looked half-drunk.

"Fuckin' Dale Sampson? Now it's a party," he said, popping a cup off the stack. "They're usually five bucks, but for this special appearance, it'll be . . . five bucks."

I handed over the bill and took the cup. Dirk stood at the keg, staring at me. I was two inches taller than him, yet he was looking down at me, one hand on the black knob of the pump, the other holding a frothy brew that he sipped from.

"Is beer extra?" I joked.

He busted into a smile. "I thought for sure you'd just wander around with an empty cup." He pumped the keg. I grabbed the nozzle and performed a terrible, novice pour—mostly foam.

"Jesus, Sampson, you pour beer like a bitch. First failing grade ever."

I scurried into the social areas of the house, trying to lose myself in the noise of the growing crowd. Blending wasn't working. Anywhere I went to stand, I was alone. I felt like I wasn't standing right, or didn't look casual enough, or wasn't drinking my beer the right way. Sweat built up on my chest and in my armpits as if the white heat of a spotlight was following me. Without Mack around, I couldn't get over the dark tingle of exposure.

I didn't know if Mack was there yet, and didn't know what it would feel like when I saw him again. Maybe relief? Was I waiting for him, hoping for him to show up, or dreading it? I didn't know. I guzzled the beer, bitter as all hell, but it was the effect that appealed, not the taste, that rebellious feeling of knowing it was an adult, forbidden thing to do.

Some basketball players were dealing cards at the kitchen table, playing a drinking game. The bump of the stereo's bass shook the bones of the old house. The treble was drowned out by the chatter of increasingly drunk teenagers. People were filing in from the porch. New guests bought cups and filled them up at the keg. I was left wandering around in silence, wondering just what the fuck I intended on doing. Regina was nowhere to be found, and was I really going to open a conversation with her by asking if she sucked off my best friend? I couldn't tell if she liked him or hated him. I couldn't tell if she liked me and had no idea what the note might mean. Mack always said it's all the same, that the girls who have hated him the most ended up falling the hardest when he turned on the jets, but hate was an emotion, a reaction, something I truly hadn't elicited from Regina. At least, not yet. I had hope. I had the note. Tonight I would know for sure. I was standing in the archway between the kitchen and dining room, feeling the eyes of a corner group tilting my way, perhaps wondering among themselves what I was doing at the party. I figured it was a good time to take an oh-so-cool swig of brew. I drank deeply, moving my throat on purpose, like in a beer commercial, to let anyone watching know that yeah, Dale Sampson was gulping down some major beer. *Check it out folks, I'm no pussy drinker, I'm not nursing, I'm not drinking for appearances. I'm here for the beer. That's how I roll.*

Someone slapped the bottom of my cup, driving it upward, sending a tidal wave of beer into my face, the burn of carbonation stinging my nostrils. The empty cup fell to the hardwood.

Beer was everywhere, mostly on me, a bib of wetness spreading on my chest, and now more people were looking.

Clint Phillips was laughing his ass off.

"Hey, asshole, who's gonna clean that shit up?" Ted said. He jumped down from his post on the counter, leaving the keg unattended. Thank God. If he and Clint got into it, I could just slip out.

"Yeah, who's gonna clean that shit up, you clumsy fuck?" Clint said to me.

Ted regarded the two of us and sighed. "Sampson, clean that mess up then get out." I could tell he didn't want to say it, but had to due to some sort of social code that dictated that he side with the disgraced senior instead of the dorky junior. I wished Mack were there. He never would have stood for this, blowjob betrayal or not.

"Where's your lover, Dale?" Clint said. "We're going to have us a little talk. I never see you without Tucker around, and that's who I mean to have words with."

"Like on the baseball diamond? Those words looked to hurt."

He pushed me, but I stood my ground.

"He didn't do anything," a girl said in protest—Joanie Herrel, a classmate I recognized but didn't truly know. A few other people who never talked to me muttered in approval, sort of taking my side, but not taking a stand.

"I'll let you off the hook," Clint said. "Just tell me where Mack is. He coming to the party?"

"Does a bear shit in the woods?"

He pushed me again. "Fuckin' smartass. You look like you need another footprint on your face."

The haze of anger built inside of me, muddling words and

images except for Clint's jaw—that naked, exposed, punchable jaw. Clint was telling everyone how gay I was, how I was quiet because the only thing I liked to talk about was Mack's dick. He spoke through a smile, the parted lips that had kissed Regina, perhaps in more places than just her lips.

"I know why you're looking for Mack," I said.

Clint stopped talking. He didn't know that I knew, and he didn't want the entire party knowing that Regina was cheating on him. I thought I had him, but guys like Clint don't get had—they'll fall on the sword before someone can stick them with it.

"Because Regina's been blowing him? That's exactly right. I should have known he'd tell his little lover. I just want to talk to him about it. Man to man. So far the only thing I found out was from Regina. She told me his dick tasted a lot like your asshole."

I cracked him with a right hook and felt his jaw shift under the force of the blow, giving me the satisfying feel of flesh and bone moving with my fist, the bundle of nerves in his chin twisting with the impact. A moan of air burst from his lungs as he fell, unconscious before he hit the ground. He was out cold, his feet twitching as he sprawled on the floor.

"Give me a roll of paper towels and I'll clean this up," I said. Ted was stunned, but he turned around and walked into the kitchen. Everyone else just kind of stared, wondering what would happen when Clint stirred.

He was only out a few seconds when he planted his hands and tried to push himself up, so I snapped another punch into the side of his face, this time catching the hollow of his orbital bone, dropping him again. He made a wheezing sound like a leaking accordion.

I backed off, hands up, signaling I was finished, fearing I went one punch too far. I created space as he tried to get up again.

"It's all cool if he doesn't come at me again."

I heard someone say, "He had that shit coming."

Clint stumbled to his feet, looking unsteady, his pupils fat, broken blood vessels inflating the flesh of his right eye. A rosy patch was on his cheek—it would undoubtedly turn into the darkness of a full bruise by morning.

He looked around. Everyone had sucked in closer to the walls and one another, as if he were giving off an invisible force that created space around him.

"Enough of this shit," Ted said, glaring at me. Clint grabbed him, trying to steady himself, intent on staying upright.

"That was a mistake," Clint said. He shuffled to the door, smiling at me. Blood was thick in the channels of his teeth. He shambled out, his footsteps loud on the hardwood, echoing in the now-silent party. I believed him. I'd met that man before, the one fascinated by playing chicken with a shotgun. That was almost two years ago. Who was he now? How close did the danger have to be before the high was gone, before he had to see and feel something far more terrible to get his high? The moment wasn't any triumph for me. Festivities resumed. Partiers still talked to one another about the incident, rather than to me. I sat at the bottom of the living-room stairs and put my head in my hands, the thrum of adrenaline hot in my fingertips. The shakes came over me as I came down from the confrontation, an urge to cry catching fire in my bones. I bit the inside of my cheek to keep myself in check. Still no sign of Regina. Once I collected myself, I planned on leaving, slipping out through the dark, making my way home without looking back.

The party continued to regulate itself back to normal. The music got louder, as if to urge everyone to move along. With the cover of the crowd, I got to the front door and went out.

Mack was in the driveway, at the bottom of the porch steps, holding on to the neck of a whiskey bottle. Two guys were talking to him. They all looked up at me.

"You cool?" Mack asked. I wanted to sob, to let the tension pour out of me in tears and heaves, but I kept it choked down, nodding instead of talking. The dam would break if I opened my mouth.

He handed the whiskey bottle to one of the guys, then waved me over.

"How'd you get here?"

"I walked," I said.

"Jesus," Mack said. "I'll give you a ride home if you want, man."

"I don't know," I said.

"So you handed him his ass," he said. We left the light of the porch. Nothing but the crunch of the gravel, the darkness, and voices heavy with an urge to mend.

"Mack Tucker–style," I said, wiping at my eyes.

"That's what I hear. Must have fucked him up good. He backed into Ted's mailbox on the way out with his truck."

We got into Old Gray, fully loaded with one headlight, a sagging headliner, and a radio that didn't work.

"No Regina?" he asked.

"Nope."

"I was telling you the truth."

I let this revelation marinate in silence.

"Why didn't you tell me until today?"

"There's no good time, I guess. I just figured you'd just move past her. Then it wouldn't matter when you found out.

I don't really like her or anything. And I know it probably hurt you, and it's going to seem stupid and pointless when I tell her I don't give a fuck about her, because that's the truth. But I'm not a good guy when it comes to that shit. She came on to me. God as my witness, she did, and then this horny part of me convinced me it was okay to say yes, to let her do it, because it would somehow rescue you. The minute I blew my load—which is an honest moment, man—I knew I fucked up. Loads reload. That's the problem with guys, especially ones like me."

I stared out the window into the tree lines and fields whispering past.

"You remember your master plan?" I said. "The twins plan? Pick one? I take one, you take the other? What happened to that?"

"Shit, it might have worked on accident. I think Raeanna likes you," he said. "Makes sense. She's a quiet one, a smart one. Just like you. She's just as hot as Regina and she's never had her mouth on my dick. It's like hitting the Refresh button on the whole situation."

"That supposed to make me feel better about what you did?"

He slammed on the truck's brakes, cutting hard to the shoulder of the blacktop road. Another car zipped past, not even flinching at the sight of a car pulled over on a road like this one—in this town, on this road, if you're pulled over at night, someone's either puking, fucking, or passed out.

"I don't want you to get hurt."

"You have an awfully strange way of protecting me." I opened the door and stepped into the high, itchy grass of the ditch. "I'll walk the rest of the way."

"It's no fun being stuck on one chick, man." He got out of

the car and jogged to catch up with me. "It was twisted, but what I'm saying is it was my bad and if you want to go after Regina, if she means that much, then go after her. Before you get all hissy, let's be honest, she was Clint's girl at the time, not yours. You said she left you a note? To tell you something? Well, do you want to hear it or not?"

"Yeah," I said. "I guess I do. Good news or bad, I gotta hear it."

"Then let's go do the shit, man. You're a walking-tall, bad motherfucker tonight. You pegged Clint your own damn self, so go unleash a little swagger. Put the Regina thing to rest, one way or another. You might even score with someone else—hello, Raeanna—before the night is over. Come on, man! Think legendary. I got your back."

He said it with a conviction that made it feel possible.

"Can I just take a walk?" I said. I needed to think about it, and it felt good to walk alone under the wild moonlight in the clean air you can only get in a country field at night. I kept walking, heading toward the dark of the tree line, trying my best to breathe and clear my mind. When I looked behind me, the parking lights of the truck glittered low and yellow in the night. I started to get close to the trees, close to the true dark. I turned back. The truck grumbled, spitting exhaust that gathered like a phantom in the darkness.

He cheered me on as I approached. I got in the truck and he started back for the party. It was really happening—we were going back. I kept looking for that sheet of dread and nervousness to settle into me, but it never came. The adrenaline, the ache of my fist, the aftershock of my anger and emotion had blunted my fear.

Honestly, I didn't fucking care—I still wanted Regina. I still liked her. I didn't mind being a third choice. I was ready to grab her by the waist and kiss her. In fact, that's exactly what I intended to do—I had seen it in the movies, and it always seemed to work well there. Maybe she'd pull away, give me a slap to the face, and then kiss me again, deeper this time. Whatever that meant. Maybe we would walk to my house that night, hand in hand, and with my mother at work, we'd make love in my very own bed, where I'd fantasized about her—about her affection, about the possibility of her, an unsoiled fantasy who would turn real before my eyes.

Mack whipped in behind the first dormant car he saw, flicking off his lights and hopping out as if sharing the inspiration of my moment.

It was a long walk back to the party. I was ready, maybe even changed. I often wonder what life would have been like if that boy had lived—the boy who just defeated the bully, the boy who was blossoming into an athlete, the boy who was rising in such a way as to threaten his overbearing best friend, the boy who had held a note from one of the prettiest girls in school. Where would he be now, I wonder?

With Mack at his side and the world unfurling before him, that boy started a long walk that he would not survive.

SEVEN

AT THE MOUTH OF THE DRIVEWAY, I STOPPED AT THE faint sound of a bell ringing out tones in rapid succession, the sound of a vehicle reminding the owner that the keys were left in the ignition. I heard the squeal of a girl but couldn't tell if it was pleasure or pain.

Mack stopped as well. I tapped him on the shoulder and pointed to the source of the noises—farther down the eastern side of the road, where more parked cars were lined up. In the distance, a dome light highlighted moving shadows in the cab of a truck. We eased closer, covered by the dark. The blacktop was a hot plate, releasing the heat of the day in invisible waves, our footfalls dampened by the sun-softened tar.

We got closer. I saw the shadow of a moving head, heard the sound of a buckle clinking, a man grunting. The moon's light was useless, blocked by the high treetops flanking the road. Where the trees gave way to open fields, pockets of white fog hovered over the earth, the coolness of the night sucking them out, trapping them until the breeze or morning sun could dissolve them.

I heard flesh rapping against flesh, the rhythm of the blows in unison with the rabbitlike chatter of the bell. More grunting.

"Someone's fuckin'!" Mack whispered harshly in my ear, urging me along into a trot so we could get a better look. I don't know what Mack was planning to do. Perhaps some sort of "gotcha" prank, but when we got closer, I recognized Clint's truck. The door was blocking his midsection—all I could see was his head, eyes closed, bobbing as his midsection thrust.

He was having sex, and I just knew it was with Regina. The realization sucked the breath from me, and I stopped, frozen in the road as Mack trotted ahead. But I needed to see for myself, so I jogged to catch up, taking a wide arc toward the truck so I could see around the door.

Clint's white ass clenched and released as he pushed forward. A pair of limp legs dangled between his own. Streaks of blood carved dark ribbons in a smooth, white calf.

My first live, sexual moment was watching my archnemesis fuck the girl I was in love with, hours after my best friend had described her skill at sucking dick.

Another squeal. Then, a half cough that stopped abruptly, locked into a gag, the sound of Regina choking.

"Shut up, bitch," Clint said, the words leaking through clenched teeth. "You got this coming."

Rape, and rage was not my first emotion. I endured a moment of absolute shame that would never relinquish its power, thankful that he was raping her, that this wasn't her choice. I could handle being a conquering hero, I could handle his fall, and I could handle her destruction as long as she hadn't chosen Clint over me yet again. I sprang into action, but Mack was already ahead of me.

If only he'd used the element of surprise, things might have turned out differently, but that wasn't dramatic enough for Mack Tucker. "Let her go, you fuck!" Mack said. He grabbed

Clint's shoulder. I was jogging toward them, wanting a piece of the heroism. The gasp unclogged and she screamed—it was Regina, all right. The warbled cry of "Help me" shook me, echoing. It echoes still. And the blood—blood sticking to her ankle, dripping from her heel, too much blood for a simple broken hymen.

Clint turned, a revolver in his hand, the barrel sticky with blood. The muzzle flashed and Mack twisted away from the shot as if hit by a meteor, corkscrewing into the ground. Clint, naked from the waist down, standing over him, pointing down at Mack, intent on firing a round into his head.

I screamed out, "No!"

Clint turned to me, his eyes hard and wild in his beaten face, the dome light a halo behind him as he raised the gun. The thickness and length of the barrel belonged to a .44, or something similarly punishing. Mack went down in a blaze of gristle, with droplets of blood and tissue creating a little puff that hovered as he fell.

The barrel gazed at me and no life flashed before my eyes, no prayers, no slow motion, just the realization that Clint had shoved that barrel into her, tearing her, goring her in ways I couldn't imagine, and the thought made me ready to die. I closed my eyes. The sound of the blast popped in my ears, then lingered as a metallic vibration, giving way to the sound of a struggle. The fact that I heard anything meant I was alive: bullets traveled faster than sound.

I opened my eyes. Regina hung on Clint's back like a wild animal, her hair frayed, the whites of her eyes big in the muted light. He tried to shake her, but she wasn't budging.

I charged him, hoping to blast a shoulder right into his midsection. I knew such a move would create an utter mess and a scuffle on the ground, but perhaps it would dislodge the gun, and with Regina and I both fighting him, maybe one of us could get the gun away.

I was two strides away when he aimed behind his head and fired the gun into Regina's eye. A quarter of her skull exploded, splattering on the dome light itself, blotting out the light. Sulfur and copper were in my nose, the warmth of her wound mixing with the harsh flavor of the spent gunshot. I finished my last stride, crashing into them, her limp body slamming into the truck, cushioning his impact.

He sidestepped enough to shed me. I lost my balance, falling, and when I tried to get up, I was looking into the gun's barrel. I saw the white of Clint's naked legs and the wideness of his eyes. Nothing could save me. My hands came up to my face and the words "Please, don't" came to me, but I swallowed them down, not wanting to give him the satisfaction. He fired.

The bullet went through the center of my hand, scattering three of my fingers and most of my ear into the night. Blood spurted from both wounds and the whir of the bullet's sound echoed deep in my eardrum. Flashing dots paraded in my field of vision. My hearing dulled and I tried not to move, hoping that playing dead might prevent him from shooting me again.

Another gunshot made me flinch, but it echoed differently, farther away. I rolled onto my side and saw the muzzle flash in the darkness, in the front yard, closer to the house. He wasn't going to waste good bullets. Screams grew in frequency. Another flash. More screams, most of them of fear, but some were awful groans of pain, cries for help, dying teenagers begging for their parents, turned almost infantile by pain and impending death. I had no doubt that Clint was gut-shooting them, and was thankful that it was too dark to see the full scale of the massacre. Kids were scattering now, into the shadows, the woods, the fields, running for their lives. Another gunshot.

I saw Regina's body lying by the truck. Her face was nearly perfect, somehow bloodless. A patch of gray tissue was sticking to her right temple, where most of her skull was gone, her head looking like a bitten apple. Seeing her that way, the gun, Clint—none of it scared me. I wanted to destroy him. I wanted to rise up, absorb another shot, and make him feel pain and loss. I wanted him to cry instead of laugh, to hurt, to wail in agony, to know what it felt like to see people you care about lifeless on a country road. But Clint was beyond my reach. Men like him are beyond the reach of normal punishment, of real justice, making their violence all the more infuriating. If he lived it would be to gloat; if he died I was sure it would be by his own hand.

Mack was still facedown on the pavement, showing no signs of life. My legs wobbled, and I knelt beside him, gunshots ringing into the country air, giving a triple crackle with each report as they echoed off the trees in the distance. Maybe Clint would come back for more bullets. Maybe Regina would stir, or give me some last words, or somehow be capable of living with her injury. Miracles could happen, couldn't they? She simply could not be dead; we had not discussed her note yet. She still had good news to tell me.

I stared into the sky, the stars masked by wisps of clouds that could not strangle their brightness. I think I smiled at how pretty it was. I heard Mack groan a little, stirring, perhaps regaining consciousness at the very moment I was drifting away.

Clint violated Regina with the barrel of his father's .44 Magnum Colt Anaconda before putting his own flesh to work.

Large-bore pistols were favorite novelty items for the hunting enthusiasts in the area, and despite the mule kick of that particular hand cannon, he handled it like a savage professional. The slugs disintegrated my hand and turned most of Mack's shoulder into tendon shreds and bone dust. Yet another slug had killed Regina, leaving three in the barrel. He calmly reloaded on his way to the party, and killed three more kids with his next five shots. With one bullet left, he swallowed the barrel and pulled the trigger. I imagined him tasting Regina's blood and juices mixed with gunmetal, the barrel burning his lips around the mix, gagging him with it, making it easy to pull the trigger.

In times like this, people ask why. They try to assign blame. I remember the look in Clint's eyes when we were banging on neighborhood mailboxes. He was crumbling inside, and when the damage was complete, he'd have the backbone for his endgame. For Clint, the humiliation of me thrashing him publicly, along with Mack besting him by messing around with Regina, had completed the collapse. After that, pulling the trigger was easy. It didn't stop everyone from asking questions, from wondering what video games he played, what movies he watched, what his parents were like. They scoured his phone for text messages, for music playlists, for Internet browsing habits. They groped for reasons, as they always did. They found nothing. I drifted in and out of a numb haze. My hand hurt like hell, each pulse blooming into an explosive throb that made me want to scream. I wanted to stay passed out, but the real truth is pain does not release you; it doesn't let go. It settles in and gets comfortable until drugs or time chase it away, and even then, sometimes it hides, whispering at all the wrong times.

I remember headlights and sirens, chatter and spotlights,

stretchers and parental screams. The flickering lamps of an ambulance. Uniformed people asking me questions I didn't answer. A medic called me a lucky boy as he inserted an IV.

I don't have nightmares anymore, but most nights, before drifting to sleep, I can't help but see her. Too many times I felt more sorry for myself than for Regina. I can admit that. I had no misconceptions about who I was. I knew something was broken inside of me, but I had no strategy to fix it and no hope of finding one.

The note she'd left in my locker stays in my top dresser drawer, but I don't know why. She's gone. All that remains is a body under a dome light staring at me with one blue eye, seeing a true part of me I could no longer hide.

EIGHT

TAPE AND GAUZE SMOTHERED MY PARTIAL EAR. MY HAND was bandaged so completely it felt like a club. Even with the painkillers, I had trouble sleeping. A nurse checked the various electronics attached to me and woke me up. I saw Mom asleep on an easy chair pulled up beside my bed, her purse on her lap. It was two in the morning and I didn't wake her. She looked terrible, tired, sick. Each day I noticed something different about her, but on that night, I noticed her breath, her ease of sleep. Perhaps it was just the emotional aftershock, but I finally knew how bad it was. My sobbing woke her up. She scrambled to my side, taking my healthy hand, sandwiching it in hers, crying along with me, kissing my cheek, our tears mixing on the palette of my flesh, the sterile, sour smell of tape and gauze blending with perfume that reminded me of cherries.

I squeezed her against me with my good limb.

"Mack?" I whispered.

"I saw him earlier. He's going to be fine."

"Fine for a normal person, or fine for him? How bad is he hurt?"

"He was shot in the shoulder," she said. "They're going to do some surgery, but his life is not in danger."

"Which shoulder?"

"The right one."

"Then his life is in danger," I said.

She leaned over my bed, her legs wobbling and weak.

"Mom, sit. I'm doing fine."

Sobs gobbled up her words. She put the back of her hand to her mouth, as if to excuse herself, then sat. "I'm sorry," she muttered. "I'm just so happy you're okay." Then she lost it, doubling over into her hands, the rise and fall of her back betraying every crippling sob.

We cried together, apart, for different pieces of ourselves that were dead or dying. I finally asked. "Mom what's wrong with you? Please just tell me."

She sniffled, breathed, then shrugged. "I'm not sure."

"Have you seen a doctor?"

"Yes. Oh yes, of course," she said, lying. She smoothed my hair, smiled at me until I fell asleep again.

The next day, I was up and around, a deep itch burning under the gauze of my ear and hand. The doctor called it normal, the itch of healing, a good sign. My hand had been operated on to clean things up, screw some things together. Half my ear was gone, but my hearing was intact. This was worse than any "healing" itch I'd ever experienced. The flame of this itch was like poison ivy blossoming under the skin, an itch that destroys your regard for your own flesh, making you want to scratch so deep there's nothing left but bone.

When Mack could take visitors, I headed up to see him. He had most of his right side wrapped in bandages. He was fresh out of surgery, his eyes shiny with drugs. We clamped our hands together and leaned into a clumsy hug.

"I'll be robotic, man," he said, nodding at his shoulder. "I'll throw the ball a hundred miles an hour now."

They had saved his arm, but he would need more reconstruction. The bullet had destroyed most of the shoulder joint, which could be patched together, but the tendons, bones, cartilage, and all the other intricacies of the joint could not be recaptured. Not the way they used to be, anyway. His arm could be saved for things like shoveling a fork into his mouth, but he'd be opening jars and doors left-handed. He would never raise his right arm over his head without grimacing. He would never throw again.

Days after returning home, the itch in my hand was alarmingly bad, so I took the bandage off and checked it myself. The doctor warned me of infection, demanding that I keep the bandages on for a full five days, after which they were going to evaluate me for another surgery, perhaps taking my whole hand away for a prosthetic, since movement in my remaining pinky and thumb was nonexistent.

I took the bandage off to reveal an entire hand, all flesh, all bone, all my fingers present, grown back to their full shape. I had heard of phantom-limb syndrome, how people can sometimes feel and move limbs that aren't there anymore, but all they needed to do was look at their stump to know the truth. Unless I was experiencing a drug-fueled hallucination, my hand had completely regenerated.

I sat on the couch and stared at the wall for a long time, trying to catch my breath. I closed my eyes, wondering if my hand would still be there when I opened them. It was still there, still complete. Even my fingernails were back. I balled a fist with no pain, I flipped off the wall, I flicked my fingers. I touched them with my other hand to assure myself they were real. I popped my knuckles and I searched every inch of flesh—looking closely, under the light, I could see a faint, white border where the new fingers had grown back, a dividing line between my original flesh and the new, regrown fingers. It wasn't a thick line of scar tissue, just a slight difference that I could barely detect.

I used my new hand to yank the bandage off my ear—the ear had also returned, though it was still a bit pink.

"Mom," I said, trying to say it loudly, but only a whisper came out. "Mom," I repeated, getting her attention.

"Coming," she said. She was lying down, something she did all the time now. We never said the C word. I kept insisting that she go to the doctor, and the subject inevitably got changed. I tried aggression. I tried to question her love for me, telling her if she didn't have the simple will to live, she was betraying her only son.

"I do want to live," she said. "Sometimes trying your hardest to stay alive isn't living at all."

She shuffled into the room, thin and gaunt. I held my hand up. She smiled. I couldn't believe the look on her face, the complete opposite of my own astonishment. I thought we'd go to the doctor and get an explanation. Was anyone else out there like this, or was this affliction completely unique?

She took my hand. After a thorough inspection, she brought it up to her papery lips and kissed it. "This is God making up for what was taken," she said. "This is God making things right."

She died in the middle of my senior year. I didn't need much in the way of credits to earn my graduation, and we both agreed I couldn't go back. Still, she begged me to walk the stage and take my diploma, if she lived that long. "There's ways to hide your hand," she said. "We'll think of something by the time May rolls around."

So I stayed home, and despite her weakness, she went to

school a few times a week to bring back classwork from fully understanding teachers so I could knock out the last of my requirements. We wanted to keep my secret until we understood what was happening to me.

She wanted to die at home, but I insisted on driving her to the hospital when the pain got bad enough. I was the only one at her side when she passed. Since Dad left, we were always a family of two, and any attempt to discuss extended family ended with her shaking her head and saying nothing.

Just before she took her last breath, she squeezed that same reborn hand, barely able to speak, her body drenched with tubes and masks and lights and cancer. Cancer was everywhere, in her bones, in her breasts, in her liver, in her lungs. I never pulled any plugs on her. I hoped that God would make up for what was taken, that He would make things right. But He didn't, and she died in front of me, leaving another empty seat for my graduation.

After she died, I lived alone. I didn't turn eighteen for a few more months, so I had to be careful. The utility bills kept coming in her name, and I kept paying them. No point changing the name since I wasn't officially old enough to enter a contract. As long as the heat and lights stayed on, no problem. The house was paid for. I didn't care that I wasn't on the title. She had no life insurance and since the bank was local, it was easy enough to empty her checking account with a forged check.

Despite her wishes, I couldn't bring myself to leave the house on graduation night, so I called Principal Turnbull and asked him to mail my diploma. Mack did the same. "I don't need to walk across some stupid fuckin' stage to get where

I'm going," he told me. He called, but rarely, and when he did, we didn't tread any tragic ground. Nothing about my mother's death, nothing about the shooting or our injuries. He came to her tiny funeral and hugged me but we barely talked. Now, only phone calls and just small talk, just because it was a habit to talk once in a while.

On my eighteenth birthday, I sat alone at my kitchen table, silent except for the tick of the clock. The fake oak didn't smell like Pledge anymore. No more waxy feel that would make your fingers smell like lemons. Just me and the diploma, a piece of fancy-looking paper hidden behind a sheath of plastic, like it was old-people furniture.

I took the cleaver from the utensil drawer. The handle felt like an anchor, and the blade had a solid heft that made me confident it could split bone. Nothing had been made right or whole by my miraculous healing. A dead mother, for what, an index finger? Regina's corpse for a useless piece of ear flesh? My friend's golden shoulder, his pride, our dreams, for what? Being able to pick up a dirty sock? Having an opposable thumb to hold silverware? Everything was taken, and I was left with a power I didn't want or even need. I didn't need my hand or ear to heal. In due time, they'd have been capped with scars and the pain would vanish. The parts I needed to regenerate, the pain I needed to subside, were deeper and there forever, untouched by my abilities. Injuries that caused nightmares and bouts of unbridled crying, of looking out the window at a sunny day and being incapable of moving off the couch.

I didn't want to accept the trade. I hated my new hand and what it represented. I gripped the cleaver. I spread my regenerated hand out on the table and chopped off my regrown fingers with a single strike. They flicked across the table as blood shot out of the mini stumps in gurgles of near-black blood. I watched with a certain affinity for the pain. I stretched the flesh of my ear taut with the thumb and pinky finger of my now-bleeding hand, and used the cleaver's edge like the bow of a stringed instrument, drawing it back and forth against the tight cartilage until a sufficient piece was severed, comparable to my original loss. I threw the fingers and ear into the garbage disposal, switched it on, then used dishtowels and pressure to stop the bleeding of my hand. I left the blood-soaked dishtowel against the wound and wrapped it with a half roll of duct tape.

For three days, I didn't leave the house, eating nothing but canned soup and cereal with expired milk. I didn't bathe, I just slept and watched television and waited, hoping that in a couple days I could remove the makeshift dressings and show God I didn't want his reparations.

Three days later, my fingers were back, my ear was whole, and the only reminder of those cuts that remained was a new set of white lines tracing the border between who I am and who I used to be.

PART TWO
DISINTEGRATION

NINE

I TOOK THE GUN OUT, A FAMILIAR .38 PURCHASED AT
our local Super Wal-Mart. At first, I kept it under the middle couch cushion and didn't bring it out for weeks at a time.
I've since warmed up to the prospect of holding it, watching
the light die in the matte finish of the barrel. When you fondle
a gun, it starts out cool and warms up, getting friendly in your
hands. Hold one long enough and pretty soon, the urge to
shoot something takes on a life of its own.

I sat on the couch and did nothing but watch TV, which is
overloaded with channels on top of channels, reruns and commercials. The car-insurance lizard thinks he's clever. Beer will
make you smile and get laid. Trucks look cool covered in
mud.

Doing absolutely nothing has its own inertia, making it
tougher to walk out the door, and once outside, the fear of my
computer kept me from wanting to come back. I had the Internet, but I feared my home page—a search engine, white and
clean, a blank slate with a single box. Type something in and
answers appear, unfolding down the page, just one click away.
It's like a cruel, modern genie that can tell you how to achieve
any wish, but doesn't do the hard work for you. I used my
computer to read the news, check sports scores, whack off to

the occasional porn video, hijack movies and music, but I avoided search engines if at all possible.

I could have set up a different home page, but even then, the search box would linger in the upper right of my browser, an oracle waiting for a visit. The Internet is like the face of God—overwhelming, incomprehensible, infinite. I lived in fear of that computer, of that search box in which I wanted to type "human regeneration," an ominous rabbit hole I didn't want to go down.

I sat on the couch with the gun resting on my thigh. One local network carried Carlton Franks on Sunday mornings as part of their religiously slanted programming block. Like any good preacher, he made loving God seem like heavy lifting, a lot of sweat in his pudgy, pink face. He always kept a handkerchief in his right hand to wipe away the sweat, the microphone trembling in his other hand. He would start each program sounding smooth and oiled, and end it sounding like he'd chewed razor blades all night.

I watched because he healed people through the television. Allegedly, anyway. He would call them by name, sweat matting his gray hair against the runny makeup on his forehead, holding his hand out. If he called your name, it was time to touch the television and get your healing. He was very specific. I would watch, waiting for him to say "Dale." He never did. And he always healed cancer and migraines and paralysis. He never once healed someone's ability to heal, so I was waiting for nothing. I just got his pixelated hand, blurry on my screen, healing a woman named Charlotte, her stomach tumor shriveling up as he belted out his passionate prayers.

For the longest time, I'd just hold the gun every day. I knew I couldn't pull the trigger. Not yet. It wasn't the fear, it was the knowledge that the gun held a clean, easy death. I hadn't earned it yet. I wrapped the gun in an oiled cloth and tucked it back into the couch cushion, then took a shower. Shaved. Put on a decent pair of jeans and a shirt that wasn't wrinkled too badly. By the time I got cleaned up and ready to start my day, it was well past noon.

My weekends evaporated with nothing accomplished. During the weekdays, I worked for the US Army Corps of Engineers, a fancy government agency, but my job title and duties were far less fancy—I was a GS-1 on the mowing crew. The other two guys drove commercial mowers; I slung a string trimmer all day. In the mornings I would get dropped off at one end of a bridge rail and over the course of ten hours, I'd try to get a couple of trimmed miles behind me. Then I'd get picked up by a white Corps truck—rangers who barely talked as I drank up the cold air spewing from the air-conditioner vents. In the winters, I did nothing. You could ration out seasonal GS-1 pay for a long time if you didn't have much in the way of a social life or hobbies and you had a paid-off house. I got myself a little car, a computer, and a prepaid cell phone that barely worked in Verner, but the house? I hated the house now. Mom was in the walls like smoke damage, every inch of it swollen with memories of her. I wanted to get out but I couldn't afford it.

Mack left Verner as soon as he could. I think it was because the town was steeped in memories of what he used to be, could have been. He carried on with his dream to party at Southern Illinois University at Carbondale, only not on a baseball scholarship. Not anymore. I didn't know if he was using charge cards or student loans, but Mack always had a way of making things work for at least a while. I had the grades for school, but college didn't appeal to me. Work didn't appeal to me. Nothing appealed to me. I got right to work wasting my days.

Before Mack left for good, we gave the announcement a moment of silence. We needed to digest the deepening distance between us, then we quickly shifted to talking about sports and weather and anything other than how truly and deeply frightening the future could look without fame, or baseball, or money, or success, or even so much as a plan.

Sometimes, when it was dark and no one could see me, I'd take a good long walk. The darkness was important. Seeing people meant those pitying looks, or worse, people asking how I was doing. I found myself hiding my hand in public, lest someone know the details of the shooting closely enough to be suspicious of my regenerated extremities. I'd see a faint dome of light to the north—Grayson, Illinois. Their population sign had four digits instead of three, they had a Wal-Mart with a floral section I'd visited once before, stoplights, cell towers, gas stations, and a selection of fast-food restaurants. Compared to Verner, Grayson might as well have been on the fucking moon, but the towns were still connected by country side roads. They cut through soybean and cornfields pocked in the dark by farmhouse lights. The kinds of roads that bubble in the summer sun, then soften at night. When it's cold, black ice nibbles the surface. Thick puddles gather where the road meets dirt, usually from truck tires denting it in, skirting the side while two passing trucks graze shoulder to shoulder, spewing gravel into the culverts and ditches that stretch out into the distance. Roads have a pulse, like railroad tracks. I could put my hand in the middle of the narrow road in front of my house and feel the fading heartbeat a hundred miles away as the blood bloomed from her skull.

Sometimes I'd walk and the questions would come—What did I do today? What difference did I make? How is the world different? Why would it miss me? Visions of *Matlock* reruns, endless commercials, empty bags of cookies, empty beer cans I acquired with sheer, illegal persistence, and half-read magazines flashed through my mind. Another wasted day.

I went home and ate an entire frozen pizza for dinner, the only non-cereal meal option in the house. When you're broke you only keep the bare essentials around—a stack of cheap pizzas, cereal, milk. A case of light beer that cost you twice as much as the sticker price because you needed to pay a stranger to buy it for you.

Rope. Razor blades. Some foam insulation, perfect for a car-exhaust suicide. When running the car in the garage, precious noxious fumes can escape through gaps in the garage door. Wouldn't want to hurt the environment. A toaster, still in the box—the preferred cliché for electrocuting yourself in the bathtub. I wonder who thought that one up—there's really no reason in the world for a toaster to be in the bathroom. Any small appliance could do the job. A toaster was random. Poetic, even.

Why does suicide get such a bad rap? Why is it considered cowardly? Take a gun and put it in your mouth, monitor yourself and feel that heart rate spike. Taste the barrel. Imagine the bullet blowing through the back of your head, shrugging away flesh and bone as it buries into the wall, an item to be examined as police scrub the crime scene for evidence, ruling it a suicide, and everyone judges you as a coward when they would never have had the balls to pull that trigger, or jump off that bridge, or tighten that noose.

Call suicide what you want, but a cowardly act it is not. If you're not blowing your brains out, you're dying by neglect. You're ignoring that suspicious mole, or smoking, or cultivating that roll of belly fat, or eating too much sodium, or fucking without a condom, or snorting coke, or driving without a seat belt.

Simply put, some deaths are acceptable because everyone loves salt, but most can't stand the taste of a gun barrel.

❦

Before I bought the gun, the empty days came and went with dizzying speed. The only person I really talked to was Mack, and even then, the calls were infrequent and sounded eerily similar to the ones that preceded them. The same versions of different stories. We danced around it. I waited, hoping that the empty days were like little air pockets that could cushion me from what happened to us. I let them build, paralyzed by how fast they could go, and it became a game with myself—how long could I keep this up? How long could I squeeze the weed whacker's trigger instead of the pistol's? I waited for the answer. I cut grass, ate, bathed occasionally, and bought groceries at odd hours to avoid people. I watched television. I ate cereal out of mixing bowls for multiple meals throughout the day. I told myself, "Tomorrow, I'm going to buy a newspaper and look at the classifieds. I'm going to get a real job and meet new people. I'm going to forget about my regenerating hand and Regina and Verner."

Mack tried to figure things out with his dick. He usually called on Friday afternoons to tell me he was on his way to a party, or orgy, or bar, or to pick up a girl for a date. We talked about the chicks he was fucking, about the spiral-bound notebook he was filling up with names or descriptions: "Janice Carter," he read. "Gloria Something-or-Other. English major with red hair and matching pubes. Stinky bitch from West Frankfurt." He went on. "I've started to give them wrestler names, like, the tall volleyball player that blew me during a frat party; she was a big one, a beast, so I wrote her in as 'Hulk Blowgan.'" He chuckled at himself. "What's up with you?"

We never lingered on this question for long. Whatever I could come up with, which wasn't much, would usually remind him of another story—a woman exploited, a fight won, a social victory, each story a grain of truth pumped up on steroids, on the fatness of obvious lies. I let him talk without pressing him because Mack needed at least one person who believed him without question. We spoke a veiled language. We told each other each Friday, in subtle code, *No, I haven't figured anything out yet, I'm not on my way anywhere, I don't know where I'm going, and I cannot let go. I can't let go. Help me.*

"I'll pump her once for you." He said this quite a bit before hanging up the phone for a weekend adventure. "Give her the shocker for me," I would say, and this was how we said, *We'll make it, you're my best friend and we can still make it.*

He never truly invited me down. He would say, "You should come stay a weekend sometime," but I never pushed the issue and he never pulled on it. His calls became less and less frequent. I never called him, always thinking he was busy with class or girls or shoulder rehab. I figured the growing lapses between phone calls were for the best—each conversation was loaded with the shadows of the past. For him, he could smell the ball diamond and hear the satisfying aluminum crack of a high school home run. He could smell the perfume of girls he actually liked before screwing them. I remembered him urging me into Regina, into a void of love and gray matter. We thought these things but never spoke of them, as if saying them aloud could make them real again.

I felt I could keep up this nothing forever, especially if I kept telling myself I was *this close* to turning it all around.

I spent my twenty-first birthday alone, celebrating by buying my first legitimately acquired case of beer. I put a note on my fridge: *Today is the first day of the rest of your life*. People believe that shit, and if I saw it every single day, maybe I'd end up believing it too. I'll wake up and take my vitamins, wash them down with a whole liter of mineral water. I'll eat a low-fat, high-fiber breakfast and keep the television off while I work out and then go to a good-paying, fulfilling job in some company that does good things for a customer base of equally good people.

Months passed and the note turned brown around the edges, the corners curling as if it wanted to ball up and die. I threw it away and replaced it with *You're one second away from turning this around. One second*. As if saying it twice made it real. Perhaps it was true. I can still star in a big movie or save a life or win a poker tournament on ESPN. What would it mean? Nothing. Everything. The suffering of human potential comes from the lack of a true pinnacle.

After that I tried, *There is no try, there is only do, or do not*. It was from *Star Wars*—sound advice from Yoda himself. Worked for Luke, so what the hell, right? Yet here came the bowl of Captain Crunch, me eating the same fucking thing to start another useless day staring at a note on the fridge. I hated that note immediately, so I figured I'd try yet again. I took a Post-it Note and wrote down the very first thing that came to mind, trying my best to not let a thought process interfere with the contents.

The result was: *If you're reading this, take this fucking note down and do something*.

So I did something. One night I put the barrel in my

mouth. How could I not think of the shooting? I tested the very brink of the trigger's pressure, knowing I was a millimeter away from death. My breath got tight. My eyes burned. I did this for three nights in a row and it didn't get any easier.

I tried thinking of Regina and couldn't do it. I thought of my mother, and still my finger wouldn't press any farther. I thought of the countless and painful days in front of me. I thought of the bank account that perpetually stayed at around two hundred bucks. I thought of trying to pick up the phone and call someone about a real job or some food stamps. Nothing worked. Finally, I thought of Doc Venhaus. I thought of a way to keep going, the only job I was truly qualified for.

Doc was one-stop shopping for medical care in Grayson. He could diagnose you, write the prescription, fill it on-site, or cart your ass into the back room for minor surgery. I remembered my mother driving us to Grayson after our usual pediatrician infuriated her by suggesting she'd allowed my strep throat to linger too long. Venhaus was casual and kind. He took one look at my tonsils and said, "It's a revolt back there. We'll have to scoop those bad boys out." He spoke with a weathered voice, a voice that conjured smoke and rocks. I remembered manicured hands and glasses and a proper haircut made of edges and angles. I remembered him giving me a cherry sucker after the visit and how much my mother liked him.

He might remember the boy who had the rotten tonsils, and if he didn't, his file would. Either way, I drove to Grayson to see how Doc Venhaus would react when he saw my tonsils had returned.

TEN

DOC VENHAUS WASN'T THE MAN I REMEMBERED. HE HADN'T aged well, his face crinkling into folds and creases when he peered down his nose and through his glasses. His hair was gone on top and cropped close on the sides, a reddish-brown dusted with gray.

"I'm having a problem with my tonsils," I told him.

He smiled, never once looking up from the chart. The flesh below his eyes sagged below the rim of his glasses. He had *jowls*.

"That's interesting," he said. "I remember you, actually. Sounds to me like you need a different type of doctor, Dale, since your tonsils are gone. They haunting your dreams, son?"

I opened wide. He paused awkwardly, but clicked his pen light on and took a look. He clicked his light off and stared at me. "What is this?" he asked.

"I need you to remove one of my kidneys to see if it'll grow back."

"Is this a prank?"

"I think I can snag twenty grand for one, but I want to know if I can make a career out of this."

"I don't think this is funny," he said.

"I don't either." I held up my hand. "My fingers have grown

back twice. Check my medical records. St. Mary's Hospital down south. You'll see I had most of my right hand shot off."

He clicked his pen a few times. We both stared at the wall. "I'm fuckin' starving," I said, snakes of hunger rolling and flopping in my midsection.

"Your tonsils are clearly there," he said, more to himself than to me.

"You got any food around here? I haven't been home all day. Skipped lunch."

"Let me look again," he said, clicking on his penlight. I opened wide. He stared into the back of my mouth until the joints of my jaw ached.

"I must have . . . made a mistake. It was a long time ago. I'll have you know, son, I've been through far too much to have a prank like this played on me."

"Why do doctors always think it's a mistake when something strange happens?"

"Because I've made mistakes before," he said, then jotted something on his clipboard. "Sorry. I shouldn't have said that."

The jotting was a signature. He was done. "I've got patients to see. Take this to the front desk. I'm supposed to be off on Monday, but we'll keep the whole day open. Run some tests. That sound okay?"

He handed me a piece of paper. I looked where he had circled my condition—infection. Antibiotics prescribed. He handed me a slip of paper with the prescription. "Don't fill this," he said. "It's a ruse. I don't want my staff involved with what we're dealing with here. Not yet, anyway."

Ah, the good doctor, keeping his little medical freak to himself. Monday I would be his own personal playground.

"How much is this going to cost me? I don't have insurance."

"My treat," he said.

"As long as we test my kidney."

"Selling organs is against the law."

"So is writing fake prescriptions."

"See you next week, Mr. Sampson. And if you're hungry, drug reps bring food here all the damn time. I'll tell Grace to give you a sandwich to go."

Grace stuck my next appointment in the computer. She was an older woman with thin, yellow hair. She had big moles on her arms. I realized that it had been a long time since a woman talked to me who wasn't wearing a name tag. She closed out my non-insured billing and I headed for the door with a turkey-and-Swiss sandwich.

When I got home, I checked my landline and saw six missed calls from Mack. That was a year's worth within one hour, so I figured something was up.

I collected myself, drank a glass of water, and called him back.

We started with the usual chatter about female conquests, only this timeline had a purpose, since the trail of girls was taking him away from Carbondale, crossing the state lines, heading west, and ending in California.

He was devoid of true excitement, as if giving a police statement.

His tone brightened when he talked about the reality television show called *Dedications*.

"There's this girl, Lori, fake tits, real hot. We've sort of been dating since March. At least she's under that impression. So anyway, I applied for the show and ended up getting a call. I'm like, okay, there's a shot here. After an interview and a few follow-ups, I made the cut, dude! The fuckers want Mack Tucker on TV!"

The dream of fame. The fastball was dead, but the dream wasn't.

"I hate to be a buzzkill, but it sounds like you're not doing the college thing anymore?"

"The casting interview was during exam week. I can get college credits any fucking time."

"Then good for you," I said.

"Good for us. Convertible trip to California, brother. I haven't forgotten. But there's one tiny complication with the casting. They want me to propose to her on the show."

"I know you don't want to get married," I said. "And you've only dated this Lori for what, ten weeks?"

"Two and a half months, fucknuts. It's a relationship, not a newborn. But they won't let me on the show if I don't propose," he said. "It's kind of the point of the show. But don't worry. I got this figured out—she won't say yes. It'll be their signature episode, where I get rejected. I can do autograph signings at malls, maybe get some momentum for a bachelor show of some sort. Chicks will feel sorry for me. Pity pussy galore!"

I could tell he never actually watched the show, which was buried on a shitty cable network that only a guy with a life like mine would run into. But the women always said yes. A typical episode consisted of Some Tool hell bent on getting married, spewing his story to Music Star during the first segment. In the second segment, Star and Tool sit in a studio together as Star writes a song specifically for Tool's One and Only Love. In the last segment, One and Only Love—who was usually a gorgeous woman who had no business being with Tool—got dragged into a restaurant or park significant to their relationship so that Star could perform the song as Tool holds her hand with tears in his eyes as he proposes.

"So you think she'll say no?" I asked. "You think any woman can say no when she knows she's on TV and being judged by a whole audience? When she has had a song from some famous, sexy pop star written and performed just for her?"

"You're right," he said. "Good thing for me my episode won't have anyone sexy or famous. I don't even know his name. Ben McSomething. It's some black dude who plays the piano and isn't blind. How good could he be? Anyway, this is a special occasion. They seemed really fucking-A pleased with what I bring to the table. This is the launch pad, bro. So I'm thinking, steakhouse. Me, you, a few pitchers. You in?"

"Maybe," I said.

"What you doing nowadays?"

I didn't want to say *nothing*. "I've got a few irons in the fire."

"Atta boy. That mean you're picking up the check, or what?"

"Yeah," I said without thinking. I wasn't in a check-picking-up state when it came to finances, but I didn't want to tip my hand to Mack.

"Good. I should come through your way early next week. That cool? I'll just holler?"

My thought was, Come through on your way to where? Mack sounded adrift. That made two of us.

"Just holler," I said. "No interesting shit going on in my world."

He screamed, "Mustang, motherfucker!" and hung up the phone.

I was back at Wal-Mart, my quick in-and-out shopping trip. I always tried to go on Wednesdays, when the store was practically empty. Mowing season was over, so I was in ration mode. After quickly filling the basket with the bare essentials, I scanned the checkout lanes for a quick and quiet exit.

I assumed that most men didn't like to check out with attractive clerks, where every item is a spilled secret—the toiletries alone advertising, *Here's what I wash myself with, here's what I think of my hair, here's the lotion I use to prevent chafing. Here's the magazines I read, the subjects I like. Here's the food that I eat. Here's the movies I think so much of I want to buy them and watch them collect dust on top of my television for the next decade.* Mine would have been, *Here's white box after white box after white box of store-brand necessities, here's ramen noodles, so yes, I'm broke.*

Clerks are taught never to make conversation about a customer's items. You don't watch a guy check out with a pack of condoms, a jar of strawberry jam, and a case of Red Bull and say, "Looks like you're in for a fun weekend." Nope, just "How are you, bleep, bleep, bleep, here's your total, off you go."

In the midst of this clerk evaluation, I saw my target, a tall, thick man who wore glasses and the kind of mustache reserved for porn stars or sexual felons. I decided to go to him, a clerk I recognized from my many Wal-Mart trips. He made eye contact with me, giving me a slight smile that was priming the pump for his official, rehearsed "How are you this morning?"

I smiled, but to avoid eye contact, I shot a perfunctory glance into the checkout lane parallel to his, and saw brown hair, the same shade as Regina's. The same nose. The same cheeks. I could see the unmistakable blue eyes, but before I could even let my mind say, Oh my God it's Regina Carpenter, my mind pumped the brakes and reminded me it had to be Raeanna.

I hadn't seen her in almost four years, not since the day before the shooting, passing her in the hallway at school. She had clutched her books that morning, almost afraid to look at me, a girl almost as shy as I was. But those four years were such eventless, empty years for me, the shooting could have happened yesterday. I looked like a dummy, staring at check-out lanes. Finally, mercifully, she looked up and said, "Dale?" I eased up to the checkout counter, a nebula of nerves firing all at once. The name tag read RAEANNA. No miracles here, just a smiley face rolling back prices.

"I haven't seen you in such a long time," I said, stacking items on her little conveyor belt. "You look amazing."

I was being slightly generous. She held most of her high school beauty, but her right eye was fucked up, the vessels thick with blood, the flesh surrounding it black and yellow, a kalei-doscope of bruising. That legendary blue iris lurked in the cen-ter. It made me think of Regina's eye hanging against her cheek after her head got blown off. Here it was, alive again, these living eyes serving as a before and after picture. Rae's skin looked tired and loose against the bones of her face.

Her lip had a scar I didn't remember. Her hair was messy, not intentionally, but forced by circumstances or time, a huge departure from her high school days when her hair was sculpted, shining, gorgeous like the rest of her.

"That's sweet of you to say," she said, her eyes down, fix-ated on her scanning chores. The messy hair was made to fall into her face, and she would brush it aside, into her bad eye, a dark curtain she kept drawn over the injury.

"So how have things been? What have you been up to?" she said. Small talk—conversation kindling never meant to ignite, rather, meant to just smolder because if we had a real conversation, it would be about the heavy ghost of Regina, and how each of us has tried and failed miserably to move on from her memory.

"Nothing special," I said.

"What are you doing around here?"

"Nothing special," I said again, staring at her injured eye. A man was behind this. Women don't get into bar fights. And no one falls down on their eye. The eye is in a concave area of the skull, designed by evolution for protection against accidents. If someone has a black eye, you can be pretty sure it was intentionally provided by someone else's fist, or maybe a stray elbow in a pickup basketball game. She didn't look like she had taken up the sport after her years of cheerleading.

She gave me my total. I paid in cash. She handed me the change and our fingers grazed, the feeling of another's flesh that she got every time she handed out change, which she then scrubs away with the hand sanitizer prominently displayed on her cash register.

Yet it was a different feeling for me because these were *her* fingers, and the blood inside them was the same blood I saw upon dark pavement. She caught me looking at her black eye and she looked away, the punctuation at the end of our brief interaction. I could have left then, but she touched her face in a nervous fashion and I caught a glimpse of her wedding ring. The diamond was tiny, which in a strange way made me feel good.

"How long have you worked here?" I asked. I already knew it couldn't have been long.

"Not long," she said. "My husband took a new job. What do you do?"

"Good question," I said, and tried to laugh off the fact I had no answer. No customers needed checking out, but she looked nervous.

"Will you get in trouble if we talk?" I said.

"I don't know," she said, brushing her hair away again.

"I'm new at this. I'd rather not get chatty on the job, at least not yet. Sorry."

I scooped up my bags and headed for the door. "Great to see you," I said.

"I get my dinner break soon," she said. "If you don't mind waiting. Or maybe we can just—"

"No, it's fine, I'll wait," I said.

I went to the snack-bar area and sat in an uncomfortable, swiveling chair bolted to the same trunk that held up the table. I bought a soda with pocket change and refilled it three times with something different at the fountain. No one else showed up at the snack bar. A single Wal-Mart employee hung out behind the counter—a young guy who changed out expired hot dogs and occasionally wiped down a glass surface.

After twenty minutes of steady checkout activity, Rae turned off her register light and left her post. She walked past the snack area and gave me a little half wave. "I just have to get my food," she said. "Be right back." She brushed her hair away from her eye again. I got a refill and when I turned around, she was sitting at my table, carefully removing a sandwich from a Ziploc bag.

The sandwich was amazing for its neatness. Neither meat nor cheese hung over the border of the crust of the white bread. The entire works was carefully spliced into two, perfectly equal triangles. She picked up a half and took a bite and you could see the entire contents of the sandwich, like a split pig in a biology class—two slices of cheap bologna, a slice of cheese that came from a standalone cellophane wrapper, and a light slathering of mayo.

"Where did you go, Dale?" she asked. "I thought you might have left school after it all happened. We heard you got hurt bad, but you never know what to believe. Someone said you lost your hand, which I can see was the rumor mill doing what it does. Then I saw you listed with your graduating class."

"Senior year was pretty much optional, credit wise," I said. "I couldn't go back."

"I went back," she said. "I didn't want to, but I'm glad I did. I looked for you."

"Why?" I said. "I was there at the end. I cared about her. I would have been a constant reminder."

"I was her sister, Dale," she said. "I see her all the time. It'll never stop. At least now when I see her, we just smile at each other."

She stared at her sandwich and took a contemplative bite. She looked upset.

"Let's change the subject," I said. "How about college. You go to college?"

"I started," she said. "Then I met my husband."

"Your husband," I said. "Who is he? Is he from our school?"

"I need to get back to work," she said.

"How long do you work tonight?"

"Until ten," she said. I caught her twisting her wedding ring with her thumb.

"Do you need a ride home or anything? Or maybe we can just hang out and talk more somewhere."

"I'm married. I can't hang out with you," she said.

"Right. Sorry." Embarrassed, I busied myself throwing away my soda and picking up my grocery bags.

She put the remainder of her sandwich in the Ziploc bag and sealed it with patient grace.

"I walk to work," she said. "I like the walk, so I don't need a ride, but if you're outside at ten I guess I can't stop you from walking with me."

I dropped my groceries off, took my second shower of the day, and searched for my least-wrinkled shirt. I wanted her to see the change of clothes and smell the soap. I wanted her to know it was important to me, because it was. Just seeing her had made it quite clear the last few years were a crucial mistake—in trying to distance myself from the death that Clint wrought that night, I had essentially executed the survivors. Of course I'd never see Regina again, but it was my fault I never saw anyone else, including Mack. Sure we talked on the phone, but the occasional phone call means the friendship is already brain dead—the only thing left is to pull the plug for good.

I squeezed my regenerated hand—a reminder that beating myself up wasn't so simple. If I returned in perfectly healed condition, it wouldn't have felt right. The questions would get uncomfortable when my condition didn't match any reports or rumors. I was robbed of the injuries I'd earned that night. I needed those scars. I needed physical damage to reconcile it mentally, to tell myself I'd paid the proper price for letting Regina die. The pain of loneliness was all I ever knew. It was the only pain I knew how to magnify.

I sat outside the Wal-Mart next to the Sam's Choice soda machine. I listened to the buzz and clap of the automatic doors opening and closing as shoppers funneled in and out of the store. People went in empty-handed and came out pushing carts loaded with plastic bags with handles that rattled in the wind, the same way that oxygen-starved cells filtered through a beating heart.

Raeanna emerged just past ten with her blue vest neatly hung over her left forearm. She paused and looked around for me. I jumped up to meet her.

"You actually came," she said.

"What can I say, I love to walk. Been doing it my whole life."

I started to cross the parking lot. "Not that way," she said. She led us behind the Wal-Mart, where it was considerably darker without the streetlights that pocked the parking lot. I could make out a dumpster and a docking area for the trucks. She led me across a grassy median behind the store and we ended up on an access road.

"You go this way, it takes you deeper into the country. Back roads," she said, pointing west. "This way is parallel to the main drag and it takes you into the residential areas on that side of town."

"You walk this by yourself at night?" I asked. I could see lights in the distance from the residences she was talking about, but the road itself had no adjacent lighting for the entire stretch. On a cloudy night, you would need the sound of your own shoes to let you know if you were on the road or had wandered off. Luckily, we had a few open patches of starlight to help us along.

"I think when I walk," she said. "Quiet is good. What, you afraid of the dark?" She took my hand. I legitimately lost my breath. It took me a few awkward seconds to say, "Of course not."

"Too bad," she said, and let my hand go.

We walked. I had to slow my normal pace to match hers. I secretly hoped she was sandbagging to give us more time together. We endured a long silence at the start of the march before she said, "Whatever happened to Mack Tucker?"

"He's finishing up at Carbondale," I said, leaving out his quest for reality-show fame.

"Good for him," she said, but she was really saying shame on us for not completing college. "He was always . . . interesting."

"That's a polite way of saying he was a prick," I said, and we both laughed.

"Regina had a soft spot for him. Lots of girls did."

"Did you?"

"Not at all," she said. "He was one of those talkers. Always keeping his lips moving so he didn't have to spend a quiet moment considering just how boring he really was. No offense, I know he's your friend."

"You might have summed it up perfectly," I said.

"Well, the quiet, smart kids usually do good for themselves—do you have a lucky lady in your life?"

"Just you," I said, hoping it would sound clever. Instead, it sounded inappropriate and desperate, a reminder of how lucky she was to have survived Regina.

"Dale! That's not the shy boy that I remember."

"Sorry, I didn't mean it like that."

"Of course you meant it like that."

We approached the cluster of houses. Porch lights and streetlights converged as we emerged from the shadows. It felt like waking up from a dream.

"I don't live far from here," she said.

"I'll walk you to your door," I said.

"You can't," she said. "Are you forgetting that I'm married?"

"Why did you hold my hand, then?" I said.

"I'm sorry about that. I just didn't want you to be scared."

"I'm not scared of the dark," I said with a self-deprecating chuckle.

"I'm not talking about the dark."

She took my hand again. My once-broken ribs tightened around my lungs and I got a little dizzy. "Are you okay, Dale? I mean really okay?"

"What happened to your eye?" I asked.

She let go of my hand again.

"I fell," she said.

"I know what that's code for."

"I can walk the rest of the way."

"You didn't even tell me his name. You haven't said anything about him at all."

"Do you really want to know?"

"I do now," I said. "Tell me about your husband. About marriage. Do you have any kids or anything?"

She walked away from me. I followed her, hoping she'd turn around and invite me back into lockstep with her. She didn't. She stared at the sidewalk as we got closer to her street. Finally, she stopped at a corner and turned to me.

"You need to go," she said. "I'm not mad or anything, but you just have to."

"Can we walk again sometime?"

"Yes," she said.

"I just can't walk you any farther than this?"

"You're already too far," she said, looking around. "If he sees us—"

"It's okay. I understand."

She thanked me for the company and turned down Marshall Lane. I waited, then peeked around the corner. I saw her shadow moving in the distance, walking faster than she had before. I wanted to follow her home. I wanted to go inside and meet her shitty husband and let him know that if he touched her ever again, I'd make him pay. I wanted her fear and my fear to disappear. I wanted to see her eyes again without the marring of bruises and swelling. But most of all, I wanted her to hold my hand just one more time.

Instead, I headed back to my car. I slept and dreamt of kissing a blue-eyed girl, as I often did, but for the first time I didn't know which twin I was kissing.

ELEVEN

FRANK WINSTON WAS THE PROPRIETOR OF THE BIGGEST crematorium in the tri-county area. He insisted on speaking in person, and said nothing specific over the phone. I took this to mean I had struck black-market gold.

Frank was a big guy, thick-shouldered with a salt-and-pepper mustache and a handshake that could crack a stone. He didn't know how I could come up with body parts, and didn't care to know.

Turns out that tissue is one of the last bootlegging frontiers in America, poorly regulated and improperly structured. Guys like Frank knew how to turn a profit, and they weren't hard to find. I just cold-called funeral homes and crematoriums, asking if I they knew how I could sell body parts. Most conversations turned incredibly uncomfortable. Frank kept it short, cutting me off. I thought he was a nonstarter, just blowing me off. However, he called me right back from a different number and, after making it clear I was serious, we decided to meet in person.

He took me at my word when I told him I could supply a steady stream of body parts, and he was more than excited to take a piece off the top in order to broker the exchanges. He chatted me up in immense detail, proud of his business, sounding more like a polished CEO than a black-market peddler.

I can only imagine he was comfortable enough to reveal layers of his operation because I had a cooler packed with ice, and inside were the dismembered toes from my right foot. Probably not worth much, but enough for him to know I meant business.

And yes, it hurt like a bitch.

One weekend a month, he had a diener with connections come in to do some disarticulation, which sounds fancy, but I got Winston to explain it a bit more simply: he found out he could make extra money selling off body parts from dead bodies he was supposed to incinerate, so he had a pathology assistant come in once a month to chop the bodies up and get the parts ready for the highest bidder. Dieners are the grunts of the medical world. They often cut apart the dead bodies during autopsies, as the pathologist gets to keep his hands clean while he talks into a tape recorder, weighs the organs, and reports the results. Since dieners aren't doctors and don't get paid like them, they're always on the lookout for an extra buck, and one corpse could be taken apart for about fifteen grand for the sum of its parts.

None of these parts went to people. They went to companies. A knee to the orthopedist medical summit, some bone to a tissue company that sterilizes it and uses it for its supply of bone paste, a foot to the medical research company looking to attract the best podiatrists in the country to a convention.

To the body-parts industry, I'm a gold mine. Demand for dead bodies overwhelms supply. I'm an income stream without the need to fabricate medical records or death certificates. I'm the legit way to get parts, as opposed to handing a grieving family an urn full of Kingsford charcoal that they think is Uncle Ted.

Guys like Frank have a big drum full of ashes stashed in the crematorium. If he cut and sold a body, he could give the family a scoop of ashes and they'd never know the difference. Ashes contain nothing that can be traced—the DNA is destroyed just as thoroughly as the flesh itself.

We discussed all the details surrounded by the comforting environs of the Winston-Day Funeral Home. His office was adorned with flowers and soft colors highlighted by ambient lighting. We sat at his desk, wooden but slick, a too-clean and glossy surface where it would be tough to pick up coins. A brochure holder displayed company literature, a picture of an every-family with a slug line that proclaimed, "Helping you honor life."

He asked me about what I could acquire in my supply chain while I looked at the front of the brochure. "Do you have a price list?" I asked.

He seemed surprised by this, but started naming off parts and their value, from memory. The brochure said, "Because your family means so much." He started rattling off the prices from top to bottom.

"A skull with the teeth in it, a little over a grand."

Family members had sat in this very chair. He would talk in hushed tones, no doubt, about the peace and tranquility they were buying for their investment.

"Five hundred for a shoulder. Skin is a flat ten bucks per square inch. A hand with the forearm attached is about four hundred."

So this is what it feels like to deal drugs or run hookers, I thought. To make money off of ruining people.

"Pull out a good coronary artery, fifteen hundred. A foot is about two to four hundred."

These were not impressive dollar amounts, considering the time and pain I'd have to endure. But it was either this or the gun, selling off parts or dying all at once.

"If the torso is already eviscerated, it's worth a lot less, but it's easier to come by." He paused and leaned closer, as if to tell me a secret. "The fresh stuff is where the real money's at. Blood, tissue, a fresh set of eyeballs to tinker with . . . If all you've got are toes, I'm afraid you're not going to make much money."

He winked, smiled, and I battled the urge to jump across the desk and choke him. Probably would have, if my foot were capable of jumping. Underneath the gauze of my fresh dismemberment, I already felt the deep, destructive itch that comes with my special healing.

"So what's a kidney worth?"

He leaned back in his chair, looking a bit uncomfortable.

"From a cadaver?"

"Live," I said. "Ready for transplant. Fresh from a healthy donor."

"I'm not the guy for that," he said. "You're talking about heavier shit than I dabble in. You're talking organ brokerage, some real dirty stuff. Cutting up bums from overseas for peanuts to give their parts to rich donors."

"How much?" I asked again.

"Depends. A bum in Brazil can sell a kidney for six grand," he said, "but that's because he doesn't know any better. But the operation? Rich-ass recipients pay around two-fifty. The broker who sets it all up and makes the connections makes an assload. He gets the recipient a mini-vacation, where they come home with a healthy kidney inside of them and a new lease on life. They don't check for that shit at customs, you know? But there's a reason it's done in shit countries. The situation can get pretty hot."

"So can you get me a broker?" I grabbed one of his brochures. "I can call you in a couple weeks."

"If you're looking to sell your own kidney, I don't want to get involved in that," he said. "There's no heat on the small stuff. The bigger stuff takes a broker with more balls than me." He walked by me, not making eye contact, presumably to show me the door.

"You can call somebody, so call them. Tell the broker it's all you can eat. I can get him a steady supply of stateside organ donors, and not just kidneys. No need to screw with permissions or medical records. I can tap the mother lode." Was I sure my organs would regenerate like everything else? No, but in situations like this, you bluff or you fail.

Winston thought about my offer for a long time. He stood up, approached me, and snapped the brochure away from me.

"I noticed you were walking like a guy who just lost his toes in some sort of freak . . . accident."

I shrugged. "Athlete's foot."

"Toes are worthless, and that's got to hurt like a bitch."

"You in or out?"

"What's my cut?"

"Reasonable. Depends on price, but expect a wedge of the action. I'm a fair guy."

"I'll have to make a few calls," he said.

"If that's the case, I need about five hundred for those toes."

"They aren't worth that."

"I'm worth that," I said. "Like I said, all you can eat."

"You're a weird little fuck, you know that?"

"And you're in the healing and consoling business. Sure."

I left, determined not to limp, the fire from my missing toes forcing me to bite deep into my cheek.

Toes, fingers, ears, tonsils. They had all returned. But organs? Knowing my luck, the only commodity I could home-grow that was worth a shit would be the things that wouldn't grow back. Only one way to find out.

I pulled out my cell phone and I heard Winston behind me.

"Wait," he said. He handed me a white envelope. "Am I lighting this money on fire, kid?"

"I don't think so," I said.

"That's not the most encouraging answer, but a gamble is a gamble. There's three hundred in there, not five. More than fair."

"Like I said, I'm a fair guy," I said. More important, it was enough to pick up a hefty dinner tab and fill up a cart with some groceries.

Mack arrived the next night, looking tanned and weathered, his hair cut shorter than ever before, his undersized shirt no match for his thickened biceps.

"Sampsonite!"

He had a backpack slung over his right shoulder, making it clear he meant to stay a night or two. I shook his hand and he pulled me into a half hug.

We ate at the closest chain steakhouse, which to us was a fancy-ass restaurant. Dinner started out with small talk and beers that went down fast. We kept refills coming—he knew I was picking up the check and I simply needed the drinks, knowing that eventually we'd have to get down to the things we never talked about once we ran out of the things we always talked about.

That moment occurred when he said, "You healed up good."

"Seems that way," I said, making a fist, then opening it.

"When were you going to tell me about it?" Mack asked.

"When you noticed," I said. "But you've never been the detail-oriented type. It's not your hand, after all."

"I noticed," he said, "at your mom's funeral."

"I wore the bandage at her funeral," I said.

"I'm talking after," Mack replied. "When everyone was leaving. I sat in my truck and hated how I left you. I mean, I hugged you and all, I told you I was sorry, but there always felt like something more to say, something to make you stop hurting. You stayed with her. By the time I got close, you were on your knees, your bare hands were pressed against her headstone, sobbing your ass off. You remember?"

Like anyone could forget a moment like that. "You left, then," I said.

"I didn't know what to make of it, what to say. I knew your hand was fucked up, but I saw it healed and whole, plain as day. Figured I might have been fucked up in the head myself or something, but seeing you now, it all came back."

"I should have told you," I said. "At least you."

"Your hand ain't my business," he said. "Truth is, I didn't want to know. Figured that God gave you the Reset button while he gave me the middle finger. Won't be the first time. Fuck that dude.

"So," he added, sucking the swill out of the bottom of his bottle, "is it time to tell me about it, or we just going to get fucked up and bang some chicks tonight?"

It was time. I told him about the hand, the ear, the tonsils. How I cut them off, and waited, and tested myself. Finally, "I'm about broke and the reason I'm limping is because I sold my toes."

Takes a lot to crack Mack Tucker's veneer, but he went bug-eyed. It took him a long time to digest that one.

"Just to try it out," I said. "They'll buy anything. But the big money is in organs—I'm not sure about those. I need a doctor's help, so that's why I'm here. I've got a guy that's going to knock out a kidney. At least, I think he will. If it doesn't grow back, no big deal, I can live with one. But if it does? I can cash one of those fuckers out for six figures or more. Set me up for life."

"Yeah, if life is a shit house, fucking ramen noodles, and ketchup," he said. "Have you really thought this through?"

"I guess."

"No, you haven't. You're a gold mine and you're sifting through the wrong parts. The hard parts."

I had already thought about what he was getting at, and didn't like the choice. "I don't want to live in a lab," I said. "It's my body; I'll portion myself out as I see fit."

"Do you get sick?"

"Haven't since I can remember."

"But you're not invincible."

"My limp should tell you that. I'm just *repeatedly vincible.* Let's just eat, okay?"

We ate. Actually, we wolfed the steaks down, tearing chunks of flesh from the bone before the knife was even through with the cut, pausing occasionally to take a swig of light beer.

"You look good, too, though," I said, breaking the silence. "Healed up and fit."

"Steroids," he said, waving his hand. "My shoulder is crap. I can barely work out. I lift more syringes than weights, but I can lift enough to get myself by. You'd be surprised how far a decent tan, a smile, and a big dick will get you."

"How far is that?"

He took it as an insult. We both knew a reality-show wannabe/college dropout with no job was just as pathetic as a regenerating parts–selling food-stamp recipient, only slightly less interesting.

"So after all this shit, you ended up with the talent," he said with a smile.

At this, I laughed. "I don't . . . do anything."

"That's the problem. If I could rebuild myself, man, what I would do."

"What *would* you do?"

He tapped his shoulder.

"Don't tell yourself that," I said.

"Why not?"

"Because you know you wouldn't have gone to the show. That shit was a high school fantasy. The gunshot gave you an easy excuse to whine and cry and say why you didn't make it. Don't make that mistake. You got lucky, having it taken from you before it could disappoint you."

"Well, fuck you, too," he said, and managed to pair it with a half-twisted smirk. "You've sort of got the right of it. But you don't get it. It's about the trying, about the ride. Sometimes almost getting there is just as good, you know? Having the shot, talking for years about how close I got. Now what am I? A survivor."

"That's not so bad."

"It can be. Look at you."

He saw right through me and he didn't even know that I handled my gun every single day without having the guts to shoot myself. That I wondered what morning I'd wake up with enough strength to finally fire it, to finally deserve it.

"You always had the talent in that brain of yours," he continued. "You know, when I was recovering, when it was all over I figured this saved you. I figured that if it didn't happen and we went on normal-like, you would waste your own dreams on mine, and try to be an agent or something, when deep down you deserved to be a doctor or a scientist or something important. Now here we are. You've got that brain and it's broken down by God knows what. Pity? Pain? You can actually, legitimately regrow parts of your body. You're a fuckin' miracle superhero badass motherfucker and instead of doing anything remotely important you're selling your toes? You're more than this."

"I'm moving up to kidneys." It was all I could think to say.

"You're more than this," he repeated.

"You just want me to go somewhere and do something so I can take you with me," I said, a bitter thing that I instantly regretted.

He sat there for a good long time and finished his beer. When the waitress came over, he smiled and handed her a folded-up bill. "Keep the change," he said, and winked. She smiled at him. Girls always did.

"I said I'd get the bill."

"You said enough." He got up. "You're right, you know. I need you to take me somewhere. I got nowhere else to go. Not even down."

He left without saying good-bye.

"You have type O blood," Doc Venhaus said. I had gone through various tests, a barrage of visits and needle pricks and questions and scrapes. I'd ask about my kidney and he'd dodge the question, just one more test, one more thing to check, we'll talk about this later. Finally I was in his office for some results. "Type-O," he said again, tossing the clipboard onto the counter-top, as if to punctuate this point, which made no sense to me.

"And?"

He sat down, loosening his collar at long last. All the recent visits had been after-hours, done in privacy after he endured a long day of sniffling kids and wheezing old people and hypo-chondriac soccer moms.

"Your blood has no antigens. You're what we call a universal donor. Compatible with all blood types. Spotless general health, not one flag. And indeed, it appears that your tonsils have regenerated."

"So what now?" I asked.

"I don't know," he said. "I kept thinking I'd find some-thing wrong with you."

He got up and stretched. "You hungry?" He brought in some drug-rep sandwiches and a six-pack of light beer. He took off his coat. I dug into the sandwich—turkey and Swiss again. Must have been a Doc favorite. The beer was cold. He was quiet and didn't eat.

"Are we going to test out my kidney or not?" I asked.

"I don't know," he said. "That's the best answer I can give you right now."

"I'll go to someone else."

"You've got to be careful, Dale," he said. "I'd almost bet you'll regrow the kidney, as nuts as it sounds. The small amount of tissue I removed regenerated, so there's no reason, logi-cally, for me to doubt those results."

"So why won't you do it?"

"It's not right," he said. "The reasons aren't right for either of us."

"Why don't you think my reasons are right?" I asked.

"Your gift can help people," he said. "It'll go to waste if you use it like this, and we'll both be at fault."

"Thank you for wasting my time," I said, and got up to leave.

"Will you come by my place, Dale?" he asked. "Let me sleep on this a few days, then I'll call you. You come over, I'll feed you and we'll talk about it."

"About what?"

"All the shit that needs talked about," he said with a wink.

The toe money didn't buy me a lot of time, but Doc was a careful man and I sensed a good nature in him. He didn't rush into my talents and didn't seem greedy to keep them to himself. At least, not yet.

"You've got three days," I said, "or I have to walk."

TWELVE

I GOT TO THE WAL-MART JUST BEFORE TEN AND TOOK UP my post near the soda machine. Raeanna shared her typical work schedule during our walk—she pulled mostly two-to-ten shifts, Saturday through Wednesday. I imagined she'd walk out any minute, see me, smile, and we'd head for the access road. The night was perfect for walking that road, cloudless and bright with a mild breeze that would help ward off my flop sweat.

At twenty past the hour, I thought she might be working late. Another ten minutes and I feared she'd slipped out a back door to avoid the possibility of my presence. I went inside to check. When the near-mummified greeter offered me a cart, I waved her off, trying to act polite in spite of my pounding pulse.

Checkout lanes one, two, and three were empty. Four, five, and six were lit up. A black woman, an old lady, and a teenage boy handled those posts. The rest of the aisle lights were dark, but I peered into them anyway, waiting for the customer service desk to come into view. A short, fat woman with black curls and too-big glasses stepped up to the counter. Her name tag said MARTHA in blue, bold letters.

"Can I help you?" she said without looking at me.

"Is Raeanna working today?"

"No," she said.

"Was she supposed to?"

"Look, sir, I'm not supposed to tell you that kind of stuff. You related to her or something?"

"Yes," I said. "Did she call in sick? Was she scheduled to work?"

"If you're related to her," Martha said, "maybe you should call and ask her."

"I'm not related to her," I said. "You saw her black eye. Right?"

This got her attention.

"I don't think she fell to get that black eye. I think she might be in trouble. What about yesterday? Did she work yesterday?"

"Day off," Martha said.

"And today, she didn't call in sick, did she? I bet she didn't. You can't explain new bruises when you're supposedly home eating chicken noodle soup."

"I didn't take the call," she said. "I didn't hear firsthand, but she didn't show for the start of her shift. She called around three to let the manager know she got in a fender bender on her way to work. She said she wasn't hurt bad or anything, just a little bruised, but too shaken up to work. Something like that."

"Thank you," I said.

"She usually walks to work," Martha said. "Doesn't she?"

I nodded. "Her address," I said. "I know she lives on Marshall Lane, I just forget her house number."

Martha looked around, as if fearing surveillance. "I'd have to look it up," she said.

"I can wait," I said.

"If it's not on Marshall Lane, I'm not telling you."

"Deal," I said. She left the desk and came back after a few excruciating minutes.

"Four hundred," she said. "Four hundred Marshall Lane."

The shrubs at 400 Marshall Lane were neglected and had a case of botanical bedhead, with wiry branches poking out in haphazard directions. A gold knocker rested in the middle of a dirty white door. Two peeling, ivory-white pillars held up a gray porch, and the mat on that porch said WELCOME!

The paint on the porch was bubbled and worn away, leaving patches of bare wood. The welcome mat was smeared with grease, and a pair of black boots with fraying laces sat beside it.

I took a deep breath and prepared to knock.

"Don't," Raeanna said, startling me. She sat on the porch swing, hidden in the dark eaves of the overhang. "He's home."

I leaned in, trying to get a look at her.

"Are you okay?"

"It's my fault," she whispered. "I never should have walked with you. I'm a married woman."

"It's not your fault," I said, kneeling beside her. Her hand rested on her thigh, and I put mine over hers. She yanked hers away. I couldn't see her full face in the darkness, but I caught enough light to see the swelling in her right cheek.

"You have to leave," she said. "If he comes out here, we're in trouble. He can probably hear us, anyway. See us. I don't know how he saw me with you the other night. I think he's watching right now."

I put my hand gently on her cheek and she let it stay there. This time, she put her hand over mine.

"If he's watching—"

"He's not watching," I whispered. "You're safe as long as I'm here."

"We're not safe," she said.

"Do you have someplace you can go?"

"I'm waiting for my friend," she said. "He's going to let me stay with her tonight. Says he needs to cool off."

"You can't come back."

"I don't have anywhere else to go, Dale. And he'd find us."

Us. What a wonderful word. I knew what I had to do.

"He's coming," she said. I'd heard it too—his heavy footfalls bounding down the stairs, approaching the front door. I wanted to kiss her, for him to see me being all the things he could never be, but it wasn't the time. I jumped over the rail and huddled in the crease of darkness between houses.

I heard the front door open. No one spoke. I heard a car pull up and saw headlights.

"Go on, then," he said in a hoarse voice. I heard the idle of an engine. I waited until I heard a car door open and close, then I heard the front door slam shut.

I took a deep breath. I went home to prepare myself for what I had to do.

When I got home, I sat at the computer and stared down the search box for a long time. Finally, I found my hands steady enough to type.

"Human regeneration."

According to the search results, I had to be part salamander. Salamander limbs are not that different from ours. Sure, the skin is a bit slimier, but there's still skin and blood. Cut off a salamander's tail, and a new one grows back. Same with his tiny legs or arms, same thing with some of his tiny vital organs. Except the heart. The heart does not grow back.

So maybe there were others like me, maybe even a long time ago, primitive humans whose hands and arms would grow back again and again until tribesmen put a spear through their heart, finally and mercifully putting them down. Maybe these ancestors became the root of vampire stories—it would only make sense that regenerating people might crave or need human blood.

But vampires were cool, and maybe I was giving myself too much credit.

The search results also revealed that many animals, including humans, can regenerate as embryos. Their healing time and durability is incredible when they're young. Over the course of development, the healing slows. After a while, scar tissue becomes the result, not new limbs. The inherent healing that these animals have in the initial stages of life naturally dissipates, leaving scientists obsessed with figuring out how to spark human regeneration. And make no mistake about it— they were obsessively searching for a spark. Articles abounded on the "key" to human regeneration—in fingernails, in starfish, in little macrophages and prions and other words I didn't understand.

When I finally made it past those results, I called Wal-Mart and asked for Raeanna Carpenter, and got a puzzled, "Who?" from the clerk who picked up the phone, who immediately said, "Do you mean Raeanna Stillson?"

You're more than this, Mack had said. *It'll go to waste if you use it like this,* Doc had said. Every superhero badass motherfucker needs to start somewhere, and I was starting with Raeanna.

I continued blazing through the Internet.

I learned that Harold, as a domestic abuser, had an eighty

percent chance of having a personality disorder. He had poor self-esteem and poor impulse control. The escalation potential of this violence was staggering. Repeating his physical abuse of Raeanna was almost guaranteed.

Raeanna, suffering from battered-person syndrome or learned helplessness, was likely in denial. Her perception of Harold as omniscient was indicative of her condition. So she was blaming herself for the abuse. All of this, combined with the loss of her sister, put her at great risk for post-traumatic stress disorder, if she wasn't suffering from it already.

Mack was an aggressive narcissist, full of glibness, superficial charm, and grandiose self-worth. He was cunning and manipulative. But I give him a lot of credit for at least wanting to graduate to acquired situational narcissism, which is brought on by fame and celebrity.

I, meanwhile, was still suffering from survival guilt, and a yet-to-be-named regenerative disorder that most people would not perceive as a disorder at all. In fact, my regenerative abilities would make me a god in many cultures.

The flood of the Internet was pouring into my living room. I forced myself to eat something with carbohydrates because soon I would need the energy—a street fight can exhaust a person in as little as thirty seconds and reaction times are faster in humans when they are nutritionally balanced. I needed to restore the glucose levels in my body so I'd have readily available energy for the fight.

Another street-fighting tip: choose a weapon that would not generate suspicion or violate any local, state, or federal laws.

I also found that survival guilt is treated professionally when a therapist makes clear alternative, hopeful views of a given situation. These views then make the sufferer believe that the death was not their fault, and they can mourn and continue with life. Simple enough. Who needs a mental-health professional when one can Google the answers and self-medicate?

The alternative to loneliness is to not be alone. The hopeful view of my situation is that because I have little to lose, I am the perfect person to carry out this mission.

I went into the kitchen and took the brand-new toaster out of the box. This was my weapon. I put a note on the fridge.

The next time you read this, you will be a hero.

Harold answered the door. Black hair, wet from a shower, stuck to his forehead.

"Is Raeanna home?" I asked, wanting his twisted mind stained with suspicion, the best kind of torture I could imagine for a man of his ilk.

"No," he said. If she was right and he had seen us together, he didn't recognize me. His eyebrows dropped and his face tightened. "Who are you?"

Harold was a tall but not imposing man, his skin pale and slack, the sagging flesh below his eyes the color of storm clouds. We might have had a competitive scrap, but the element of surprise is too great an advantage. Another advantage is that I have been hit before, so the threat of violence held no fearful sway over me.

And I had a weapon. I swung the toaster by a thick handful of wound cord. The corner of the toaster crashed into his cheek first, a blunt cutting edge that inflicted maximum damage, dropping him to the floor. He clutched the wound, blood spurting between his fingers. I stood over him as he recoiled, then took another swing. The flat side of the toaster mashed the top of his head, sending toaster parts flying, leaving me holding nothing but a frayed cord.

Harold cried out, curled in the fetal position, muttering "Please" through his blood-stained hands.

I knelt down and drove a hard fist into his midsection. Instinct caused him to drop his hands down to protect his middle, and I looked into his ravaged face. The cut went from ear level to an inch above his chin. Blood decorated the room in glistening, abstract squirts.

"You won't find this toaster test in *Consumer Reports*, will you Harold?" I punched him in the lung to let him know an answer wasn't necessary.

"Two things," I said in a harsh whisper. "Never touch her again, and when you go back to work and people ask what happened to your face, tell them you fell."

I backpedaled toward the door, keeping my eye on him in case he mustered the energy to jump up and mount a reprisal. I backed right into the coffee table in the middle of the living room, and heard the telltale rattle of pill bottles. Lots of them. They rolled around at my feet. Was Rae sick?

Harold was still moaning, clutching his broken face.

I stooped, picking up two bottles in my right hand, looking at them just long enough to see the name of the medication, something with an x in it, which wasn't very helpful. All medicines seemed to have x's, y's, and z's in the name. I turned the bottles until I saw Harold's name, but the more interesting name was right above it—Dr. A. Venhaus.

I thought of taking the bottles, but stealing prescription meds was an unnecessary risk. I dropped them and headed out the door, breaking into a sprint. My movement was covered by dusk. I ran long and hard, waiting for my muscles to spasm and my lungs to burn. It never happened. I maintained my full sprinting speed all the way to my car, which I'd left in the Wal-Mart parking lot. I had sweat and I felt the lactic acid of

a long run, but it never hit me hard enough to slow down. I
didn't know if it was the adrenaline or if my regeneration as-
sisted with endurance.

Once home, my fleeting confidence gained traction. I pulled
out my revolver and checked the chamber. Six bullets. Blood
had dried black on my hands, almost matching the gunmetal.
I removed one shell, my reward for delivering justice to Harold Stillson. A tiny chance of survival. Six bullets felt so final,
having that one out, earning that empty chamber would make it
much easier to eat the muzzle and let 'er fly if the time came.
But that time felt further away, blurry even. I spun the chamber. Why stop? There were five more chambers to go. I put a
note on the fridge: *The meaning of life is practicing the will to live.*

THIRTEEN

YOU SHOULDN'T NEGOTIATE IN ENEMY TERRITORY, BUT there I was, sitting at the kitchen island at Doc Venhaus's house. We drank beer out of frosted glasses. Earlier in the evening, I met his wife, Lucille. He sold me as some local college student job-shadowing for a semester. Lucille was about ten years younger than he was, with a fake rack but a legitimate smile. I sensed both love and concern when she spoke of her husband.

His daughter, Samantha, was a couple years younger than me, blond and good-looking enough to have me staring at my shoes to avoid eye contact.

Doc grilled on the patio. We ate chicken and potatoes and corn on the cob. Samantha had that youthful distraction of having better things to do, not wanting to spend time at the dinner table. I had only witnessed this type of behavior on television, and seeing it in person plucked a string of regret inside of me. Jell-O came to mind. I'd eaten some Jell-O at Mom's deathbed. I kissed her good-bye with red lips and cherries on my breath, the last thing she ever smelled before the last bit of life and soul smuggled themselves out of her, riding a long, final exhale that wouldn't have blown out a candle.

After dinner, Sam's friends picked her up. She said bye to "Dad" and bye to "Lucy" so I knew then that Lucille was a stepmother.

After some customary post-dinner small talk, Lucille said she was going to bed to read for a spell. She actually said "spell." I wondered if maybe they were all putting me on, trying to show me some wholesome family that deserved the fame and fortune that would come with Dr. Allen Venhaus's amazing discoveries, thanks to my miracle tissue and the thing he was presumably looking to score that evening—my cooperation.

To be fair, I liked the guy and I'd accepted the invitation knowing damn well I might have to tell a man who could have been my friend to fuck off. He had an earthy appeal to him. He talked like a guy, peppered in the occasional swearword, and he was plain about things. He was the proverbial "kind of guy I'd like to have a beer with," so there we were, testing it out, one beer at a time.

The sun went down. We wandered outside to the patio, where I could smell the aromatic, fatty smoke from the now-cool grill. A swarm of insects danced around the patio light. We sat in wicker chairs with crickets chirping in the distance. Humidity clung to the beer glasses. Lightning bugs winked around us.

The black outdoors, waiting to be filled with the words of men. I thanked him for dinner.

"Have you thought it all through, son?" he said.

So here it was. Small talk had smoldered for days, and he was done with it.

"Nice night out here," I said. "I like your place."

"So let's say I take out your kidney and it comes back. Like your tonsils. What then?"

"A fire pit would be sweet out here."

"I'm not offering to do it. I'm just asking," he said.

"You lived here long?"

He took a long, slow drink of his beer. Three gulps, each one sounding a hollow chirp I could hear in the dark silence.

"Some people think things happen for a reason. You one of them?" he asked.

"No. Things happen *because* of a reason."

"A cause-effect man. Explain your little gift to me then."

"Nature fucked up," I said. "Some kids get three arms or a cleft palate. I got a superpower," I said.

"You hit the birth lottery then, kid."

"Sure," I said, and finished my beer. "Can I get another one?"

"Not yet."

We sat drenched in quiet for a long time.

"I don't want to be a guinea pig," I said. "No experiments. I don't want to be some missing link. I just want to know if my kidneys will grow back."

"To sell one," he added. "Right?"

"No. To sell a bunch of them. To get the fuck out of here and take someone with me."

"Where?"

"Wherever she wants to go. Wherever's safe."

"You're quite the idealist."

He got up and went inside, and came back with two more beers. No glasses. Presentation time was over. We drank straight from the can.

"So you haven't thought this through," he said. "How much do you anticipate earning for a kidney?"

He knew the answer. I played along. "I'm thinking six figures," I said.

"A medical center would give you that and more to simply

study and test you, and it would be far safer. It's a better deal for you."

"So you got divorced?" I asked.

He drank to this, then glided past it.

"Plus you would be helping people. One kidney saves one person. There's sixty-three thousand people on the waiting list. Most of them are going to die waiting."

"The person I'm wanting to save isn't on that list."

"Kill two birds with one stone, then. They'll pay you. Start a bidding war if you want. Get an agent. Get confidentiality in writing. Whatever's going on inside of you is pure hope. You get that?"

"Whatever is inside of me only seems to wake up when I get cut or beat on. If that's hope, hope can go fuck itself."

"Sling your organs then. You heal, but you hurt. Organ removal isn't a wet kiss, and you want to repeat it . . . how many times?"

Being hospital property seemed like I was selling not only my body, but control of it. Living in a sterile room with chrome and that God-awful powder blue. "I still have to find out if my body can pump out a kidney."

"To hell with your kidney," he said. "For the record, I think things happen for a reason. I think God sent you to help a lot of people. Including me."

The moon played hide-and seek-behind fast-moving wisps of cloud. On the far horizon, blinks of lightning, but no thunder. Not yet.

He told his story without interruption. He talked slowly, carefully, a surgeon's talk, as if he could linger at the moment his life changed and make it different. The pieces of his story stacked up just-so, blocks of the unlikely building up, tearing out bits of his life to make room for their rise. But I was the most unlikely of all. I was the one who could make things right again.

🖤

After his residency, Doc settled down in Minnesota. He didn't say it was rural, but it felt that way—I imagined snow and wind and icy lakes and chains on everyone's tires. He was the only surgeon for miles around, and worked everything from car-crash trauma to tonsillectomies.

He got married. He had Samantha. He helped people get better, and people who knew him called him Doc. A doc is a friend—a doctor is a guy who does not appear to give a shit. I tabbed him as a doctor at first, but he was about as doc as a medical professional could be.

Then came the inevitable Big Regret that all men of a certain age seem to have, the girl with the bad gallbladder, Angie, twenty-two, skinny, with a whole cliché-filled life ahead of her. Gallbladder problems made me think of old, fat men, but it turns out that girls are six times more likely to get gallstones. Birth control increases the chances, as do multiple pregnancies, or rapid weight loss. Angie was a trifecta—pregnant, scared, lost the baby, went on birth control, crash dieted to lose the weight. Doc talked about her as if she were vibrant and perfect, as any older guy perceives someone in their golden twenties, I'm sure.

Gallstones are typically harmless, but Angie got a stone caught in her cystic duct. This is a cause for at least one-fourth of gallbladder removals.

"It was my job to know this," he said, and I knew the fuck-up was coming.

He had removed a gallbladder as a resident, but none since, and this surgery, this story, is what he invited me over to hear, I was sure of it. He talked about the surgery like Mack would have talked about one of his historic home runs—the kind of moment that nestles in and stays. The memory that you can smell and feel, it's not just runny paint on the canvas of a bored mind. It's there, whole, and can be delivered into your reality just like a newborn.

I could see the blue smock, the steel, the drapes and scalpels. I felt the cold, brown coating of disinfectant slathered on Angie's stomach. His scalpel blade blew through flesh and yellow fat, but dissected no farther. Modern medicine is not about the blade anymore. It's about cameras and vents and ports and carbon dioxide, and all the other white-noise details that he talked about, reciting them to himself more than me. I could barely follow until he slowed down and talked about the major risk—the main bile duct. The gallbladder and liver are quite the tag team. The bladder itself is tucked under the liver. Severing the main stalk to remove it means treading carefully around the main bile duct.

"Injury to the main bile duct causes death twenty percent of the time," Doc said. "The rest of the time, the bile backs up and destroys the liver. The damage is permanent."

He didn't have to say any more, but he did anyway. This was his penance. I waited for him to destroy the main bile duct.

He stripped and searched, trying to reveal the point of the gallbladder, which he could sever to remove it. A stem peeked.

"I stopped," he said. "I looked at the screen. Everything was as big as boiler-room piping. I announced where I would be cutting. No one said anything, they were just ready for me to get it over with and get them the hell out of there. It was all routine, you see? Lap choles are done hundreds of times over in hundreds of hospitals. It's batting practice for a surgeon. There was only one mistake to avoid." We stared out into the dark together. I waited without speaking. "I struck out in batting practice," he said finally, chilling me with the baseball metaphor.

He was just about to cut when he saw a bead of fat near the incision point. "This is not an issue unless it's obstructing the incision angle or vision, and it wasn't. Still, a jolt went through me that something might be wrong. But I went ahead anyway."

That bead of fat could have saved both him and Angie— had he flicked it away, had he been completely thorough, he might have exposed the rest of the area. He might have seen that the duct that he was cutting to remove the bladder had a fork in it, that the real and safe incision point was above the fork and he was about to not only injure the main bile duct but clip it off completely.

He was telling me this story in Grayson, Illinois, because he did not see the fork. He cut off the main bile duct and with it, he extracted his wife, Minnesota, his reputation, and untold thousands of dollars from his life. In its place, he transplanted the guilt of knowing Angie would be worse after the surgery than she was going in.

Surgeons make this mistake in one out of every two hundred lap choles, one-half of one percent. But it is still a severe surgical mistake, one that lured him into the realm of lawyers and malpractice and seeing a sick and yellow girl tethered to a waiting list of over sixteen thousand people wanting new livers. And out of that list, who knows how many died waiting.

Angie's image stood out for him among a host of Minnesota images—his wife packing, his now-empty office, the small-town talk making its rounds and coming back to him through the channels of his trusted friends. He was damaged.

Marked. Broke. Malpractice insurance drying up, bank account draining, daughter getting ridiculed at school. There is no privacy act for bad doctors. There are no heroes on television explaining that doctors make mistakes, that they are not infallible. We expect our doctors to be perfect. No mistakes. No confusion. Crucify the bad ones, and by bad . . . one mistake is all it takes.

His story had left him, rising and vanishing into the night air like a coil of smoke, leaving quiet behind. The night was cooler but still humid. The last swig of my beer was warm, the can sweaty. He waited.

"She died waiting for a liver," he said. "She was young, high on the list. But she was tough to match, and rejected her first transplant. Graft-host issues."

His cards were on the table and the hand was pity. He explained a few connections he had, old friends who could transplant organs with the lights off, guys with research credentials. But at the end of the day, this would be Dr. Allen Venhaus's discovery—the surgeon's mistake made right again by work the world would never forget.

In short, I had him.

"I have a connection working the black market for my kidney," I said. "I can call him and opt out. Tell him it's game over. Get on your team. We work on helping people, then. But on my terms, and first, I need something."

"I don't have any money," he said.

"Not money. Harold Stillson. He's a patient of yours."

Venhaus drew back and away from me, almost shrinking, the burden of medical privacy laws and ethical dilemmas swirling around us.

"I saw a lot of medication at his place. What's wrong with him?"

"You know I can't talk about this."

"You made a mistake once," I said. "Make another one and then we'll wipe the slate clean."

"Dear God, why?"

"Less to do with him and more to do with his wife. She's an old friend."

"This isn't going to work," he said. "Call your crooked funeral director. Winston. It's not a big town, you know. I know that piece of slime is who you're talking to. You're two of a kind."

I thanked him again for dinner and got silence in return. He stared off into the blackened woods, glued to his patio chair, and I went home. I wondered just how long Doc would sit there having a drink, thinking about that fork and where to cut, how many hours he had spent on that porch reliving that surgery,

Now he was thinking about my offer. All I had to do was wait. He'd convince himself it was his duty to do it, that it would be worth denting his honor one more time to deliver me to the world.

FOURTEEN

I GOT HOME AFTER DARK, MY LITTLE PIECE OF NEIGH-borhood morphing into a collection of porch lights and streetlights and shadows and the occasional bark of a dog.

As I approached my front steps, the back of my head took a blow that sounded like distant thunder, sending me face-first into the porch. Pain danced with dizziness, but before I could sort it all out, I was getting kicked with boots and struck with something—definitely not a toaster, but a club of some sort. Something hard and thick—enough to press skin and tissue into my bones, leaving tattoos of scorching hurt. The toes of boots found their way into my legs and sides, my ribs and neck.

Angled against the porch, one of those boots dropped like a piston, giving me an old-fashioned curb stomp, driving my mouth into the edge of the step, blowing out teeth and gums and lips. I felt jagged stalagmites of shattered tooth jutting from my jaw, the rest of the shards mixing with globs of blood and spit. "Clint?" I gurgled, knowing it wasn't him, couldn't be him, but his face is all that I saw in the dark.

Panting breath, club shots, kicks. The feel of bones giving way, of skin splitting, my head thrumming, my adrenal glands opening up like a boat throttle.

I tried to roll and flail, to no effect—it just revealed fresh places to get hit. I tried to curl up, fetal-like, but kicks and strikes cockroached their way into my softest areas. The goal might not have been to kill me, but it was a side effect my attacker wasn't worried about.

The violence stopped all at once—that serene calm that is made more still by the chaos of the storm that came before it.

"Tell them you fell," he said. I couldn't see him smiling, but I could hear the way it shaped his words.

I started crawling into the yard. I didn't have a destination, I was just moving to move, to feel like I was getting away. I had no idea if Harold was still lording over my fallen body, ready for more. The grass was wet with dew, slipping through my fingers. I got to the sidewalk by the closest streetlight, then I turned onto my side and reached for the cell phone in my pocket. The pain in my forearm crackled with each move of my fingers—a broken arm for sure.

Black fluid seeped from an oblong crack in the screen, the bubonic plague of a fractured display. Then a boot dropped, crushing the phone and most of my hand against the rough surface of the concrete, my fingers twisted and snapping like bubble wrap as he twisted his foot.

I figured the best thing to do at that point was just play dead. I went limp and closed my eyes. I scanned my body for pain, finding it everywhere, my brain throwing its hands up and saying, "Fuck picking a spot; you're totaled."

Observant, I heard fading footsteps. The clop of running boots. Would he tell Rae about this? Maybe I would die here, on this sidewalk, a noble death dealt out because I couldn't stand her having a black eye.

So I closed my eyes and waited for something or nothing to descend upon me.

The fog of sleep lifted. Maybe I was emerging into an after-life. The secrets of the universe would be mine.

Cold steel surrounded me—smooth tile, jars on the countertops, no clutter. Each heartbeat was a beacon that lit up spots of pain inside of me.

Maybe it was heaven. Maybe God was a doctor, and we would die and wake up in His care, and He would fix us up and then we would get our "Welcome to Heaven" party, complete with a smoked pig and barely dressed girls and Jesus making water into wine and beer and Hawaiian punch.

But this wasn't heaven, it was just an all-purpose medical room, and a vaguely familiar one at that.

A big piss burned in my abdomen. I wanted to move, but I was swollen and sluggish, my blood feeling as thick as used motor oil.

"Hey," I said, a whisper at first, my throat full of rust and croak. With subsequent tries I gained some throat traction. Louder, but not loud. I banged on the side rails of the cot. Another futile "Hey."

I wanted to swing my legs over to get up, but then I noticed I had a piss tube stuffed into my johnson. This helped me scream a little louder.

Doc Venhaus came through the door and shushed me. He wore street clothes—jeans, sneakers, a polo shirt.

"Don't rush yourself," he said, standing bedside, his mere doctorly presence enough to drive my head back into the pillow. "You've got a broken leg, among other broken things. If breathing hurts, it's from rib breakage—and you have been lucky enough to have your lungs intact after breaking your ribs. Again."

"You definitely did your research on me."

"Of course." He did doctor things, checked things, wrote things down. He was monitoring me, but from the feel of my injuries, I belonged in a hospital. This wasn't an altruistic act that Doc Venhaus was doing; he found me and decided to bring me to his office because he wanted me all to himself.

"Damn lucky I came along when I did," he said. "Healing's one thing, but I don't know if you have nine lives yet."

I had never thought about the possibility, but it would have been just my luck to be immortal and suicidal at the same time.

"So did they do the toes, or did you?" he said.

I pointed to my own chest.

"That's why they're ahead of the curve then."

He pulled the blanket back and raised my foot to show me. They were whole, completely regenerated, except for the pinkish color and the fact that the nails hadn't grown completely in yet, making them look queer, like a face without a nose or eyes.

"When did you find me? What day is it?"

"You've been out for about thirty-six hours."

I felt around my mouth—tips of new teeth were already ascending. My split lip was sealed up into one piece of flesh instead of the two curtains I remember from the beating.

"I'd like to take you into X-ray again in the morning. Seems there's no need to cast your leg at all—I have observed the bone mending perfectly on its own."

He'd arrived at my house to continue our discussion. "I couldn't sleep," he said. "I needed you to know I couldn't betray the trust of a patient. Not even for you. I owed you that answer in person."

Sadly, he was still a few minutes too late to save me from the latest entry in the Dale-Beating Hall of Fame.

"Did you call the cops?" I asked.

"No one knows you're here."

"You should have taken me to a hospital. Right?"

"If you were normal, yes. But hospitals have access to things like medical records. One look at a chart that says you should have half a hand and only one ear, and you'd soon have every doctor in America poking around inside of you for answers."

"As opposed to just one. Am I on painkillers right now?"

"No. I didn't want to interfere with your natural process."

"Well, don't be stingy. It may heal fast, but it hurts like fuck. How about your best painkiller cocktail? And when I wake up, I'd like some soup. Vegetable beef."

Doc juiced me up until it felt like a pat of butter was melting on my brain. I dozed off, wanting to sleep through my healing until it was over, like it were some boring car ride that I wanted to end as soon as possible. Healing might come with positive connotations, all these images of light and warmth and hope, but in reality, healing hurts like a motherfucker.

Two days later, Doc let me go home. My broken leg was nothing but an annoying limp. My teeth were back, whole and slick and white as a glass of milk, untouched by years of food and abuse. My split lip was a true laceration, the flesh parted by blunt force, but the wound had already fused back together. Splints held my fingers straight as they mended clean, which didn't take long.

The pain of broken bones vanishes until you try to move them, so my healing became a game of keeping the broken parts still. Bruises melted away from my skin, draining away the pools of tenderness that lurked underneath. Lumps on my head receded. The abrasions probably hurt the worst—they were deep rashes on the back of my hand, on my arms and legs, on my right cheek. The skin was scrubbed away by concrete and boot soles, removing the epidermis and exposing the nerve endings, where even a cool breeze across an undressed wound felt like the sizzle of a grease fire. Even the subtle pulse from my beating heart pounded the rashes like a drum. I felt my cheek get hard and crusted-over. When those scabs fell away, leaving patches of gloriously restored pink behind, I knew I could take off the bandages from my arms and legs. I think the pain was worse because I was so engaged in it, monitoring myself for the healing I knew would come, but it's hard to describe because pain is like a bad dream—your recollection of it never matches the actual experience.

My cell phone got smashed in the brawl, so I called from my home phone to order a new one and asked the clerk how to check my voice mails from a landline.

Shockingly, I had three of them. The first was Frank Winston, who wanted to talk to me about "that thing," like I were some drug-running gangster. He left a callback number. I saved the message.

The second was Mack. He sounded downtrodden. "It's me," he said. "I just figured since the shit has simmered down for a while now, we should talk it out. Hug it out. Punch it out. Whatever. Call me." The message was a day old. I wondered if he thought I was blowing him off on purpose.

The third one was Rae. She just said, "I hope you're okay" after a long breath, and hung up.

FIFTEEN

I WENT STRAIGHT TO RAEANNA'S HOUSE IN BROAD DAY-light. Fuck Harold, I thought. If he was worth a shit he'd be at work anyway. Still, I parked down the street and walked most of the way, the limp from my broken leg slowing me down. I was healed-up, but not all the way. I had patches of pink all over and all the bruised places were still a subtle shade of yellow. My broken bones had mended, but I still had a day or two before they stopped hurting. I was limping on a broken femur after just a couple days of recovery, though, so I couldn't complain.

Rae wore sweatpants and an old fleece top, her hair flick-ering in the cool wind as she watered the mums lined up in front of her porch. She saw me limping down the sidewalk, and she choked off the water hose. I caught a look of relief in her eyes, maybe even happiness, but it vanished quickly, gone in thick, molten drops, showing me fear and panic with such stark clarity that a tingle of my own fear gave my lungs a hard squeeze. She went from fear to anger, the seasons of emotion changing in her face. She walked up to me, her lips clenched, and slapped me across the face, waking up the heat in the healed abrasions.

"That was for the neighbors to see," she said. "Meet me behind the Wal-Mart in thirty minutes."

Raeanna was there, as promised. She was edgy and nervous, pacing by the recycling dumpster. She got into my car.

"Drive," she said. "West, on the country roads. I can't be gone forever. He'll be home soon and . . ." She stopped mid-sentence, squinting as she looked at me. "He said he smashed your face into a stair."

"I don't bruise easily," I said.

I thought we'd talk about her escape from Grayson, how we'd leave together, where we would go. I left my hand on my right thigh as we drove, hoping she would hold it. She was married. I barely knew her. Hell, I barely knew Regina and took a blind dive into that one. I could have bailed on the whole rotten situation. I could have said, *Dale, you learned your lesson. Quit that stupid job and move out of your mother's house. Go somewhere and do something. Meet someone. Get to know them. Ask them out. Then, when it's a date, and only then, hold hands. Maybe kiss at the end of the night.* But this wasn't courtship—this was heroism. I left my hand on my thigh and continued to hope.

"Harold is involved with drugs," she said, tilting the conversation in an unexpected direction.

Harold used to run meth—cheap and dirty, toxic and destructive, made from farm chemicals and over-the-counter medicine. Southern Illinois's drug of choice. One dose could start a brushfire of human rot and addiction, turning skin and teeth and hair black and green, building a zombie stench in addicts one could smell from a mile away if the wind was right. But he was smart enough to never sample the stuff himself, which Rae told me with palpable relief. Harold was rotten enough to begin with, so I could only imagine his violent impulses magnified by the paranoia of being a tweaker. Meth addicts are among the most paranoid, dangerous, desperate, and reckless motherfuckers you're ever apt to come across. Crack heads were mild by comparison—they would sell their mom's DVD player to get a fix, but a meth head would blow up a church with their mom in it just to pick the loose change from the collection tray out of the ashes.

We were on an old road in Grayson, Jasper Bridge Road, which felt safe and secluded because the corn was high and unharvested and the potholes made it clear that only a few people ever drove this road on purpose.

So I stopped the car. She kept breathlessly getting me up to speed on Harold. She was afraid he would call in some old connections, tried-and-true tweakers who would do anything for a fix.

"If you stay, he'll keep after you," she said. "All he has to do is dangle a bag of crank and you'll be in a ditch some-where."

"I don't care about any of that. Forget it. I'll manage. I need to tell you something." She was breathing hard. Nervous. She looked up at me. "Rae, I wasn't in love with Regina," I said. "Christ, I was a kid."

"And he works in insurance and he just got promoted, so he can look things up and know—"

"Rae, dammit, listen to me. I wanted her but I didn't love her. I give myself too much credit, as if she cared for me more than she did. Time has made this into a great tragedy in my own head because I don't have anything else."

"It never feels like you're really talking to me," she said.

"I don't know what that means," I said. "But we could just

pick up stakes and get out of here. Leave Harold behind to punch walls and sell crystal."

"If I wanted that, I would tell you to keep driving," she said. "I wouldn't even bother to pack or call anyone."

"Right now, then," I said. "I don't have to go home. I'm ready to punch the gas and get us both the hell out of here."

"It's a nice thought, isn't it?" she said. The wind rustled in the high corn. The heat battered us through the windshield. I had the air conditioner turned down low so we could hear each other, and sweat was bursting out of her forehead. I saw it gather at the base of her neck and felt it crawling down my own cheeks in fat drops.

She looked at me and I could tell she was about to say no. I leaned in to kiss her and she recoiled, pulling her head out of range.

"Dale, please," she said, and there was that hand again, on my face this time, gently pushing me back into the driver's seat.

I turned around without saying another word. We got back to the dumpster, the drive back spent in total silence. I kept the car idling as she walked to Wal-Mart's service-entrance doors. She stopped and doubled back to the car. I rolled down the window to accommodate her.

"There's nothing to wait for if you stay," she said. My head felt suddenly heavy. I let it drop and stared at the Chevy bow tie in the center of my steering wheel. "I'm sorry if I gave you that impression. If you don't leave, the only thing you're waiting on is him." I didn't answer her. Her fingers rested on my car door and I waited for her to move so I could roll up my window and bottle myself up in air-conditioning and white noise.

"Look at me!" she said. It took me two long breaths, but I looked at her, looked into the blueness of her eyes and they made me regret every one of my wasted days. "You need to leave," she said at last, and she was right.

I pulled into my driveway and found Mack Tucker seated on my porch, a backpack slung on his shoulder and a weak smile on his face.

I got out of the car and just stared at him. I felt ready for the .38, almost excited on the way home, hungry for the relief it would offer me, but now it seemed I'd be living a little while longer, at least until Mack was gone.

"Well, Sampsonite, you were right, man. The producers had us all set up in a piano bar for a nice, romantic date. My only job was to get her there at a certain time on a certain night without tipping her off. She asked about the cameras, and the waiter just said a famous piano player was performing. I knew it was Ben McCann. I met the guy when we taped the first segment of the show."

I knew how *Dedications* usually went. Mack and Ben would go over all the ways Mack loved Lori, all their special times together. The second segment would be Ben torturing himself artistically, coming up with an original song dedicated to Lori that incorporated all of Mack's bullshit.

"Anyway, when I met him, the entire time I'm thinking, Who the fuck is this guy, he isn't any famous musician. So we're at dinner and the fucker comes out onstage and the place erupts. I'm, like, the only guy there who doesn't know who this fool is, and he starts tinkering on that piano, says it's an original song, says Lori's name, says my name, the cameras come in tight, and I about puked up my steak, I swear to God, because I saw it in her face right that second. I saw the 'yes' in her throat just waiting to come screaming out of there."

"So she said yes?" I said.

"Just like you said she would. I'm engaged." He dropped his backpack and kicked it.

"Tell the producers you don't love her," I said.

"I can't. They like the episode. They like me. Hell, they even want to tape the wedding. They think the song's going to be a hit: "My Life for You." Nothing huge like those other reality shows, just a small thing in a small church to show that we're so in love we couldn't wait for a bigger production."

"So you're going to get married to a woman you don't love to stay on TV? I mean, not even to get on TV, but just to stay?"

"I won't be on TV if I break it off. They won't air the episode if they don't have the wedding to go with it. That's all I got, man. I wish I could tell them to eat a dick, but I can't. You got your regeneration thing, right? We should use that instead."

I didn't budge from my spot in the driveway.

"I didn't mean it like that," he said. "Like, *use* you. But you should use the talent you've got. I've been thinking though, if it really works, it could be like a makeover show. You could help people, like that blond prick who builds poor people houses every week."

I just laughed. "You're insane. And I'm still pissed at you."

"I admit it, our conversation shouldn't have gone down the way it did last time. What do you say about dinner, huh? A night out? Shit, it's my bachelor party, man. You know, you can be my best man at the taping. You should come with. California's the shit, just like we always thought it would be."

He smiled, for real this time—that Mack Tucker grin that melted hearts long before he broke them.

We went to a joint called the Rio Grande Steakhouse the next evening, just another McSteakhouse, a clone of all the others, complete with the heart-stopping fried-onion appetizer. He wore jeans and a tight-fitting compression shirt—worn mostly by professional athletes and even then it's under their uniforms. A shirt so tight it looked painted on, which would get most men laughed at, even the chiseled ones who filled it out with cuts and bulges. Not Mack. He looked like a man striding around in a five-thousand-dollar suit. We sat down and drank Coronas, then ordered massive steaks.

"So, what's new in your world?" he asked. I was shocked. Mack hardly ever started conversations by asking about someone else. Maybe a little humility did the body good.

"I got curb-stomped by a former drug kingpin. I healed fast."

He laughed. "I'm sure you did. So am I whipping this drug lord's ass?"

"It's complicated."

"What? He's got a whole army of henchmen?"

"Sort of, but that's not the issue."

"Don't beat around the bush, then."

"He's Raeanna's husband," I said. He almost spit out his beer. "She lives in Grayson now. Works at the Wal-Mart. He hits her."

"So," he said, "me and you getting a chance to save at least one of them twins. That about it? You in love with this one too?"

"I don't know."

"I don't understand this, man."

"You will never understand," I said. Mack felt like an artifact of the self I was supposed to be, that supposed-to-be Dale who sits at a bar with his best friend, drinking a beer, lusting after promiscuous women as we closed out our college days. That Dale spends his entire paycheck on shots, beers, and greasy food. Mack matches him, wearing a suit with the tie loosened after a day of abusing the rubes as part of some hotshot investment firm. That Dale probably works in something financial, but something solitary—accounting, probably. By the time the night ends, he pukes in the toilet and keeps drinking to wash the acid out of his mouth and nostrils, then ends up finishing the evening suffocating while a girl of questionable age sits on his face in the basement of Mack's three-bedroom house, of which only one bedroom has an actual bed; the other two are converted into a guest room with a shitty futon and a workout room. That Dale wakes up with the young, nameless girl beside him and a hangover thudding in his head and his dick stuck to his inner thigh, and he and Mack laugh about it, and take all day Sunday to soak themselves in Gatorade and aspirin to get ready for Monday, the workweek, the grind, but when Friday comes they do it all over again.

"I don't think you understand what I've been going through, motherfucker," Mack said. "It's not all about you, so let's not be slinging guilt and pity just yet."

The next day, that supposed-to-exist Dale and Mack would eat greasy McDonald's breakfast food, knowing full well it's deadly, and they tell stories about what happened in the basement, what happened in Mack's bedroom, and they laugh and high-five. On the way home regret settles in the same way a cold comes on, stealthy, not knowing if it's there until it's there for good, and the regret moves supposed-to-be Dale further into manhood and responsibility, not by the example of his parents or role models but through the mistakes introduced by the element of Mack Tucker.

"Then tell me," I said. "Explain to me just why in the hell you distanced yourself from me so much after high school."

And the element of Mack Tucker would mellow with age. And soon the regret filters out and we just have those stories that we tell late at night, after our wives and kids have gone to bed.

"I can't really explain it," he said. "No huge things, just a bunch of little things. Throw enough pebbles in a bucket and soon you can't carry that fucker anymore. I needed to clean out my bucket. By myself."

"Fair enough."

We finished our dinner. He stared at the dinner check. Things felt awkward. This must be how a date feels, I thought.

"You're still my best friend, man," he said. He gave our waitress his credit card. "I think she's got big enough tits for a twenty-percent tip." On the Mack Tucker gratuity scale, that was the top tier.

"So I'm not sure what to do," I said. "Well, maybe I know what to do, but it's one of those things—if I do it, there's no going back from it. So I have to be sure."

"That's a lot of vague shit you're saying," he said. "But this is a bachelor party, man. Let's hit a bar, have a mojito or two or three or four, and talk this shit over. Among other things. Maybe even drag some chicks back to your pad. Sound like fun?"

It sounded like a something on a Saturday night where there had once been only nothings. His proposal was actually petrifying, but he had just bought me dinner and he was still my best friend, and I now know that had I not gone with him, I would have died that night one way or another—either by my own hand or Harold's—so all things considered, I made a damn good choice.

We drank and talked until the bar closed. The bartender—a brunette named Kyla, with a lot of freckles and bright lipstick, invited us to an after-party. Correction: invited *Mack* to an after-party. By then I was swimming in booze and the last thing on my mind was suicide. The world seemed muddy and small and completely harmless.

I woke up in the backseat of Mack's Jeep Grand Cherokee, squeaking against the synthetic leather, yellow streetlights turned gray by the tinted windows. Too late to be night, too early to be morning. Gray time, when anything that happens feels like a dream. I stumbled out the door and vomited hard on the curb.

"He's alive!" Mack proclaimed. I walked toward the dark blur of people on some random front lawn. Someone handed me a Bud Light. I popped the top and drew a deep swig to blot out the acid taste of vomit to the sound of light applause.

Mack was standing next to a blonde. "Sampsonite, Tosha. Tosha, this is my main man, Sampsonite." He seemed less drunk than before. Tosha had to be the alpha female at the gathering—tall, blond, Mack-approved tits. He must have traded up from Kyla. Tosha smiled at me with teeth so white they almost glowed. Kyla continued to hang around them, a bee fluttering around the flower of Tosha. Kyla looked at me, the forgotten friend, as if to say, *Don't you just hate it when this happens?* As if she sensed that I knew how it felt. And she was right.

Mack wasted no time leading Tosha into the bowels of a strange house that smelled like an old quilt. Crow's-feet texture on the ceilings, tan walls, baseboards that were high and white, except for a line of dust that had gathered at the caulk line. Family photos on the wall. Tosha was in them. An only child with an old father and a mother who looked to overdo the tanning bed.

Kyla turned on the television. She put on some random ESPN feed featuring thick Germans lifting cars in those strongman competitions that only ran at three a.m.

"We don't have to watch this," I said. "You can change it."

She sat in the recliner. I sat on the couch. An ocean of green carpet separated us, the shag tamped down by foot traffic.

"Come on, now, I know you like ESPN. You're a guy."

"I prefer old reruns," I said.

She laughed.

So ESPN was some sort of olive branch. We watched the Farmer's Walk competition, grunting men in tank tops sweating in the sand, their straining eyes hidden by Oakley sunglasses.

"Your friend is quite a character," she said.

"He makes an impression."

"Not necessarily a good one."

"We're here, aren't we?" I said.

"What is that supposed to mean?"

"It's like a vampire thing," I said. "You invite them into your home, you get bit. I doubt you'd be upset if you were in there with him. Correct?"

"Touché. But fuck you all the same." She smiled. "You want a drink?"

"Yes," I said immediately. God yes. Sweat gathered in my palms and armpits. A girl. An empty room. She was smiling at me. She wanted to have a drink.

She brought a bottle of vodka and a carton of orange juice

from the kitchen, one in each hand. She took a swig of the vodka, then chased it with a swallow of OJ, then held them out to me. "Screwdrivers. Your mouth is the mixer."

I stared at the offering.

"Don't worry, I don't have cooties. You scared of a girl's spit?"

My answer to that was three swallows of vodka, big ones, and I guzzled juice to keep myself from puking it up.

"What a trouper," she told me. "My turn."

We took turns. The bottle emptied so fast, I didn't even know I was getting drunk again until she fetched another one.

I didn't remember falling asleep, but I went from drinking to suddenly waking up on the couch with her head on my chest. My mouth was so dry it felt fossilized. My eyes felt small and tight from dehydration. My hand was on her waist, against her skin, the love handle, where her shirt had curled up slightly from the waistband of her jeans. An erection ached against the side of my leg and I had to piss.

I peeled her off of me. She moaned a little but didn't wake, curling up tight against the couch cushions, stuffing her face into the crevices.

I had passed out first. I was sure of it. So she had cuddled up to me and slept. Kyla. Pretty enough. Clever girl, and maybe a bit lonely. I looked out the bay window of the living room. Dark, with a tease of light on the horizon. Four thirty-ish.

I was not steady on my feet. Just an hour of sleep had blunted the massive drunk that was settling into me, a drunk that had perhaps not fully gripped me yet. Sick and dizzy and thirsty and I wanted to wake her up and ask if we could talk again sometime. She'd say yes. She liked me. This is what it felt like, to have a girl want you.

I heard the fridge close. Mack was in the kitchen, guzzling a bottle of water.

"Dude, you look fucked-up, like one of those telethon kids," he whispered. He threw me a bottle of water. I split the cap and drank the shit out of it. "You ready?"

"For what?"

"To get the fuck out of here."

I looked at Kyla. Something must have been on my face, I'm not sure what, but it got Mack's attention.

"Say, hey, did you hit that?"

I shook my head and then I remembered: *You're not Raeanna,* I told her when she started kissing my neck. The kissing stopped.

"You have a girlfriend?" she asked.

"No," I said. "Maybe."

"Don't tell me, it's complicated. Well, you're a keeper. Most guys pick getting laid over telling the truth."

"I wish I knew the truth," I said.

"She doesn't like you?"

"I think she does, but there's different kinds of like."

"Oh crap, she's got a boyfriend. Doesn't she?"

"She's married," I said.

Kyla started shaking her head. "You have to let her go," she said.

"If I let her go," I said, "I got nothing else to hold on to."

"Oh, honey," Kyla said. She hugged me. I didn't want to hug her back, not at first—it felt like an admission that I needed it. No one had even attempted to comfort me for anything since my mother died. I hugged her back and tried not to cry, but failed—two narrow streams of tears funneled onto her shoulder. We held each other until we fell asleep.

"Same old Sampsonite," Mack said with a smile. "Couldn't get laid in a monkey whorehouse with a bag of bananas."

"I think I'm going to throw up. Again."

"Well, be polite and do it on the lawn."

I stumbled out to the front yard and retched in the grass, the faint tang of orange juice mixing in with bile.

He slapped me on the bottom, a "good game" gesture from our baseball days. "Good thing for you, I banged myself sober. I'll have you home in time to serve me breakfast in bed."

Giving Mack Tucker access to a one-night stand was just like putting Popeye on an IV drip of spinach—you can almost sense the strength and confidence billowing back into him. Still, he was just an imitation of his younger self. Everything looked and sounded the same, but his antics were glossed with wistfulness that made it all an act.

Mack drove and the sky went from black to blue, an evolving bruise in the distance, an orange glow flickering up ahead—but it wasn't the sun.

"What the fuck?" Mack said.

The glow was punctuated by the flicker of lights, of blue, of red, of white—a kaleidoscope twisting in the blur of my blotchy sight.

Fire trucks blinked around a huge fire. As Mack pulled up, I saw a pack of neighbors, that nosy pack of fuckers who wanted to know exactly what was going on, but any blind man could see the flames popping out of shattered windows and the caved-in roof. Any person with decent hearing could detect the whoosh of hungry flames and know that someone's home was burning down.

My home, my mom's home, owned by a guy with no money and no insurance, and to make matters worse, I now had no car, either, because it had burned in the driveway, the tires melted, hot and waxy against the concrete.

I just got out and stared. Mack said things like "Holy shit" and "What the fuck, I mean what the *fuck*" over and over again because, really, there was nothing else to say except for "Did you leave the oven on or something?"

No, I didn't. I just fanned the flames of Harold Stillson.

"I don't know what to do, man," Mack said. "I can't leave you hanging, but I've got to be in L.A. on Monday. I've got that wedding thing. Come with. Fuck this shit. Fuck Raeanna and her weird-ass husband. This is a sign."

"Not a sign," I said. "When will you be back?"

"We never got this far during our talk last night, but hopefully I'll never be back, man. I want to stay there. It's all sun and sand and it's so far away from this place. Grayson, Verner, Meeker, all these little shithole towns, man—fucking nightmares. They've been nightmares for years, and I only realized it the first time I hit the skins on a California beach at sunrise."

We watched my house continue burning. No one bothered us. We stayed quiet for a long time, the parting of ways feeling imminent, maybe this time for good.

I held my hand out for a shake, but he pulled me into a hug.

"You're my brother, Sampsonite. I love you like a man loves a perfectly grilled steak." We kept the hug masculine and tough with hard claps on the back. "Let's get that Mustang," he continued. "I'll sell this Jeep and charge the rest. I'm fucking serious. Just come with. Caution to the wind. Walk away from this ash and this town and Raeanna and all that bullshit. This is God telling you to get the fuck up out of here, and this is me telling you we can blow up the West Coast. Just me and you, tearing shit up. We can reverse it, the way we always dreamed—you can be the famous one and I can help you handle your business. Think about it—why sell your kidney for a few bucks when you can give it away on TV? You'd be the biggest story in human history. You'd never have to buy a drink again. The world would fucking love you. You could have whatever you wanted. Just come with me."

"Whatever I want?" I said. So he wanted to save me and I wanted to save Rae, and Rae had already failed at trying to save me from this, from the beating and the fire. And Regina was still dead. We were all failures at saving people. We all held little lockboxes of hurt that might get a bit smaller if we could just do one good thing. One right thing.

"No. I've got to stay."

"You can't be serious. For what?"

"Business."

"You know I love a good fight, but you aren't winning this one. Drugs and thugs. This isn't a fistfight on a baseball diamond. This is real. This is—"

"It's Clint Phillips stuff. Right?"

I sensed the Mack Tucker hate gland filling his eyes with liquid steel. "Suit yourself. But it's time to let that shit go. It's a big world out there. You should join it sometime."

I stared at the fire.

"You need a ride somewhere?" he asked.

I shook my head. He lingered for a moment, and then he was gone, the Jeep curling away at the stop sign at the end of the block, the brake lights fading from view.

When the fire was out the sun was barely up. The cops took my information for their report, the firemen had done their work and left, and the neighbors were done asking if I needed anything. I went behind my house and laid down in the wet grass of my stamp-sized backyard, smelling the cold air made humid by the char of the house, pieces of soot falling, black snowflakes in an open sky, unblotted, nothing between me and the universe.

Sleep came. I woke to the sound of an idling truck. The sun was high and I felt filthy, the way you feel after burning leaves all day. The house was a dark canker sore on the block now, the remnants of the studs jutting up like abscessed teeth. The car was the color of rust, aged a million years overnight, surrounded by a skirt of broken glass, the rims locked into the driveway by hardened puddles of rubber. My stomach grumbled, expecting breakfast, or lunch, or more water to help chase the thud of my hangover. My skin itched for a shower.

The FedEx guy stood there with a small box, staring at the remains of the house. I shambled toward him.

"Dale Sampson?" he said sheepishly.

"Yeah," I said, and signed for my new cell phone. I walked to Grayson. I checked in at the Allsop Motel, a cheap and dirty place where the rooms made me think of semen and blood and suicide and moths and Bibles. My gun remained in the ashes of my burned house. I left it there, where it belonged.

SIXTEEN

AFTER TWO NIGHTS AT THE ALLSOP, THE MANAGER TOLD me my check bounced. No surprise there. I drained the account right after I wrote the check, buying a digital camera with a video clip recording function and a pair of bypass loppers, cashing out eighty bucks for food. I didn't argue with the guy. Turned out another night at the Allsop would not be necessary, so that was one stroke of luck.

The argument held me up enough to get to Doc Venhaus's office later than planned, but I still got there on time. It was only day three of my stakeout at Doc's, and I hit pay dirt. At nine thirty, Harold's GMC Sierra was one of the few parked vehicles in the lot. The sun was weak that morning, allowing the frost to linger on windshields longer than usual. The black paint of the Sierra appeared icy and dull. I went into Doc's building through the back door with the key that he had given me for all of our after-hours appointments.

It was game time with Harold on neutral turf. I went inside, entering into the main hallway that connected the exam-room entrances, and Doc Venhaus was looking at a chart. He looked at me, shook his head, and put the chart back.

"Get out, Dale." I'd ignored his calls and never gave him

an answer about letting him get me into clinical testing, but it looked like he was expecting me.

"I need to talk to Harold," I said. "I'm sorry I haven't gotten back to you, but if you didn't know, my fucking house burned down. I've been busy."

"Busy, but you're here," he said.

"I've made a decision. I'm not going to sell my organs. I deleted Winston's messages. I'm out. But I'm not in with you, not yet. One day, though. On my terms and my timeline."

"You think it's your decision?" he said. "It won't be for much longer."

"What the fuck are you talking about?" I said.

He slotted his chart into one of the exam-room doors. "Follow me." The door at the end of the hallway was clearly marked as an emergency exit. He pushed the bar on the door and we stepped into the cold. His white coat flapped in the sharp morning wind. Water gathered at the corners of his eyes and blood rushed into the capillaries of his nose, turning the tip cherry red.

"You've obviously been staking me out, waiting for Harold," he said. "Did you happen to notice a young man in a naval uniform come into the office yesterday?"

As a matter of fact, I did—he was carrying a briefcase. Something about a uniformed soldier carrying something so uncharacteristic caught my attention.

"Well, he's not in the Navy. He's from the US Public Health Commissioned Corps, under the direction of the CDC."

"That's a real thing? You're not shitting me?"

"There's not many of them. They're deployed in national emergencies—or by request, depending on the department and situation."

"He asked about me?"

"No. Not yet, anyway. He simply asked if I encountered any patients with particularly unusual symptoms."

"That vague?"

"He was feeling me out. They know, Dale. Make no mistake. I have no idea how, but with the publicity surrounding your original injuries, it's not surprising you couldn't hide your regeneration forever. I told him none that came to mind, but I'd have to check my charts."

"And he knew that meant you were stalling for time. Deciding whether or not to sell me out."

"There's no leverage here, especially for me," he said. "They don't need me. If I'm not complicit, I don't have a superpower to hold over their heads."

"I mean, what's the worst that could happen? What could they do?"

"In the interest of national public health? National security? Anything they wanted. Unless you cooperate. Unless I cooperate."

"What are you going to do?"

"I think that's a question you should be considering yourself," he said. "I'm supposed to contact him today. I would imagine they want me to corroborate your ability, give them your records."

"And use my trust in you to convince me to cooperate."

"Possibly. But if you trust me, Dale—you'll cooperate if they confront you. There's no longer an alternative."

"There might be," I said. "But I'm not leaving until I talk to Harold Stillson."

"If you insist on complicating all of this even further, I'm not going to stop you," he said. "But if the police are called, you overpowered me to get into that room, got it? So it would just be best if you said your piece and left. He's in Room Six."

We went inside. He joined Grace in the administrative section of the office. I opened the door to Room Six and found Harold lying on the exam table—tired, gaunt, and stricken, his eyes retreating back into his skull, his fingers skinny, his skin looking as frail as parchment. He saw me and just smiled, absolutely unsurprised. Instead, he looked as if he were perversely amused by my presence.

I pulled up a chair and tried to act calm.

"Fancy seeing you here," he said. "Unarmed, surprisingly. I figured you might have a coffeemaker or a microwave or something." He laughed weakly, his hands clasped over his belly. They rose and fell with each slow breath. The stitches were gone from his face, but a red trail crept from his ear to his jaw.

"My armory burned with the rest of my house, but maybe I can find a magic bullet to jam up your ass."

"Unfortunate, about your house. Did you have insurance?" He smiled. Of course, the fucker worked in insurance. He knew I didn't have any, probably checked to make sure when he was looking into me. He knew damn well how catastrophic burning that shithole would be.

"So why all the pills, Harry?"

"Chronic bronchitis. Every fucking year. Never fails." He sat up and coughed. "So what kind of ambush is this? Does Allen know you're here?"

Allen. He was on a first-name basis with the good doctor.

"I just needed to talk to you somewhere neutral, where I didn't have to look over my shoulder for the next dose of retribution."

"So talk."

"What will it take to get rid of you?" I asked.

"What? For me to leave you alone?"

"No. For you to leave Rae for good."

He closed his eyes and leaned his head back. "You don't have a clue, do you?"

"Seems like everyone feels that way. What is it, Stillson—money? You got a price?" I said—but what if he did? What if it was more than the eighty bucks I had left?

"I've got no use for money," he said. Then, after a long silence, "She still has nightmares you know. About her sister. I know you were there. You're in them sometimes. She talks in her sleep."

"If you don't leave her, she's going to leave you. I promise you that."

"Cross your heart?" he said through a fragile smile.

"Guaranteed."

"We should just ask her, then. She's in the waiting room. Should we call her in to settle this?"

The thought of her just beyond the walls gave me the first rattle of our mini confrontation. I had built a precarious frame of hope inside, one that depended on Rae having a buried disdain for her husband just waiting to burst out, a fire I could build slowly with logs of money I didn't have, fame I didn't want, and affection I didn't completely understand. It already felt impossible. If she came inside and sided with Harold, all would feel lost.

"She's going to get tired of you," I said in my best hardass tone. "She won't stay for all your tomorrows, no matter what she might say today."

"I'm not leaving her," he said. "She's not leaving me. She took a vow. You're going to be disappointed. And for what you've done here today, I just might go home and give her a backhand right across her face. Tell her it's from you."

Now, that was certainly designed to get a rise out of me,

and it worked, but I had to breathe myself back down. I liked Doc, and a brawl in his office would make things tough on him.

"I'll say it slower," I said. "She's . . . going . . . to . . . leave . . . you. I'm giving you a way out. You can keep your pride."

"So you give me something to leave. Like what? Money?" he said, and laughed. "What do you have, Dale Sampson? Nothing. I saw your credit score. Or lack of one. You don't have a house, and that was your only paltry asset. That and a shit car that's melted in your driveway. Maybe you should have sprung for full coverage on that, huh? And where you going to take her? The homeless shelter? The soup kitchen? You have nothing. You don't even have a real job. Are you hiding an emergency fund in a Folgers can buried in your backyard? No? Then let me say it slower. You . . . have . . . nothing."

"Not yet," I said.

"'Not yet,' he says. I've got a little piece of marital gossip for you. You've earned it after all this—but Rae has nothing either. Sometimes she says she's leaving me and she'll go to her good friend's house for a night or two then return and say she's sorry, even though she's got nothing to be sorry for. I let her say it, though. It makes her feel better. That last time, after I saw her with you, she lied to me about you. Eventually I got the truth out of her. I always do. When it turned out you were . . . you, I admit it, I felt a little jealous. What a relief to see you had nothing. Just total relief. So if you have nothing and she has nothing, that makes me pretty powerful in this little situation we have. Being the only guy with something, and all."

"If you love her, let her go."

"I love her plenty, and you certainly don't understand the

secrets between a man and his wife. You see, Dale, she hasn't told you half as much as you think she has. You're filling in the gaps with that hopeful little erection of yours. You're a boy and you'll always be a boy, to me and especially to her. But I've told you enough. What's your move, Dale? What next? You going to hit me and force me to burn your nothing down?"

I walked out and made a straight line into the waiting room. Rae was reading a magazine, glanced up, saw me, and damn near turned to stone.

"I'm asking you to come with me right now," I said. "Right now, because I'm leaving and I'm never coming back."

Her face was painted with a hurt I didn't understand. "Dale, I'm so sorry," she said. "What he did to you. What I did to you." And that was all she said about that. "Certainly, don't come back. It's best for everyone." She couldn't look me in the eyes.

"You'll look for me one day," I said. "It may be tomorrow, it may be a year from now, but just call me or show up and I'll be there for you. I'll get you out of Grayson, for good, and we can leave him behind to rot. So when you're ready to take a stand, I'll be there."

"I am taking a stand, Dale," she said. "Good-bye."

I went back to the motel and set up the camera. I switched it on and took my place on the bed, where the brand-new bypass loppers rested, those big-ass garden shears that can effortlessly cut through a two-inch tree limb with disturbing ease. The sticker was still on the handle, the jaw of blades still oiled and tight.

Reluctantly, Doc had given me a syringe full of lidocaine. I jabbed the needle in the flesh between my metatarsal bones on the top of my foot. A cool, sufficient numbness spilled into my toes. I pressed Record.

"Mack . . . I'm not sure how your *Dedications* experience is going, but tell your producers you have an idea for a show. One man gives his organs away to needy families. The same guy. Because his organs keep growing back. I know you believe me . . ." I held up my right hand. "Tell them about what happened to my hand, and what it looks like now. What my ear looks like. But just in case, I figured I'd show you this."

I took the bypass loppers and raised my foot into the frame. I put the jaws snugly against my second toe and snapped the loppers shut. My toe popped into the air, then fell onto the dirt-smudged motel carpet.

Thanks to the lidocaine, I didn't even wince.

"I'm on my way to Los Angeles," I continued. "This tape will beat me there in the mail. But the next time you see me, this toe will have already grown back, and you'll know it's real because I don't have a special-effects budget. And if you don't believe it, I can do it again and again and again, until you or anyone else has no choice but to believe it."

I turned off the camera, then jotted *Watch this as soon as you can* on a piece of paper, signed it, and dropped it into an envelope along with the camera's memory card. I addressed it to Mack Tucker, care of the *Dedications* production company. I threw the envelope into a mailbox slot on my way out of town. I walked west with my eighty dollars in my pocket and no intention of ever coming back.

PART THREE
EVISCERATION

SEVENTEEN

THE TEMPERATURE WAS PERFECT BECAUSE LOS ANGELES has subtropical weather patterns. According to the Internet, there is an average of thirty-five days per year where there is a recorded amount of precipitation. The immediate connection I make is to the movie *Chinatown*, to water shortages, to old movies on an old couch with a gun stuffed under the cushions.

Inside Tracy Pike's office, it was a perfect seventy-two degrees. The chairs were leather. Mack wore jeans that cost more than a month at the Allsop Motel, along with his wedding ring. I wore one of the five decent shirts in my closet rotation, a gray polo.

Tracy, the producer who championed our idea, had a towering wit that gave her hustler approach an intelligent gloss. She wore black-framed glasses and I had a sneaking suspicion they were vanity frames and her eyes worked just fine. She never seemed to have them on; rather she used them as a prop, as punctuation to her too-polished gestures when she talked. Her black hair was always perfectly shaped, straight from a shampoo commercial. She would have been a skinny girl in Grayson, but in L.A., some would say she had ten pounds to lose. She dressed for business at all times, wasn't much for pleasantries, and barely ever smiled. But she had a nice smile

175

when it escaped, and I imagined her to be some hayseed from the Midwest who came to L.A. to prove she could be better than everyone else. But what the fuck did I know? To me, the Midwest was the only real place and L.A. was a distant solar system, the type of place where light and screams and dignity could not escape.

"Sit," she said.

We obeyed. She was a perfect match for the pitch, because like everyone else in that town, she wasn't happy with her own role, her own success. Everyone wanted to be something else. Writers wanted to direct, music stars wanted to be in movies, movie stars wanted to release albums. Producers like Tracy were still grunts. She wanted more clout, a production company of her own—autonomy, creative control. For those dreams to come true, I needed to be real, and to prove I was real, that I was useful, I had to regenerate a kidney.

Getting the surgery covered was actually pretty easy. She found a transplant center that would cover the expenses on the extremely rare "non-directed" donation I was making. I simply went in, got evaluated, and let them take a kidney and give it to whomever I wanted. When the surgery was over, I ditched the transplant center's follow-up care to meet with Tracy's handpicked physicians. I had a feeling getting all of those advanced medical tests without much in the way of paperwork had cost a shitload of money, cash that she might have even put up herself. Not easy to do, considering that all logical signs pointed to me being an incredibly persuasive fraudster. Hell, I wasn't even sure myself that an organ would regenerate. Life and death and scar tissue. Cash that might be gone forever, an organ transplant that might not take, a kidney that might not grow back and fuck everything up.

But the kidney had grown back. Dr. Reynolds, the great-looking, fame-hungry lead doctor of Tracy's little team had already confirmed that, but the big chiefs wouldn't order more episodes without making me sing and dance for their own medical team. They verified my records with the transplant center, and more doctors tested me, only these fuckers were less Hollywood—old and skeptical and completely annoyed they had to mess around with the bullshit they were absolutely sure I was slinging.

The results were in. Tracy threw an envelope into my lap, a stiff manila one that must have contained medical films. "Full medical workup. This one is from their doctors," she said. "You've got two kidneys again. They still didn't believe it. Hell, I don't believe it. It's like they want to open you up and see for themselves, and I wouldn't mind a peek myself."

Mack pumped his fist. She smiled, a rare artifact dusting off before my very eyes.

"They picked it up?" he asked.

"They picked it up." She confirmed. "I still think the network thinks it's a ruse, but they can't seem to uncover any evidence that proves it. And if it's real, they just can't say no." She took a long, deep breath. "This is the world we live in now," she said. "An honest-to-goodness superpower, and instead of putting a mask on, you're taking it to reality TV."

"It is my mask," I said. I'd already explained it to her, the true importance of the show. Of course, I said nothing of Raeanna; I said nothing about hoping for the money and the platform to lure her from an abusive relationship. But I did tell Tracy that I needed the show—if I was famous, if I was known, if I was helping people, then the CDC and DHS and DOD and whoever else couldn't make me disappear. I had the leverage back, as long as I could duck them while the show was getting off the ground. So far so good in that regard: Doc

Venhaus hadn't agreed with my plan, but he had no other alternatives, so he agreed to cover for me. He handed over all the charts and files related to my treatment to the USPHS officer in charge, Capt. Lyle Hayes, and he gave an honest statement—all except the part where he knew my whereabouts. The transplant center eventually gave away my location, but by the time they found me, I was ready.

"We've got to start right away," Tracy said. "I'll be working twenty-four-seven. The budget isn't huge. I'm hoping insurance companies will work with us to cut overhead for the first season, but if it takes off, we can start paying for the surgeries out of the production budget. Really dig deep into the donor list where people not only can't find an organ but don't have the coverage to get it transplanted." She kept looking at me. I hadn't found the proper channel of enthusiasm to jump around or hoot or smile. My kidney incision had hurt for three days before closing up.

"Dale?"

"Sorry," I said. "I just don't have the words to describe how awesome this is."

"Well, if you start to forget the level of awesome, just remember, we are filming a pilot, but *you* are saving someone's life."

"I'm pretty damn sure I filmed a pilot, Ms. Pike," I said.

"For the last time, it's Tracy. I'm your producer, not your mom."

"How many surgeries are we talking?" Mack asked.

"They ordered six episodes. Two months during the summer. Ambitious, considering the logistics involved. Fucking actual surgeries, paperwork and waivers from all hell."

"And I just wait?"

"You just wait. You both go celebrate if you want, but me?

I've got to get story editors chasing leads on the waiting list. We'll shape up some treatments and Dale can make the final call."

She'd pulled off a hell of a trick with her contacts, getting access to the lists. But the real trick was something only I could deliver—directed donations were legal, of course. I could give anything in my body to anyone, whether I knew them or not, but it was explicitly illegal to take money for an organ. The regulations themselves prohibited money, specifically, and also threw in "valuable considerations." I figured TV fame or the success of our show made the directed donations we had planned illegal. Unless I could get some people to look the other way if some heat came down, but that wouldn't be a problem. I figured some government officials would let me save a few lives if they got a seat at the table.

"We'll mix it up," she continued, "but we simply must have some donations that are uncommon, visual, the type of thing no other human can give. I mean, I can give a kidney. We need to make sure we get an arm off of you. An eye, maybe. Not sure. I'll give a list to the medical team—a medical team, mind you, that doesn't exist quite yet. The pilot was a skeleton crew. Now we can give out actual jobs, and casting the doctor is going to be key."

"How much dough are we talking?" Mack asked.

"Not the time to talk specifics," she said.

"It's kind of like the exact time to talk specifics," I said.

"Can you both do me a favor and chill the fuck out? Go have a beer or something. Kill a few days off because pretty soon, we're going to be balls to the grindstone for a few hard months."

"Lucky for me, my balls are tremendous," Mack said. "Resilient and supple. You'd love them."

Her phone rang. "That means leave," she said. We did, but

not before Mack blew her a kiss, blowing it off of a hand with a platinum wedding band from a very special *Dedications* wedding that was taped but never aired. Apparently, the women in focus groups hated Mack Tucker, leaving him with a legally binding marriage and no fifteen minutes of fame to go with it. Pretty much any woman old enough to vote saw his charms as a slimy, arrogant prick who'd say and do anything to ride his benevolent best friend to fame.

The network settled on a title, *The Samaritan*, and focus groups loved the pilot episode, especially middle-aged women. Not for anything exciting, like me being good-looking or dynamic. Just the opposite—I was tender and broken, a beaten puppy they wanted to take home, and somehow, from this cesspool of patheticness, the world's most amazing superpower was emerging.

Hollie Clarke was the recipient on the pilot episode. She was a single mom, struggling to make ends meet. She had end-stage renal disease, but more than anything she had problems with living; deep down, I could tell that she thought her life insurance policy would do her daughter more good than her juggling two jobs to keep them above the poverty line.

I was in recovery from that surgery when I woke up to find two men in naval uniforms at my hospital bed. Most of the footage was in the can, and even as they stood there, the cameras were rolling. Negotiations were easy. We got access to the donor lists, free rein to pluck whomever we wanted, and I had my freedom—except for a few "to be scheduled" stays at Research Triangle Park in North Carolina, and a spot for a commissioned corps medical officer as an adviser and analyst on my medical team.

THE HEART DOES NOT GROW BACK | 181

Home for us was an apartment so small you could take a shit in the bathroom and cook dinner in the kitchen at the same time. Even though I'd signed with the show for enough dough to afford a better place, living in a shithole was a familiar taste of home. The entire way home, Mack had touted his intentions to celebrate. But I sat down and turned on the television.

"Christ, the TV again? Seriously? It's Thursday, we just got our big break, and you're just going to sit on your ass all night?"

"Forgive me if the prospect of getting sliced up for the next few months doesn't excite me. I need my rest." So far, we'd only filmed the pilot. The recovery was fast, but far from instant. It hurt like hell for the few days it took the kidney to grow back, and while everyone else was astonished by my improbable recovery, I was simply waiting for the agony to subside.

"It's far more exciting than letting your life evaporate like a puddle on a hot road, that's for damn sure. You're going out. Getting fucked and fucked up, man! This is all because of you."

"I wish I could point to the moment of responsibility for what my body does. The reason that it's my doing. It isn't. It's like inheriting money. I don't do anything other than breathe every few seconds. I don't even do it on purpose."

"I have no clue what the fuck you're talking about," Mack said. "If you don't hit the town with me tonight, I will have this apartment so full of ass and booze that you will shoot loads of excitement on your precious little television."

I turned up the volume.

"I'm gonna go polish the body up a little bit, so you have about ten minutes to make the right decision."

I made the wrong decision. But he accepted it, knowing he

didn't have to babysit me or worry about me dragging the night down. He finally had a role on a television show, even though it was small and mostly behind the scenes. Mack was officially an associate producer, but his only job was to basically hang out and be my friend. Tracy and her real staff did all the heavy lifting. She was putting the finishing touches on the schedule. It wasn't just about shooting the footage, of course; she had to consider surgery logistics, recovery times. Me? I kept waiting for Rae to call me, as I had for six months. She never did. I still thought about her, mostly during the waiting—waiting for Tracy to call, waiting in offices and hospitals, waiting in lines for takeout, waiting for taxis.

During commercials, I turned down the volume and picked up the phone, dialing Rae's number except for the last digit. I let my touch linger just above the last one, and then hung up.

This is what teenage boys did. This is what it had felt like to call Regina while she was alive.

But if I could just dial that last number, maybe I would talk to her and find that things had changed. That I wouldn't have to go through with this. If she had left or Harold had gotten blown away by a tweaker I wouldn't have to lure her away by saving strangers on national television for fun, fame, and profit.

I hung up and dialed a different number instead. Hollie answered.

"It's Dale."

"Dale Sampson?"

"Yes. Are you doing all right?"

"You know I am, Dale. Nothing's changed since last week. Still ticking. That's a damn fine kidney you gave away." She chuckled, but nothing felt lighter. The phone was greased with palm-sweat, the mouthpiece moist with the condensation of breath.

"That's good. Real good. Melissa?"

"She's great. Growing like a weed, and I'm going to see all of it thanks to you."

I didn't talk, expecting her to hang up. She didn't.

"I just keep thinking it isn't real," I said.

"Me too. Every morning I wake up, I have to convince myself it wasn't a dream."

"Dreams would be nice."

"You don't dream?"

"Nightmares."

She didn't ask about them.

"Has anyone told you about the show?" I said.

"No. I don't care about the show, Dale. I got a kidney out of it already, so forgive me if I'm not exactly rooting for it to air."

"It got picked up a few weeks ago. We have a schedule now. Once we're done shooting, the pilot's going to run."

She was quiet for a long time.

"There's something we didn't tell you," I said. "Not that it matters, but you should know. I shouldn't tell you over the phone, either. Would you consider meeting me?"

"Of course I'd meet with you. You can come by or—"

"I don't want you to think it's a date or anything," I said.

This sort of startled her. She collected herself and said, "I wasn't taking it that way. I doubt we're good dating material. We're already about as intimate as two people can get."

"I'll come by sometime, then, if a time or whatever works for you."

She didn't answer immediately. I let her think, listening to her breathing on the phone. I could almost hear her processing what I meant to her, forming what she should say next very carefully. She ended up surprising me.

"Why don't we go out to dinner? My treat," she said. I didn't know which sentence was harder for her to spit out, but it was such a sweet and innocent gesture I almost cried.

"Yes to the first part, no to the second," I said. "A gentleman always buys."

"You've done enough," she said. "Honestly, I have to do something to make it up to you."

"Be a good listener. I have a story for you. A whopper. Do that and I'll get the check. Deal?"

She thought about it and said, "Deal." She was a thoughtful, careful conversationalist, this one.

"Thank you," I said. "You pick the place and the time."

"Skaf's in Glendale," she said. "Good and not expensive. Are you free tonight?"

"I can pick you up in two hours," I said.

When I hung up, I wished immediately that I would have said good-bye in a more chipper tone, the kind of immediate regret that snaps like whiplash right after a conversation with a girl that you wish had never ended, and right then, I knew I was in trouble.

I didn't tell Mack where I was headed, but he could tell by the fact that I'd dressed half-decent and combed my hair it was something important. He let me borrow the Jeep and on the way there, I tried to figure out just why exactly I was doing it again—why did I find myself infatuated with a girl for no discernible reason? Again?

Finally, I decided to tell that question to fuck off. It's just a stupid question. We don't know why we like or love anyone until we discover those parts for ourselves, and what draws us in deeply enough to discover them is different for everyone.

We'd already shared something, and I wanted so badly to help scrub away her tension and fear. When you're always worried about bouncing checks and scraping together electric-bill money, that shit settles into your face and shoulders and stays there. Whether it was Raeanna or Hollie, saving people always seemed to cost money—money I didn't have. Instead, I wanted to give her the only currency I had to spend, which was the truth about my kidney. I didn't want her to see the episode on television and wonder why no one told her, or to find out from someone other than me.

She lived in a little one-bedroom deal, with the only window visible from the street barred up. The city was technically Van Nuys. That was a weird thing about Los Angeles. I kept thinking a city was a city, but you were just never in L.A. itself, at least not for the human stuff, like meeting a double-shifting waitress for dinner.

She answered the door and I could tell we either weren't leaving the house, or weren't leaving on time, anyway. She was a tall woman, with big lips rich women paid out-of-pocket for, big green eyes, and hair that looked blond half the time and red the other half the time, depending on which angle the light was hitting it. She could have paid the rent in a dozen different ways, but she didn't have those L.A. aspirations. She never talked about acting or modeling or the screenplay in her bottom drawer. She told *The Samaritan* chase producers about her life in such a straightforward, powerful way, without a hint of complaint or a hint of seeking pity. When I saw her footage, I immediately wanted to pick her from the shortlist they gave me. I wanted to save her life without ever meeting her daughter, Melissa.

I still wouldn't get the chance, it seemed—Melissa was gone, but the entire place looked like an archaeological dig for long lost toddlers. Toys were everywhere; every wall had pictures of a red-haired, gap-toothed little angel. She was a good smiler. The fridge was covered with pages ripped from coloring books. I could see the kitchen and bedroom from the open doorway. The house was probably smaller than my apartment, but reminded me of my palace in Verner.

She fiddled with her earring for an uncomfortably long time, faking a smile, finally saying, "Well, come on in."

I looked at the pictures of Melissa and said, "She's cute," and I wasn't even bullshitting to be nice.

"Thanks. She's at my sister's tonight. Believe it or not, I have to work at ten."

"I believe it," I said.

Her hair was still wet from the shower and I couldn't tell if she had makeup on or not. That she would answer the door in such a vulnerable state was sort of touching.

It was already closing in on eight. "Do you think we'll make it to this place and back in time?"

"No," she said. "Wait—did you really want to go out to eat?"

Now she had me all screwed up. "Well, I wanted to talk. You wanted to go out to eat."

"I thought by talking . . . I mean, you really want to eat dinner?"

"Oh, Hollie," I said, the truth dawning on me. "It's not like that."

"Don't get the wrong idea," she said. "I don't treat myself like currency. I'm not like that and I've never done anything like that."

She sat down on the couch and said without looking at me, "I don't have anything else to give you. I thought this might be what you wanted, and you sort of deserve it. My body, in a strange way, belongs to you."

"Hell, my own body doesn't even belong to me," I said. "I'm glad you're sitting down."

I sat down next to her and she started to cry. I put my hand on her back and felt the dampness of her skin through the thin silk of her dress.

"My God, what you must think of me," she said. "I just don't know how to handle all this. I thought I was going to die and now I'm not and it's because of you, and I don't know how to thank you."

"Three things you gotta know," I said. "First, I'm a virgin. So as awkward as you just felt, how about *them* apples? Second, I think you're one of the prettiest girls I've ever seen. And finally, that kidney I gave you? It grew back."

That dried up her tears in quick fashion.

"What?"

"I can regenerate my organs and tissue," I said. I held up my right hand. "Did you ever see the Verner shooting covered on television?"

"That one in the Midwest, at the high school party? I think I remember," she said.

"The guy blew this hand off. It grew back." I tugged my ear. "My ear grew back. My tonsils? Removed when I was a kid. They're back. And that kidney I gave you—I have it back again. So if you think I own anything in your body, that's just not true. It's all yours. All I sacrificed was a little pain, and hell, they have drugs for that."

"That's about the weirdest thing I've ever heard," she said. I took her shift in body language as a cue and took my hand off her back.

"You don't believe me, which is fine," I said. "The show is going to start airing and every week I'll be giving things away. You may not believe it even then. You and a lot of other people will think it's TV magic or some shit."

"It's not possible," she said.

"That's what I thought too," I said. "Now that it's all on the table, let's just say fuck it. Let's process it on our own terms, okay? I just want to hear you say fuck it and smile, and give me the number of your favorite local delivery-food source. Then I want you to go get some sweats on and let's wolf that shit down so you can get a nap in before work."

She smiled and said, "Fuck it, then."

"Louder," I said.

"Fuck it!" she cried, and laughed out loud.

We split a large pizza and drank Coke out of a two-liter bottle with almost no ice cubes, the best damn way to take it. You can really guzzle it down when it's not too cold, just drink it so fast the bubbles hurt your nose. She talked about Melissa. I nodded and said "That's nice" in all the right places, and just like that, my first-ever date was in the books.

On my way out, this tall, beautiful girl with her hair in a bun and a faded Raiders T-shirt kissed me on the cheek and said, "Thank you."

And I didn't think there was much to say to that, only things that could ruin the moment. I left and took the long way home, the way people do when there's a moment worth savoring just a little while longer.

EIGHTEEN

I GOT HOME RELATIVELY EARLY AND THE TELEVISION lulled me to sleep. Later, the sound of a giggling girl woke me up. I was getting better at sleeping through Mack's late-night entrances, no matter how loud his conquest for the evening was. But the muted giggling, a hidden-secret giggle, eased me out of slumber. I knew this sound. Tickling and foreplay, soon to be replaced by grunts and heavy breaths that always sound strange if you're not the one having sex.

I tried to sleep. The heavy crash of flesh kept me awake, a smacking sound louder than the laugh track of the *Cheers* rerun on TV. Thankfully for my sanity, Mack's weakness was his endurance. The noise wouldn't last much longer, and it didn't, and I fell asleep to the image of a strange and slender arm draped over his chest, wondering if that was as comforting as television made it out to be, or as annoying as it seemed in my imagination.

I never heard the girl leave, and woke up to Mack cooking his "I'm guilty of keeping you awake all night with my adulterous banging" waffles with microwaved sausage links, and we ate, squinty-eyed, standing at the countertop, washing them down with Gatorade straight from the bottle.

"You tell that one you were married?"

He smiled, his mouth full, and held up his hand, wiggling his platinum wedding band with his thumb.

"This motherfucker is money. It's like a filter that wards off all the relationship-wanting chicks. If they see this thing and give you the time of day, you know it's fuck, suck, and duck the fuck out. I mean, look at this; is this heaven? She didn't even stay for breakfast."

Another huge bite. Loose syrup dripped onto the counter-top. "I feel used, I tell you," he said. "Used! Like the rubber on the nightstand."

"I'm eating."

"Hey, you know why she didn't stay for breakfast? She was sick and tired of putting sausage in her mouth." He punctuated this by taking a bite out of a sausage link.

As far as I could tell, Mack hadn't seen his "wife" in months. Everything was fake about *Dedications,* except for the marriage, which was legally binding in the state of California. He might have even filed for divorce, but kept the ring for "ho-filtering," as he put it. He never spoke much about it. Could the relationship have actually damaged him? I wondered. Impossible. The pain must have been reserved for something entirely unrelated.

"You dial Rae last night? Do that stupid shit where you jerk the phone off, wishing you had the balls to call her?"

"No. I called Hollie."

He shook his head. "Hollie? Christ, dude, you need to get *laid.* You get that? You get sucked into these busted-up chicks. You insist on drinking swill from someone else's bottle, dude. Plenty of fresh beers in the cooler, ones that don't have Harold Stillson's cigarette butt floating at the bottom."

"I'm not getting zapped."

He picked up the phone. "What's Rae's number? I'll call the goofy bitch. Seriously."

"Not happening."

"Then, here." He slid the phone to me. I stopped it with my palm before it went into the sink. "Call her. Tell her to fuck or walk."

"That doesn't make sense. She's already walked."

"You're one frustrating motherfucker. She's already walked? That's what I've been telling you for months. I'm telling you to call her finally because then, maybe, you can finally get to moving on. Personally, I'd tell her to walk off a short fucking pier with a hundred-pound bag of meth tied to her ankle."

He grabbed a balled-up T-shirt from the top of the couch, put it on, and picked up his wallet. "You've got your privacy for a few minutes. I'm going to get condoms and toilet paper." He stopped at the door. "This show will never work if you're a mope-ass on TV. I'm shocked they picked it up, the way you were when the cameras were on. You're saving a life and it looks like your fuckin' dog died. Move on. For both of us. I wouldn't be giving you so much shit about it if I didn't care."

He left, and I'll be damned if he didn't connect with a sort of twisted sense I understood. Months had passed. No word. The time had come to at least dial that last digit. If I didn't, in some weird way, I felt like I was cheating on my promise to Rae if I kept talking to Hollie.

So I dialed, my finger hovering over that final "8," the tip sticky from syrup, the smell of maple and grease in the air. The apartment was shadows and coolness, the shades drawn, the light falling on the floor in creases. I pressed the number. I listened for the ring without bringing the phone to my ear, contemplating hanging up before anyone could answer, but a voice said "Hello" on the second ring. I brought the phone close, tight against the cove of my ear.

"Hello?" the voice said again. A woman, not Rae.

"Hi, I'm looking for Raeanna Stillson."

"You're not the first one," she said, and chuckled a little. "This must be their old number."

I hung up without another word. She was gone and it hurt like I didn't expect it to hurt. And I knew *The Samaritan* would happen then. I finally wanted it. I wanted to be on television and look into the glittering eye of a camera and know she's out there, and I was here, saving people, and one day I would look into that camera and say her name for millions to hear and she would feel the mistake she had made become hard and sharp inside of her, and she would call, and I would think about not picking up—not picking up would be such an option for that future me, I was sure of it—but I would wait for three rings at least and then pick up and go from there.

"Your hands?" Hollie said. "That's insane."

"Feet, too," I said. We were finally seated at a real restaurant, some white-tablecloth joint called Providence. You can always tell a restaurant is fancy when the price-to-portion ratio is something completely asinine. I got a piece of salmon the size of a deck of cards with some sauces randomly smeared on the plate, artistically presented next to a haphazard alignment of fruits.

"Quadruple amputee. Old guy got a blood infection. Sepsis? Something like that. Should be good stuff for TV; he sure knew how to talk to the cameras. Stuff about finally touching his grandkids' faces."

"That's what I was to the show-running people?" she said. "Stuff?"

"Sadly, yeah. But not to me. I promise, not to me."

"I know, Dale," she said. "But the joke's on them. I held the good stuff back."

She was eating some chicken contraption with a glass of red wine, and took a long drink.

"You can tell me," I said. "But not if you don't want to. I understand the value of keeping things to yourself."

"No, I can tell you. You're the kind of guy you can just tell things to. But after I tell you, let's just say fuck it and eat, okay?"

"Fuck it, indeed," I said. "Shoot."

"I tried to kill myself," she said. "Pills. Melissa, God bless her—she dialed 911. I have no idea how your people didn't find out about it, but even if they did, they wouldn't know that I prayed every day I wouldn't get a call about a donor. I wanted to die in the worst way because I *love* that little girl. I'm worth over a half million dollars dead. Young and dead, anyway. Even when I was so broke I had to skip meals, I paid my premiums. I knew it was the only way to protect her. And we drive by this place in actual Los Angeles, a beautiful place on Raymond Avenue, brick with a green roof, green steps. Perfect landscaping. It's close to everything, including a good school. It's not a dream home but any home is a dream for me."

"How much?" I asked.

"That, I shouldn't say," she said. "It seems like I'm trying to play a future celebrity for a handout."

"I'm just curious," I said.

"Something like four-hundred thousand," she said, and punctuated it with another gulp of wine.

"She'd have a mostly empty house and maybe some money left over for college," I said. She nodded. "But no mother.

And that money for college? It'll evaporate, Hollie. Life does that to money. She'll be so young, some handler will drain it off for property taxes and repairs and utilities."

"My sister wouldn't—"

"She wouldn't care as much as you," I said. "But you're here now. Right?"

"I'm here now. And I'm calling fuck it," she said. "So, if you do that amputee guy and your hands and feet grow back, what next?"

"The one after that should be easier. I'm going to give a pancreas to a diabetic war hero. They say this guy might win the Medal of Honor. His battalion was pinned down for an entire day, one of his comrades dying just out of reach. He was stuck behind the husk of an old truck, his ammo low, radioing every few minutes for permission to extract the injured soldier. He kept getting negatives, and he kept refusing opportunities to pull back to safer ground. When he was down to his last clip, the tide finally started to turn, and he radioed again for permission, getting an exasperated "affirmative." He didn't hesitate, and the injured soldier lived. But alas, our hero got diagnosed as diabetic, got discharged, and already had a kidney transplant. He ended up with serious complications and needs a pancreas."

"A pancreas sounds easier than hands and feet," she said, and giggled a little. "Sorry, I don't mean to laugh, but you treat it like a long day at work."

"That's sort of what it is," I said, and took a sip of water. The waiters had actual fucking assistants, one of whom immediately refilled it.

Hollie watched, fascinated. "How hard you think it is to drink this water to the bottom?" she said. "Do I have to chug it?"

"Easy now, you're driving," I said.

The rest of the conversation was relaxed and full of laughter. The only time we returned to anything resembling heavy conversation was at the end of the night, on the sidewalk, as I tried to hail a taxi.

"Can I come see you?" she asked. "In the hospital?"

I wanted Hollie with me, of course, but I didn't want her cast as Regina in my head. It was too much.

"I don't want you to see me like that," I said. *It didn't work out so well for the last girl,* I almost said, but didn't.

"You're going to be 'like that' for quite a while, aren't you?"

"Yes," I said. "But it doesn't mean I won't call you or that I won't be excited as hell to see you when the taping is done."

A cab finally pulled up to the curb.

"So it may be a while," I said. I started to say something else, but she interrupted me with a kiss—a real one, her lips alive on mine, her mouth aggressive and warm, tasting like wine and, somehow, honey. I felt the wedge of her slender hips pushing against her black cotton dress and I was too scared to pull her any closer. I just enjoyed the feel of a woman in my arms, kissing me.

When the kiss was over, I was too stunned and amazed to say anything. "Can't have you forgetting about me while you're working," she said. I watched the sway of her body as she walked away. When she looked back, I thought of Regina leaving me at the hospital. I should have been overwhelmed by the joy and excitement of the kiss but instead, waves of dread lapped at me until the cabbie finally honked.

I got in the cab. I was the Samaritan. I could make people complete, save them, and be no worse for wear. Tissue returned. Bones mended. Organs rebuilt themselves. But for all my powers, a single kiss could crush and bewilder me. One look from Rae could move the rudder on my life's entire course. A note in a locker, a phone number hand-scrawled on a piece of paper, a "Get Well Soon" balloon, blood on a truck's dome light—my memories, like my flesh, could never be destroyed. If they never formed scar tissue, I would always be myself. I would never be the person who could benefit from the electricity of that kiss—the man Hollie deserved.

I meant to call her. I truly did. But after the surgery took my hands and feet, I woke up and Mack visited. He didn't say much. I kept expecting Regina to walk into the room and check on me. I kept imagining that my missing right hand was due to gunshots and not the careful blade of a surgeon.

He sat there and read sports news on his new smartphone and kept asking if I felt any healing coming on yet. I didn't. My eyes kept flicking toward the phone on my nightstand.

"Jesus, you call Rae yet, or what?" he said.

"I actually did," I said. "She's not at that number anymore."

"Thank the fucking gods," he said without looking up from his phone. "Look at this shit. Like, seven NFL coaches got fired. You're still a Bears fan, right? Who you got for their next coach?"

I used to love watching football. I think ignoring it was part of the self-flagellation I'd made a habit of since my hand grew back.

"Ditka," I said jokingly. "Mack, I think I'm into Hollie. Quite a bit."

He still didn't look up.

"I know. We sort of had this talk. My concern is that you're both having a little pity party. She's going to fuck you because

you saved her life; you're going to fuck her to forget about Rae.
I give it two months."

"Thanks," I said.

He was wrong. It didn't even really start. It didn't last a
moment after that conversation.

After the operation, once my hands grew back, I looked at
Hollie's number a few times but I couldn't call. Phones and I
got along just about as well as me and luck, or me and women.
Regina's spirit was so heavy as I cycled through those hospital
rooms—from pre-op to post-op to recovery, I could almost
hear Regina telling me to not inhale the helium in the balloon.
And when I saw Regina's face, I saw Rae's. That was the worst
part—that my adolescent love was controlling my adult desires.
I needed Regina, even if the relationship made zero sense and
was destructive and dysfunctional. My desire for her was sus-
pended, and Rae woke it up. I couldn't control it. Only Rae
could fulfill it now. I wasn't strong enough to let it rot and
finally move on.

If it weren't for that desire, happiness might have been a
phone call away. I knew Hollie liked me, and not in a pity-
party sort of way. I knew she was waiting. Finally, after a
month went by, she called. I let it go to voice mail and she
didn't leave a message. She did it again a few days later and
that was it.

The next few months were a haze of drugs and blood, of
Mack hovering over everything, of Tracy's stern advice and
relentless energy.

My meals were shit glopped on trays from hospital cafete-
rias. I thought of Regina, of Rae, of Hollie, of what my life

would be like if only I had the guts to be happy. One after the other, I was smothered with affection from recipients, compressed in hugs, drenched in tears, showered with proclamations of my generosity, feeling like shit the entire time, always in pain, always wondering, wondering, wondering. I had no doubt they were thankful, but on those days, I was usually weak from recovery, feeling constrained while wearing normal clothes like jeans instead of blue, assless hospital gowns, thinking all the time of Hollie fake-smiling during her double shift, putting on a show at a table to assure a solid tip. I thought of Rae and wondered if her eyes were black, considering where her heart finally settled. Maybe she'd left him for good, but needed a fresh start without me. Maybe she was still there, dodging punches.

Then, just as I told Hollie I would, I gave away my pancreas to a guy who was also named Dale, only this one had guts and balls. He had a limp from shrapnel that was unrelated to his latest act of heroism, the one that did, in fact, lead to the Medal of Honor. He was one of the few living recipients of the award, and Tracy was psyched. Nothing like free publicity, I guess. He mentioned me in all the press related to the medal, like if he deserved one, I deserved ten of them. He was wrong—he only had one leg to give. He was capable of sacrifice. I was not. In any case, I didn't get to know the guy that well during shooting. I didn't like to get emotionally involved with recipients after Hollie, and it showed on television—the only part of the show that focus groups keyed in on as a negative.

I was inaccessible, but that was by design. Capt. Lyle Hayes was the Commissioned Corps officer who shadowed our medical team. The corps, as Doc had told me, was under the umbrella of the United States Public Health Service, but

Hayes made it clear he represented interests in the CDC and the Department of Defense. The rules were simple: any footage with his likeness in it couldn't appear in any public forum. My exposure was limited to the show, filtered, controlled, and edited, and he personally approved all footage that appeared on television. Typically, Tracy would be fighting like a pit bull to get me on the *Today* show or a sit-down with Oprah, but she didn't fight the blackout. "You? In an unfiltered interview? It'd kill the show." She didn't elaborate, but I could tell she was taking an order from Hayes and shaping it into her own decision. Our communications mostly consisted of him glaring at me, pissed that he had to be out of uniform so much on my detail. He was a post-op fixture, though, hovering over me, clinging to his charts, riddling me with a barrage of questions, his pencil smoking as he spoke.

I gave away four organs—five if you include bone marrow— to Kimmy Higgins, a nine-year-old who had a myofibroblastic tumor that encircled her entire blood supply. She got the platinum maintenance plan—liver, two kidneys, pancreas, marrow—all at once. She lived, and somehow, so did I. It was simpler than it sounds—I just let machines do the work for me until I regenerated enough to wake up. Sometimes I'd spend time in comas—black and dreamless, just days and sometimes weeks flicking by as if I'd just blinked them away.

Dr. Reynolds stayed on as the leader of my medical team, but he never did come to grips with my ability. He seemed constantly amazed. "If this didn't kill you, nothing's going to kill you," he said before almost every surgery.

I did a double-lung transplant next—two Dale lungs, two different recipients. A double feature. Tracy kept saying it smelled like a season finale. My last surgery of the taping schedule was pretty basic. I gave a college athlete a liver and some bone marrow. He had severe aplastic anemia, and had endured a year of chemotherapy, infections, blood transfusions, a bout with pneumonia, and was almost always in the hospital. Greg Moseley was the guy's name, just a few years younger than me. We had a long talk off-camera about hospital stays. For once, a "contestant" I had something in common with.

"You're in the hospital, just thinking about everyone who's not in the hospital, wanting to be with them," he told me.

He made me feel silly and humbled and I almost called Hollie, but I didn't. I couldn't.

When they discharged me from that last surgery, I'd have months to go before my next one, and that was only if season two became a reality. We needed ratings. Everyone was left to prepare for and get nervous about the premiere, but I was me again, free to do whatever I wanted, so after that last checkup and surgery, I sat outside the hospital on the bench and cried. Even though most of my body was different, I was still the same goddamned Dale.

NINETEEN

WE WATCHED THE SEASON PREMIERE OF *The Samaritan* at Tracy's house, our first opportunity to relax after months of taping.

Two projection screens were set up in her living room—a cold space, the furniture white and hard, the walls mostly glass. Her entire house looked carefully staged, torn straight from a trendy catalog, an uninviting place with furniture that could be traded in for a car and curious decor with no functionality: glitter-spackled balls in a basket, wiry-looking tree things, candleholders that held candles with black wicks but no melted wax, so she must have lit the wicks to make them look like they were used often even though they weren't. Everything in there was either fragile or attracted fingerprints, giving the entire place a repellant, don't-touch vibe.

Mack drank a lot of beer at the party and when people asked him about his involvement with the show, he happily told them "associate producer." Everyone seemed appropriately impressed. I figured Mack Tucker wasn't the first guy in L.A. getting by on a useless job title. He was nervous—the next step was to have a hit on our hands. After enduring multiple surgeries over the past few months, I really didn't care if the first episode was a train wreck. I was almost hoping for a ratings stink bomb that would land me on the safe padding of the Hollywood blacklist. At least then, the decision would be made for me. If it was a hit, if they asked me for more, I couldn't say no. The show employed people. Mack was happy. Rae was out there, watching.

People I didn't know were getting introduced to me by Tracy. I would shake their hands and smile in all the right places and thank them for the congratulations and forget them the minute they walked away.

"Nervous?" Mack asked.

"I wish this thing would start already. I'm sick of these smiling pricks."

"Hey, I'm smiling."

"Yeah, but that's because you're the one who's nervous."

"Touché," he said, and finished his beer.

The show began with a voiceover, the Big Voice Guy opening the show with the words "In a cruel world, where being on a donor list means hoping to live while waiting to die . . ." Which was punctuated by images of crying families. Hugging families. Sick-looking people. To viewers, they were just montage images meant to set the mood. But they would meet these people. I had met them. I knew their names. I had saved them. Big Voice Guy continued, "These families are praying for a miracle. Dale Sampson is that miracle—blessed with an incredible and unexplained ability to regenerate his organs and limbs, his mission is to use his gifts to save as many lives as he can."

Then me, walking the streets of Los Angeles, looking nobly at random things in the distance. In every shot, the streets were wet because dry streets don't photograph well. Our crew had guys with hoses spraying them down. I can't watch a movie anymore without spotting the wet streets, even if it's a night scene in a film set in a dry climate.

It took me ten takes to look noble in that shot. I kept asking what I was looking at. Turns out it didn't matter.

Then the montage flashed to me off the streets and in a hospital gown, getting toted away. Hugging families in slow motion. Mack pushing me in a wheelchair, smiling down at me. Dr. Reynolds casually putting his arm around me. You see, he's more than just a doctor, he's my *friend*. The magic of television. I hated him. I wanted Venhaus instead, but Hayes shot that down. He assured me the good doctor was living his normal life in Grayson with no repercussions, and I believed him—they wouldn't want to piss me off. Not when I was co-operating so splendidly.

I was smiling directly at the camera to close the montage, and this shot had taken nineteen takes to get right.

All the while, Big Voice Guy summed up the hook of the show for our viewers at home. "The stories are real. The surgeries are daunting. But Dale will risk it all in order to be . . . *The Samaritan*."

At this point everyone at the party cheered. Corks popped, Champagne frothing onto the floor from multiple bottles. Tracy handed me a glass.

"They're ruining your carpet," I said.

"If my hunch is right, I can afford new carpet." She winked. "And you'll be hosting the next party."

"Fuck yeah," Mack said, and took the Champagne flute, knocking it back with one flick of the wrist.

"I can't drink," I said, smiling. "I'm on a pretty strong cock-tail of meds, and a little short of breath."

"Still recovering from the last one?" she asked.

I nodded.

"What was that one, the—"

"Double lung transplant," I finished. Two recipients, one

Dale Sampson, one surgery. Two lungs would mean certain death, right? The ventilator kept me alive. They planned on showing the time-lapse footage of my new, pink lungs blossoming into existence. Oh, the intrigue.

"Just relax, then," Tracy said. "Make yourself at home."

I trudged through all the congratulations and found a comfy place on her sofa next to Dr. Reynolds. He was definitely not a "doc" type. Smooth and good-looking, his ambition was never hidden. For him, this series was about becoming the expert on my condition, getting the assist for saving lives, building his legacy, not as a doctor but as a television personality. A guy who could stamp his approval on foods and diets and sell trendy health books. I could feel the memoir notes collecting in his little head. His contract even stated that at least one episode had to portray him saving me and the recipient from certain death. A few legal things had to be hashed out, but I was on board with it.

The first segment of episode one followed that winning formula, the time-tested showbiz axiom of "Give me the same, but different."

The first act of the show introduced the recipient, their family, their situation. The longer the odds, the better. The more tragic the story, the bigger the impact. Seeing Hollie on television, so long after I had first met her at home in Van Nuys, made me realize that I was a total fucking moron. Part of it was my longing and regret, but she looked beautiful, even at her sickest, which she was at the time of the taping.

In a tearful testimonial, on camera, Hollie described getting that phone call, the one where the Samaritan was going to ride to her rescue. Pictures of Hollie and Melissa, a mother struggling to raise her girl alone. A mother who struggled with diabetes that had turned into full-fledged end-stage renal disease, landing her on the transplant list. The average wait time? Ranging from a year or until death. In America, death usually comes first.

Commercial break. Silence in Tracy's living room. A sniffle or two. "Holy shit," Mack whispered. "This is fucking gold."

In the second act of the episode, I meet Hollie. I watched myself on television, a surreal feeling, the incisions flanking my rib cage still hot with pain days after my final surgeries of the season. Lots of silence in the room. Most of the people there, even the crew, hadn't seen the full episode yet. Maybe they snuck a peek at the sizzle reel—the six-minute teaser of this pilot episode that had kept the funding coming and the execs buzzing—but never this. Never my lack of charisma, my stone-cold and unemotional looks and tone, my inability to shed a tear, the awkwardness of my hugs when Hollie hugged me, sobbing, thanking me for a miracle. She said I was sent from God.

I believed that assessment to be wrong, and I was the only one in the room who realized she was putting everyone on by acting relieved. Only I knew that she'd wanted to die. I should have told her about the gun, about how much I wanted to do the same thing, but for no noble cause. Not for a daughter, but for pure cowardice, for pure exhaustion with a world that had no place for a freak like me.

The third act covered the surgery. Enter Dr. Reynolds, who clearly explains the procedure, and the drama heightens, thanks to the craftsmanship of the story editors.

The story editors, edit producers, and post-producers were by far the most important elements of the show, the overlords of manufactured tension, logging hours of interviews with the surgical team to mine the best quotes to splice into the broadcast. Their descriptions of dangers and complications could be sprinkled into the action, creating drama where there really wasn't any to begin with. If I gave you a picture of a focused doctor working steadily on his patient, and a voiceover doctor said, "This surgery has never been done like this. We're treading new ground. And it's not a matter of *if* something will go wrong, it's *when*"—cue dramatic music and cut to commercial, and you're done. Simple.

We glazed over the surgery, since kidney transplants are basic and frequent. The last ten minutes chronicled Hollie's recovery. She smiled during this part of the show. She spoke with relief and better skin color during the episode's final moments, Melissa playing at her feet. Melissa, whom I had yet to meet, but could have met. If I'd just made a phone call or two. If I could just move on from the twins.

Then, a strong focus on my recovery. As Tracy put it, showing me in healing mode drove home the fact that I could regrow these organs, and highlighted the extent of my sacrifice.

When the episode ended, the party remained silent. These were folks who had been in the trenches with us. Maybe it was the emotion of seeing how lives had changed, or the relief of seeing a glossy final product, the fruits of many hours of work. Who the fuck knows?

I just know that I didn't cry, I didn't know what the big deal was. What exactly had I given up other than a few days of pain? Days I would be well paid for?

"We have a hit on our hands," Tracy said, finally, breaking up the tension. Silence turned to cheers and applause. "I feel it in my bones. This just . . . lands inside of you."

The party regained momentum. Music fired up. People drank. They danced. Mack danced with Tracy, who looked to be drunk. She was in trouble, I knew that much. Both of them were drunk with fantasies of overnight ratings. And also, Champagne.

Nothing for me. I half expected Hollie to be at the party. Tracy told me she was invited, but she didn't show up. Too much of my life involved waiting for girls to show up at parties. She had her piece of me, but over the last few months, I basically told her through an uninterrupted, awkward silence that I wanted no piece of her. That wasn't the real truth, but I just wasn't strong enough to be that guy yet.

With the show over, I picked up the remote control and turned on one of the projector screens and found some of my favorite reruns on an obscure cable channel. Nobody objected. Nobody even seemed to notice.

The overnights for the first episode were strong, encouraging, but by no means explosive. Eight million or so viewers.

I could walk the streets of Los Angeles without much notice. I would walk with my eyes down, directly in front of me, avoiding cracks when I could, slicing through the throngs of people with a quick turn of the shoulders.

I had no agent, but I had Mack, who I think had an agent, but Mack worked directly with Tracy. He wouldn't say as much, but she would filter her advice to me through him, and he would regurgitate it to me as if it were something he discovered on his own, as if the credentials and clout and knowledge and legal acumen were gifted upon him in a dream.

I stayed in the apartment and did not watch the second episode, which drew ten million viewers. According to Mack, this upward tick in viewership was a huge sign, and we were one step closer to a fat contract for the second season, which would guarantee us houses "so fucking hot there's a basket near the door for chicks to leave their panties in."

Viewership climbed in week three and week four. Buzz built up like plaque. We were the number-two show on television. A second season lurked on the horizon. My likeness was featured on magazine covers. The legitimacy of my ability was debated on talk shows. Interview requests piled up, none of them granted.

I waited for them to ask me about season two, and it didn't take long before they wanted more from me.

Mack invited me to a steak dinner he insisted on paying for. This wasn't our typical McSteakhouse. The waiters were better dressed than we were. Crumbs and half-empty water glasses were not allowed. The lighting was low, or as he put it, "If I were gay this would be romantic as fuck."

Tracy was supposed to meet us, but later. We ordered some beers.

"That's okay, right? You feeling nice and recovered? One hundred percent?"

"Good to go," I said.

He kicked back the first one faster than usual. Something was up.

"You having marital problems or something?" I asked.

"What marriage?" he said, still wearing his ring. "I imagine her hanging out somewhere, just waiting for me to make enough money to bother with divorce papers. I'm not too worried about it. No worries, man. No regrets." He said that like a man with regrets.

We asked if they had one of those big fried-onion things. They didn't. So Mack told the waiter to bring more bread.

"Tracy isn't going to be here for another hour," he announced. "She's got the framework for a season-two contract."

"And?"

"And I want to know if you're on board."

"Are you asking me or telling me?"

"I'm asking, you socially backwards prick. If Tracy asked, you couldn't tell her no. You'd just nod and off we would go into the wild blue yonder. You ever wonder why you're not allowed to do interviews? You depress the fuck out of me sometimes."

He flashed two fingers at the waiter, who had fresh glasses of beer at the table before Mack mustered the words to continue.

"I think I'm sort of famous. And Rae still hasn't called."

"Fuck her and fuck Hollie. Look, bro, you fucked up the Hollie thing on your own, and I call that progress. But I'm glad that shit's all over. I told you, that Hollie thing had 'busted' written all over it. I'm not sure if you can handle real heartbreak, kid. It sucks. Having your sort-of-true-love blown away is a great goddamn tragedy, but let me ask you something—what if the thing Regina wanted to tell you at that party was to leave her alone? That she wanted no part of you? No puppy-dog looks, no more bullshit. How would that have fit? You dodged heartbreak by dodging Hollie. Trust me."

"Maybe heartbreak is exactly what I need," I said.

"Well, if you knew what was good for you, we wouldn't be here having this conversation."

"I thought this is what you wanted?"

"Yeah, for me. Not for you."

"I never thought there would need to be a season two," I said.

"Right. You become famous, Rae shows up at your

doorstep and you live happily ever after. But in the real world, where this is about business, I gotta tell you—season one only writes the check, motherfucker. Season two cashes it. But I'm not here to convince you to do it. I'm just here to ask you about it."

I ate bread instead of answering.

"And what would you have me do, best friend?" I asked.

"Honestly, Dale? We don't have to do this," Mack said. "I thought about it. I mean, really did, and there's money and bright lights out there for us, but I wonder if you'll wear down like a battery one day. My agent says we can get work off the steam of season one. Make bank in other ways, ways that aren't cutting you open. I even offered up another angle for the show, a way to transition you out but keep the concept. I wanted to try a different kind of episode, but we don't have the capital for my episode request. So no season two. I can't believe I'm saying it, there's some real money here and we have all the leverage, but I'm saying no."

This hit me, a cold jolt of wind blasting into the nerve of a sensitive tooth, the ice of the truth seeping into me. This was the grade-school Mack on that playground who'd spurned the girls to pick me up off the blacktop.

"I'm not saying no," I said. "Not yet."

"Do it only if it's what you want. Not for Raeanna. Please, sweet Jesus, not because of her. You haven't talked in a year for God's sakes. Fuck, man, you make me sick. Do you realize I could have your virginity cashed in tonight? With hot chicks, too. Not skanks. You have to ride this wave, brother. Let her live her little self-destructive existence and go about your fucking business."

"I'm still me," I said. "I went through all of this for nothing."

"Nothing?" Mack said. "Those people you helped would

be dead by now, and you can't even let yourself feel good about it?"

"We could do whatever we wanted in season two," I said. "I don't need to find Raeanna to talk to her, and if I talk to her, maybe that loop closes. Then maybe there's something with Hollie, or someone else, even. Maybe I'll be who I have to be for once—strong enough to find what I need to find."

"It's your decision, brother. I don't think it's the right one, but I got your back." He raised his glass. "To season two."

Our glasses clinked and we guzzled our beers until our eyes watered, the waiters hovering over us, ready to refill them instantly. We let them.

We were half-drunk when Tracy got there, dressed a little too sexy for a business dinner. She sat down next to Mack. She had a briefcase stuffed with notes and paperwork and parameters for a season-two agreement.

"You're going to need new paperwork," I said. "I'm doing an interview this season. At least one. It doesn't have to be on a talk show or anything, we can even make it an episode so there's some measure of control, but it's got to be live."

"You really think the government acronyms that are up our asses are going to approve that? Get real. And I've been more than happy keeping you out of interviews because you have the social skills of roadkill. Nothing you can say comes across as likable. It's what you do that matters. What you say can only screw things up. The answer is no."

She ordered a Chardonnay. I sensed Mack's hand on her leg under the table. He winked at me.

"I'll get Hayes to budge," I said. "If he doesn't, you can find another fully regenerating human to take my place. And maybe the next one will even have some social skills."

"Fine," she said. "You get Hayes to budge, I'll sign off on it. One interview, our episode. I approve the questions in advance."

I was fine with that.

She looked at Mack. "You tell him yet?"

He shook his head. "Nope. I told you I knew the answer. But fuck it, hear it from him. Sampsonite, what's your stance on religious partnership? You care to sign up as, say, a walking messiah for your local Christian megachurch?"

"Pass," I said.

"You should think about it," Tracy said. "It's not different than endorsing a brand of sneakers. You just show up for a few Sunday services, we put out a press release, nothing huge. It'd boost the show and you would get some positive publicity out of it."

"If I could make water into wine, I'd get into the liquor business, not the religion business."

"They're willing to pay," Tracy said. "More than your show salary. It would shut up the ethicists out there, the ones that think this whole show concept is immoral, that we're taking fame in return for saving people. They don't think it's something Jesus would do, so you could use a little Jesus on your side."

"You talk to Hayes about this little idea?" I said. "You ever think about the consequences if I legitimize a world religion? I don't think that would do the scientific community any favors, but he'd be far more concerned about the consequences in the Middle East. They're not exactly mild-mannered when it comes to shitting on their particular brand of theology. Besides, if I always vowed that, no matter what, I would never send Carlton Franks or anyone like him a dime. Not unless I was healed through the television, then maybe I'd consider. But endorsing them? That would be even worse. As for the ethics police, I can't say I don't agree."

"Organ donations are up," she said. "People are remembering to sign their driver's licenses and become donors. Nondirected donations are at an all-time high. That's our shield against any puritans out there saying you're soiling the institution of donation. And how did you know it was Carlton Franks who contacted us?"

"Who else could it be?" I said, trying not to act surprised. "Anyway, I'm not finished. Demand number two: I want Allen Venhaus on my medical team, like fucking today, or there's no season two. Period."

Tracy stared at her Chardonnay. "Why can't you be this decisive on television?"

"You got the check?" I said to Mack. He nodded once. "See you later," I said, and got up to leave.

Of course I was assured my demands would be met. The only concession was "reunion" episodes during my downtime, my healing time. They needed more episodes for a season two order, and our taping schedule could only accommodate four to six surgeries when you factored in recovery times for me and the recipients. Getting a second season taped would take a while as they scooped me clean, my organs like crops to be rotated, only worth a hell of a lot more. An "update" on people I've helped through reunion episodes would be cheap programming that could draw viewers, an idea that Mack came up with, probably as he was concocting ways to keep me out of the operating room.

I went home and pretended the camera was rolling behind the bathroom mirror. I needed to practice—if I got my interview episode, where I could tell America anything I wanted. I drew a blank, stopping, starting, wondering. I had no plan. I just figured when the real camera was rolling, I'd find the right words and Rae would be watching.

TWENTY

CAPTAIN HAYES WANTED TO TALK TO ME BEFORE GREEN-lighting an interview episode. Tracy gave me a coffee-shop address and a time. I got there five minutes early, and Hayes was already seated in a booth, wearing civilian clothing, but his khakis had crisp pleats and his dress shirt didn't have a single wrinkle. No pieces of stray lint clung to its surface, and the points of his collar looked sharp enough to draw blood.

"If you're trying to look civilian, it's not working," I said, sitting down across from him. "Your posture is too good. Your clothes look like I can bounce a quarter off of them."

"Since we're being frank here, I think I should express that the initial novelty of your little healing tricks have worn off, your act is wearing thin, and I do not like what you have chosen to do here."

"Good."

He dismissed me with a careful sip of coffee. I could smell its blackness and strength from across the table.

"This won't take long. We don't have to give in to any of your demands. You walk away from this show, it doesn't make a difference to us."

"Compliance is the difference," I said. "I want the interview. You want compliance."

"You haven't complied from the start," he said. "Days of research on you take months with the breadcrumbs you've given us. You get the interview, you get approval on Venhaus, you get one more season. After that, we get six months, on campus, at the Triangle. You'll be an honored resident. After that, we'll see."

"Sign off on the interview, sign off on Venhaus as a gesture of goodwill. *Then* we'll see."

"Listen here, you little shit, compliance can be forced. We can only smash a terrorist's toes once, but yours we can put on an infinite loop."

"I think you're familiar with the story of the golden goose? Putting your hands around my neck won't make me shit the golden eggs any faster. You're either with me, or you're against me."

"I want my hand on the Dump button," Hayes said. "I won't press it unless you talk about religion, or US government involvement. I'd advise you to be vague about the extent of your powers. Keep the focus on the show, or whatever girl it is you're drooling for."

"No," I said. "You have my word I won't mention you or the government, and I won't be inflammatory when it comes to religion, but anything less than a live feed and you'll have to kill me to research me, I promise you that."

He couldn't help but laugh. "I didn't know you had this kind of grit in you, boy. On TV you come off as a pussy."

"I think everyone's a pussy to guys like you," I said. "That's not a compliment."

"It's close enough," he said. "All right, then. Live feed and you can bring Venhaus in. I think it's worth noting I'm going out on a limb for you here. I'm trusting you. Also, we haven't been the hardasses we could have been. Your medical team is adequate at best because TV people picked them instead of us. They haven't picked up on a little something that only you and I know."

"My healing's slowing down," I said. "Running down, like a battery." Mack had called it.

"One more season. If you hold up. If I have to put a stop to this whole carnival, I'll do it, no matter what you think you can hold over us. Studying a dead body is better than studying the boy who got away."

He got up. "I didn't pay for that coffee. Put it on the show's tab." He grabbed his jacket and left.

A few days later, Tracy called me with news on Venhaus—he was in, but he wanted to talk to me, alone, before signing any releases.

I finally had some creative control, some clout. Nothing would be said about Doc's ancient error for the purposes of dramatic backstory. For the purposes of the second season, he would just be a concerned doctor, a great doctor, who decided to join the team. I would repair his image and that would be plenty of payback for the patience and advice he had given me.

He came to L.A. to see me in person. A year had passed since I last saw him. He looked haggard, older, the edges on his face and neck a bit harder, the creases and folds of his flesh solid as bent metal.

Tracy gave us her office, the new one. Glass and light, space and skyline. Comfortable chairs. Doc wore a suit that looked like he dug it out of a closet for just this occasion, one he hadn't worn in years. It even had the leather patches on the elbows; all he was missing was a pipe and monocle. It took him a long time to look me in the eye. We shook hands.

"I'm sorry I dragged you into this, Doc," I said.

"Don't be sorry," he said. "But this, all this is wrong, Dale. Even you can't save all the people on those lists by yourself."

"Organ donations are up."

"You're whoring yourself. This is just as bad as selling organs on the black market."

"But I've got some leverage with the feds now, if the allowances I've squeezed out of them are any indication. You're here, aren't you? We can make you right again. A famous doctor. You can get in on the ground floor with whatever it is I can do with my body."

"Angie's dead," he said. He walked over to the window. "It's my fault and nothing can change that. Nothing you can do makes that mistake go away."

"We can fix it all up," I said. "Show everyone you saved someone, anyone. I'll just have them pluck someone off the list. Hell, you can pick if you want. By the time they're done with you, they'll want to give you a medal."

"They?"

"They."

"No way to slice me out of what I live in," he said. "We're made of cells and tissue, veins, bones, and blood, but reality doesn't transplant. You can't cut and paste a soul."

"So why the hell did you come?"

"Not for what you think or expect. I just want to see for myself that they're treating you right around here."

"Well, you're in," I said, without hesitation. "Under one condition—you're my guy. You don't listen to surgeons or producers or Captain Hayes or anyone else, not even Mack."

"Why do I get the feeling you have something planned that may not be in your best interest?"

"'Best interest'? I'm the guy who lops off toes for fun."

"Fair enough," he said. "So do you still think things don't happen for a reason?"

"You one of these nuts that thinks I need to choose a religion?"

"That's not an answer."

"I don't know, Doc. Maybe they happen for a reason. A bad one."

He chuckled, then opened Tracy's mini fridge and grabbed a bottle of water, looked at me, and smiled. "She won't mind, right?"

"I'll have one of my television slave drivers send you an agreement. But you may be docked for the water."

When I heard a knock on the door, I thought it might be Hollie. Mack never knocked like that. He usually tried the doorknob first and if it was locked, he'd just let himself in—even though he'd moved out once the checks started rolling in, he kept a key.

Excuses to explain myself to Hollie started forming in my head, the most honest of which was, "I'm just not ready, I've lived my life scared and I'm still scared and I'm just not ready to let you know how much I care about you," and then I opened the door and it was Raeanna.

Suddenly, I couldn't say jack shit. I was used to the way L.A. people looked, especially the girls—perpetually tanned and teeth so impressively white you wanted to scream, all of them puking their way to rail-thin figures. To see Rae holding a cheap purse, wearing a JCPenney sweatshirt even though it was too warm for it, her hair tied in a simple ponytail, it was mostly a visual exhale for me.

She looked beautiful to me in a way that Hollie wasn't, not

that either of them was prettier than the other. Rae was shorter and she carried a little more weight on her cheekbones, giving her a full face highlighted by those sparkling eyes.

"You left him?" I said finally.

She hugged me for a long time. When it was over, she shook her head without looking me in the eyes. "Technically, I'm tagging along with my best friend to New York," she said. She was too clothed to check her properly for signs of abuse, but her face looked perfect for once. "Harold expects me back on Monday evening."

She had two days in L.A. I wondered what she meant to accomplish, but didn't ask.

"You know, this is a pretty crap place for a TV star," she said, trying to lighten the mood.

"I'm saving for retirement," I said. "And crap apartments here buy you mansions where we live." *Lived*, I meant to say. Past tense. I wasn't in Illinois anymore and I wasn't going back.

"I guess. I stopped for a coffee on the way here, and even in a convenience store, it cost more per ounce than my perfume, I think."

She was here. Finally here, and I found myself thinking of what Hollie was doing, where she was working, what she might have thought of me after so many months.

"I thought about you a lot, even before you were on TV," she said. "It's dumb. We're completely toxic for each other at this point. I can't be sure if I thought of you because you're you, or because you're not Harold."

Another curse, this one shared by everyone drawing a breath: we know what we feel, but never why. We get the raindrops but never peek inside the clouds.

"I just want you safe," I said. "All of this, the show, L.A., all of this sprang out of seeing you in that Wal-Mart checkout line."

"It looks hard to be superhuman in real life," she said.

"I wish I had the scars to show it, but I remember them. I look at a spot, like here," I said, pointing to my rib cage, "and I remember the incision and how much it hurt for days afterward."

"If you were to feel like you saved me, would you stop?" she said.

"I don't know," I said. "I think so. It started out feeling that way, like you'd see me on TV all the time, wonder about me. About us. Maybe one day leave him and let yourself pursue something better. But even if that notion was crazy, even if I didn't meet you in the checkout line that day, I had to run, and the public eye was the only safe place. I didn't want to be here, and I don't want to be here forever."

"It's a nice notion," she said. "But when were you planning on letting *yourself* pursue something better? What if I didn't show up?"

"I got approval to do an interview episode. I hadn't heard from you; I was going to use it to tell you I still cared and that I wanted you to leave him."

"In front of millions of people, you'd embarrass me like that?"

"I never thought of it that way," I said.

"That is just so . . . Dale," she said, smiling. "If you promised me that you'd stop the show, I'd feel better about asking you what I came to ask you. Even though I'm not sure I can ask you."

"I promise I'll stop," I said, blurting it out without thinking.

"Thank you," she said. "But I don't want to talk about it right now. I don't want to ask you. I can't. Not yet."

"Sure," I said. "You hungry? Thirsty?"

She nodded. I didn't have much in the kitchen, but wanted to impress her by actually cooking something. I made pancakes and bacon, the perfectly incorrect meal for three p.m. She ate an entire short stack, using so much syrup I thought she'd get diabetes before the meal was over. I knew what stress eating felt like anyway.

When she was finished, she asked to lie down. I darkened my bedroom and tucked her in. She touched my face and smiled. "I feel like I haven't rested in weeks," she said. "I'm just going to sleep, if you don't mind. I may sleep right through the night. Would I be putting you out or something, if I stayed?" I shook my head.

I sat on the couch and turned on the television. Raeanna was here, sleeping in my bedroom. I didn't feel any kind of victorious rush. I thought of Hollie. As usual, I couldn't let myself have a perfect, happy moment. There was no silver lining I couldn't strip away to find the darkness within. I couldn't let that happen. Not this time. I had only one chance. Only then did I have the strength to break my inertia and dial Hollie's number. It didn't go to voice mail—I heard the distinct sound of someone picking up, then hanging up.

I found a *Cheers* rerun, one of my favorites, the one where Sam and Henri have a contest to get phone numbers. I think Mack would have beaten them both, but maybe I was biased. When Sam walked out at the end, triumphant not in phone-number volume, but in having three lovely ladies on his arm, I dialed Hollie again and got the same result.

I looked in on Rae, who was slightly snoring. Her shoulders were naked and I knew she had taken her shirt off, probably even her bra, the quilt lying just over the top of her breasts, which were no doubt pooled underneath in that sexy way I'd only seen on Cinemax movies.

I watched more television and fell asleep. I woke up after midnight, and Rae was snoring louder now, lying on her side.

I went outside and it was like someone turned on the lights and volume of my existence. No city ever truly sleeps. This one never even got drowsy. I hailed a cab and had it drop me off at Hollie's house.

Bugs harassed the naked, yellow bulb on her porch, looking like electrons, flying in smooth, practiced circles. All the lights were out. She and Melissa would be asleep, but I was here and just needed to ask her a question to see the answer in her face.

I knocked. I heard the rumble of footsteps in this simple house, the air bursting with the smell of night and dew, the sound of wind strumming trees.

Lights turned on, emitting a soft glow behind the drawn curtains. A man cracked the door, keeping the chain latched—a fit, good-looking man, with no shirt on, with abs, with stubble. His eyes were kinked up with sleep, and he rubbed at them, muttering, "Who the fuck are you? You know what time it is?" through a sticky mouth of not-quite-morning breath.

What could I really say to the guy? I found myself crushed to have him answer the door. A part of me exploded with self-hatred, with regret. It fought with the part of me that was relieved that another decision had been made for me. If Hollie had answered the door, if she let me in, if she forgave me for ignoring her, what would I do? Luckily, women like Hollie moved on. Maybe women like Rae did too—it just took them a hell of a lot longer.

"I need to speak to Hollie please," I said.

He yelled for her and yielded without another word, either knowing who I was or just not caring. Hollie came to the door wrapped in a robe.

"Dale?"

"I have to ask you something."

"Come by tomorrow, please, if you insist. This is just inappropriate." She rubbed her eyes and the yellow light glinted off of a ring. On her left ring finger. An engagement ring.

"I know it's inappropriate, but it won't take long. Now, if I didn't give you a kidney . . . listen carefully, okay? If I didn't give you a kidney, and you met me without the whole *Samaritan* thing, would you have liked me just the same?"

Her eyes flickered behind me, past me, through me, anywhere but upon me.

"You're a nice man," she said. "I hope this isn't a romantic question, because I'm—"

"Engaged. Sure. I get it. I didn't call for months. I'm a prick. I'm an asshole. But if we met and just talked like this, small talk, normal talk, without the kidney backstory, would you smile at me? What kind of person do you think I am?"

"Generous," she said. "Good night, Dale."

"No. I said if I didn't give you a kidney. You wouldn't know if I was generous or not. What would you think of me?"

There. Pity. Of course she wouldn't say anything. I couldn't make her forget what she had gained from me, but I refused to admit I had given her anything, anything at all. But she must have wanted to humor me. Honor me with some truth. Or at least kill my urge to ever call her again.

"I wouldn't have given you a second thought. Okay?" she said. "I'm not happy to say it. Don't you remember when I almost fucked you out of guilt?"

"I remember when you kissed me," I said.

"You might have remembered, but you didn't care," she said. "You never called."

"Is he good to you?" I asked.

She closed the door behind her and stood with me on the

porch. Me and porches and hospital rooms and random beatings—Jesus, some things I could just not escape.

"He's fine," she said. "He's a good-looking man with a good job. I've given up on some scorching romance that changes my life. We'll marry while the sex is still new to him, then I only have to work one job. Then he'll either stay and take care of us, or get tired of me and move on, but I'll be better off thanks to whatever settlement he leaves behind. Melissa will be better off. And I have to do it because of you."

"Me?"

"You, Dale. I told you—I didn't want to live. I truly didn't. Now I have to live like this. Mel has to live like this. I have to endure business decisions instead of real relationships so I can drop at least one shift and be with her, try to wring some sort of value out of the time I've got left. Time you forced on me. God was going to take me away and replace me with a fresh slate for her, and then there was you. You, Dale."

I bit the inside of my lip to stop it from quivering. "You don't have to put yourself through that. You can wait for the right man. If you need some money to wait, some money to be happy, just—"

"Fuck you, Dale," she said. "I don't want your money. Not a dime of it. I already have a scar that makes me think of you. I don't want to think about you anymore."

"I just wanted to help," I said.

"Saving people doesn't necessarily mean saving their lives," she said. "Good-bye, Dale. Oh, and what we just talked about was fuck-it talk, okay? That's the last we speak of it. I owed you the truth. I owed you that much."

I nodded and she went inside. The old Dale might have taken everything she said at face value, but I was finally sure about how much she cared about me, about how much it hurt her that I disappeared. She didn't believe in love anymore. She didn't believe she deserved it. Here I was, the world's most inexplicable marvel, saving lives at every turn with impossible abilities, and I'm the one that made her stop believing in miracles.

I stood on the porch until she turned the lights out, leaving me in the dark.

I smelled coffee in my hallway and knew it was coming from my apartment. When I keyed myself in, the lights were on and Rae was standing in the kitchenette, spooning sugar into her mug.

"I hope you don't mind," she said. She took the coffee to the living room and sat on the couch.

"I was just out . . . visiting with someone," I said.

She smirked. "We're not married. I don't care if you went out for whatever it is you went out for. It's not my business."

I sat down near her, but not next to her, leaving a vacant cushion between us.

"You going to sleep?" she asked.

"I don't sleep much. I certainly can't sleep with you in my apartment," I said.

"I think that's a compliment?"

"Yeah, it's pretty-girl-at-my-place nervousness, not murdering-thief-in-my-midst fear or anything."

She drank coffee and picked a channel. We watched syndicated comedies I never got into, like *Seinfeld* and *Home Improvement*. She laughed out loud so much I figured it was on purpose, a way to break the tension, the silence. She had something to ask and I could do nothing but wait.

After a couple of episodes had passed, she said, "What's the sunrise look like around here?"

"Looks like someone slowly turning the contrast up on a television," I said.

"You ever go to the beach around here and watch it?"

"We're on the West Coast, Rae. The sun rises over the city, not the ocean."

"Yeah. Right."

I realized she might have been poking me into a little date of sorts. Hell, I didn't know. I didn't know anything anymore.

"What's the hardest part?" she asked. "About all the surgeries?"

I knew that answer immediately. I never tried to form it into words, but I tried for her.

"I'm not sure if you knew this. Do you remember when my ribs got broken by Clint?"

"Yeah," she said, looking disappointed for some reason.

"Regina drove me to the hospital and stayed with me for a while. After Clint stomped the shit out of me, I woke up in a hospital room and she came to see me. She brought a balloon. Now with every surgery, every time I wake up, I keep finding myself hoping she will be there, and all over again, the reality of her death sets in. It's like when you wake up after a good dream and it takes a few moments before it fades away and reality wrecks it, and you have this little moment of disappointment. For me, the disappointment stays a little longer. Usually until I get another dose of painkillers."

Rae stared into the rim of her coffee cup.

"God, Dale, I can't fucking take it anymore."

"What?"

"In the hospital room? That was me."

It was like my blood suddenly couldn't find the places it needed to be. My breath got short.

"But Regina gave me her number."

"Because I was too shy. She said she'd get you to call, that she would help hook us up."

"And after that—"

"It was all me. Always me. At the baseball diamond when Clint hurt you. Driving you to the hospital. Giving you the balloon. You just kept wanting me to be Regina and I couldn't say anything. I was shy and scared and didn't want to see you be disappointed that I wasn't Regina. The way you looked at me and talked to me when you thought I was her, I kind of loved it. No one ever talked to me that way."

"The party. The note. 'R.' That was you?"

"I'd finally got up the courage to tell you the truth. I left the note in your locker. I wanted to tell you at that party, that it was me.

"If I'd said something earlier," she continued, "if you knew that Regina didn't care about you but I did, who knows how things could have been different. I should have been at the party. We were going to make things right that night, Regina and me. I was going to walk out of Ted's party with you holding my hand and she was going to crack the façade of Mack Tucker and leave Clint for good. God, Clint—he never would have pursued her as hard as he did if he hadn't known how desperately *you* wanted her. She was nothing more than a way for him to fuck with you, fuck with Mack."

The twins were no different from Mack and me at that age, plotting a perfect outcome, the path to a utopian future. The next day, the next year always feels like it's going to be perfect, so we fuck up the present waiting for it to rearrange itself, but of course it doesn't.

"If I never let you believe it was Regina, if I didn't beg her to let me tell you on my own time . . ."

"How?" I asked. "She fucked around with Mack. That's why he went off. You had nothing to do with that."

"He went after her because *you* liked her. If I'd just told you sooner, maybe he would have shifted his focus to me, and who knows how that might have turned out."

"It might have ended up with you in that truck," I said.

She stopped short of telling me that she would have taken that outcome, but I could tell that's what she was thinking.

"You don't stop guys like Clint," I said. "Something else would have pressurized his crazy ass and the pop would have been just as loud and deadly."

"I just keep going over it in my head," she said. "I gave you the note. I was ready to tell you the truth. Regina was relieved. She kept telling me it wasn't right, keeping you mixed up. That night, God, Regina tried so hard—I mean she physically tried to pull me out of my bedroom and get me to that party. I just couldn't do it. I was scared."

She feared the big reveal, when someone you care about might look you in the face and tell you they don't give a rat's ass about you. I knew the power of that moment. So did my mother—it's easy to convince yourself you're not dying of cancer when you avoid the doctor, but you can't dodge the truth forever. We can only postpone it, sometimes for so long that the truth doesn't even matter anymore.

"You had nothing to be afraid of," I said. "I would have loved you."

Memories of Regina were dying in my mind. I had to recast her in my brain as Rae, and it felt strange, but the girl I'd fallen for all those years ago was suddenly alive, on my couch, drinking my coffee.

I took a breath so I could move again, and closed the gap between us, sliding onto the middle cushion. I put my hand on her forearm, and she took the cue and put down the coffee, and held my hand in both of hers.

"It's not your fault," I said. "Not her, not Harold, not any of it."

"I know. I just can't make myself believe it."

"Believe it. It's not your fault."

"Say it again," she said, her hands clammy.

She leaned in and kissed me, hard. I kissed her back and it all seemed to happen while I was on the cusp of passing out, her sweatshirt hitting the floor and her breasts in my hands, the way she commanded me, pushing my head and my hands into soft places. She seemed to know I was a virgin, to sense it, and it should have been beautiful but I was done before we got started, so to speak. I tried to apologize, but she shushed me and waited, taking me into her hands and waiting for me to get hard again, smiling, getting on top of me. Sweat started to blossom on the small of her back as she worked, and this wasn't exactly what I thought it would be, this love thing, and that's what this was. She pushed away the coffee table and got on all fours and helped me inside of her. "I love it like this," she said. "This is ours," she said, and I knew it was a way that Harold had never done it, a way he hated, and I knew it was love because Mack had always said love is a feeling you wish was forever, you never want it to end, and feels best from behind.

I stared at her back, her hair, the way she turned to try to see me. She reached, touching my hip with her hand, urging me along and I looked at the television because it was on, and who can look away from a television? It's like trying to stare at a word without reading it.

But the people on TV were pixels, not flesh, not real. Rae was real, and we fucked away a million pounds of guilt and regret and frustration and fear that night.

We slept on the living-room floor and woke each other up with kisses, followed by wordless, greedy sex. We ate more pancakes in our underwear, then had sex again. Later that day, we ordered takeout and fucked until the delivery guy knocked on the door—I paid for it while wrapped in a blanket and put the sack of Chinese on the coffee table, where it got cold as we finished our latest session. We were sweaty and hungry, eating from white boxes while staring at each other, wanting each other. I ate so fast I almost vomited while she was on top of me.

We went straight through the night, enduring rug burns and chafed skin. We had sex half-asleep, and then I woke up with her mouth on me, limp, trying to suck-start me into another roll and by Christ I was game.

She had to fly home in the morning and she still hadn't asked whatever it was she wanted to ask. I didn't press her, but I wanted her to hurry up and get to it. I wanted her away from Harold. I wanted more of her, all of her, nights and days filled with nothing but her.

We lay in bed as the sun rose, waiting for our bodies to oblige us one more time.

"So when are you leaving?" she asked.

"Leaving?"

"Leaving's the only word I have for it. Going on hospital tour. Doing your Samaritan thing again."

"Another week or so," I said.

"What are you going to do with your little interview episode now?"

"I don't know. Propose?"

She held up her hand—she still had her wedding ring on. I hadn't noticed until right then.

"Bad form," she said.

"Well, maybe I'll just use it as a platform to retire. As long as your ring is gone by then."

She didn't say anything. Her hands did the talking and the rest of the early morning was panting and light sleep. Finally, deep sleep took over as the sky outside turned gray. When I woke up, she was gone. Full sun peeked through my drawn shades and I suddenly wasn't sure what day it was.

I shambled into my living room and Mack was sitting on the couch, holding the remote in one hand and a beer in the other.

I froze.

"I had to make sure you were breathing," Mack said. "I pounded the fuck out of the door before I used my key. You look positively post-coma, and that's coming from a guy who's actually seen you post-coma."

"What time you get here?"

"Not long ago," he said. "Two beers ago? Shit, son, it's almost dinnertime. We going out or what? It's almost season-two time. You better get your strength up."

"Yeah. Let me get ready. Hey, you see anyone?"

"Like, where? Here? You holding out on your boy? Some hot call girl or something? They usually run a two-dick discount. You should have called."

"Never mind," I said, and got ready. We did our normal steakhouse thing, and I waited for Rae to call and ask me whatever it is she came to ask me, but she never did.

TWENTY-ONE

BY THE TIME THE FIRST SEASON WAS DONE AIRING ITS limited run, *The Samaritan* was the number-one show of the summer, and the number-three show overall. The next step was to crush the singing competitions, and by measure of publicity and buzz, even I could see that when the next season finally hit the airwaves we'd be number one.

The strategy of keeping me from doing interviews had some unintended consequences. I became the Holy Grail for the paparazzi, and I barely left the house, making pictures of me even more in-demand. I was a mystery, a blank slate allowing columnists and bloggers to flood the Internet with ruminations about my motivations, my personality. To some, I was a humble man using one of the only outlets modern society could offer—television—as a platform to share my gift with the world. Others thought it was a disgrace to besmirch my gifts on a reality TV show. Then there were the extremists, the religious nuts who either thought I was Jesus or a conniving Antichrist looking to influence the world with my black magic.

The debate also included how we were manipulating the donations system. Purists correctly detailed how we were violating the law by getting "valuable gain" in the way of TV ratings and publicity, two things that translated directly into mountains of cash. The false-flag nut jobs actually came up with the right answer for once—that the government was turning a blind eye in exchange for my cooperation in testing. They even had unique ways of coming up with conspiracies of my power being weaponized. One blogger wrote a jarringly specific article about an unstable chemical weapon that caused a fast, fatal necrosis, arguing that I was the key to stabilizing the compound for military use.

My defenders came back strong, citing the increase across the board in altruistic donations—blood donations, organ donations, directed donations—all at record highs. More people were checking their driver's licenses to make sure that they were donors. I even filmed a PSA urging people to donate.

The final debate was more specific to me: What was my responsibility? Should I give and give forever? What if I stopped? What if I wanted to retire and stop enduring the surgeries? That was a messy one for even me to consider.

At the very least, the hoax angle died out. Our network put up a million-dollar reward for anyone who could prove that I was a hoax. The other networks had a more vested, monetary interest than just the reward—everyone craved having the number-one show on their channel, and if the other network had it, tearing it down was just as effective as beating them with programming of your own. I bet that Hayes secretly hoped the hoax rumors would persist, but he signed off on a live Internet stream of one of my surgeries and recoveries—the double-lung transplant. They time-lapsed it on television, but that particular surgery had dozens of in-person medical witnesses and millions of viewers livestreaming online, via the network's website, which was a pretty cutting-edge thing at the time. I guess Hayes and his superiors wanted the world to know that what America had in its possession was one hundred percent legit, but streams can be doctored and those who didn't believe still didn't believe. The skeptics were a vocal minority, drowned out by my various champions in the media. But that was it for live streams— both Hayes and I figured once was enough, and the network didn't want to water down the show itself by broadcasting the footage from the tapings.

All of this resulted in the tapings of season two getting as much coverage and buzz as the episodes themselves. The tapings were like nested dolls from which the smaller, more concentrated version of reality would emerge—heavily edited, of course.

In the first taping of the second season, Patrick Debrobander, an eight-year-old burn victim, was the star.

Patrick had no parents. He lived in an orphanage in the desolate, corn-fed state of Iowa. One of the boys at the orphanage was a couple years older and was a known bed wetter and animal torturer, leaving him just one merit badge short of the serial-killer trifecta. He earned it on a Friday in September, rolling up Patrick in a blanket and setting it on fire. He called the game "human log" and they found him putting a marshmallow on the end of a coat hanger while Patrick thrashed and screamed to escape the flaming blanket.

Third-degree burns on his arms, straight to the bone. Second-degree most everywhere else. Barely a patch to harvest a skin graft to get his cheeks one bit closer to flesh-toned. His blue eyes twinkled in a mess of pink and red, his nose, luckily, had shape, but no flesh. His hair, scalp, forehead, and eyebrows were all fine, making him the perfect makeover candidate for our show. Obviously. I wouldn't have met the boy if the story editors couldn't deliver a happy ending.

Dr. Reynolds tested my ability to regrow skin by removing a patch on top of my thigh. In three days, it returned, no scars, just a barely visible line where the incision was made. "You scar," he had told me, "but barely. It's imperceptible."

This episode would definitely need a "Warning: Graphic Content" voiceover after every commercial break. Seeing Dr. Reynolds pull out a pink glop from my guts, as he had in past surgeries, looked neat compared to this massacre. Two surgical teams worked, my skin getting yanked off in big patches still orange from iodine, then getting carried to another surgical room, where they shaped Patrick back into a flesh-colored human being.

Considering the amount of blood and gristle that was spilled, the outcome startled even me. He had suture lines and the shape of his lower face wasn't quite right, but the world could be his again. He smiled and hugged me at the end. This hug took place a month after surgery, after I had recovered in a sterile environment, protected from the media, while my skin slowly crawled and expanded over craters of itching rawness, making me new again.

After I checked out, Doc Venhaus insisted on driving me home in his rented Chevy Cobalt. Rae had gone silent. I could do nothing but wait. For once, I knew what Hollie felt like. But Doc knew something about Rae and Harold, and the more I hammered him for information, the more he kept his distance during the tapings of the surgeries.

"So what's your complaint of the day?" I asked him.

"Did you tell them about your healing timeframe, compared to your healing in my office when you first met me?

Not that it matters. I can't be so stupid as to think someone as sharp as Reynolds hasn't noticed."

"I think he's noticed. He just doesn't care. Without me there's no show, and he lives for the show."

"So *you* know. You just don't care."

"What's your family think of you being attached to my hip in L.A. for six months?" I asked.

He turned up the radio and we didn't talk again until he pulled up at the curb in front of my apartment.

"Why did you bring me out here, Dale? Did you think I'm another person you need to save?"

"If you aren't, then why the hell are you here?"

"Same as you. I don't have anywhere else to go."

"What the hell are you talking about?"

"You left and didn't tell me where you were going, so I didn't have any information to give them when they finally came on strong."

"They?"

"It seems that Hayes is a proper representative of 'they' in this affair. The surveillance was keyed in on me at the time, like I was the one laying the foundation of some massive hoax. It's a lucky break for you it was that way, otherwise they probably would have sniffed out your plans to come out here with your friend."

"You would have told them I was out here, if you knew. Right?"

"You're goddamn right," he said. "Anything they had planned is better than this carnival you built out here. They would have treated you better than you're treating yourself. Better than they treated me."

"Which is how?"

"Hostile. Evasive. Even though I wasn't either myself. I

gave them everything on you, every piece of data I had. Detailed statements about my evaluations of you. I signed affidavits. I passed lie detectors."

"And they still wrecked you," I said.

"First, they took my license because I gave you prescription lidocaine with no legitimate medical purpose."

"That's bullshit. How did they even know?"

"Because I told them in a statement. But don't worry, if it wasn't that, there's only a thousand other reasons they can conjure out of thin air to revoke a medical license. Without the license, my practice was quite obviously gone. My income. Then our credit cards went dry. My bank accounts were frozen. My house descended into foreclosure. Lucille tried, and wanted to stay, but I was damaged goods. The divorce was my idea, to keep her from circling the drain with me. Samantha went to live with her mother."

"So what did you do after all that?"

"Government aid, if you can believe it. They gave me an apartment and a monthly stipend. All I had to do was sit by the phone and wait for you to call, and when you did, I had to cooperate."

"So you're spying on me right now?"

"Yes," he said. "And I'm supposed to put pressure in the right spots because you trust me. But I say fuck 'them,' and fuck Hayes. When I became a doctor, I took an oath and I'm going to keep it for once. You'll get nothing but the truth from me. They can't do anything more to me than they already have."

"Sounds like you do need saving," I said.

"You more than me, Dale. Did you know surgery causes depression? Have you been given psych evaluations?"

As a matter of fact, I had. Weekly. A psychologist traveled with us. I had a clean bill of mental health, proof positive that the psychologist was either incompetent or knew where his bread was buttered. Like the team doctor on a pro football team, the goal is to keep the star player in the game.

"You seem to be the only one who cares about my psyche. Let's hope it's in good working order. I need to figure out a way to get the heat off of you, and I'm beginning to think there's no clean way out of this for me. Not without a toe tag. And Rae Stillson—she was out here, you know. She had to ask me something but never got around to it. How's her husband doing? Do you still treat him?"

"Not anymore," Venhaus said. "He's dying."

Episode two was the first living-donor, full-leg transplant in history. A Spanish doctor had performed the first full-leg transplant just a few years before. But living donors weren't apt to give up their leg—and no one insane enough to want to would get past a psych consult. Luckily for me, the playing field was rigged in my favor.

Chop-chop.

Jack Bryson ran a family farm of three generations. He got his leg caught in a hay bailer. The hay bailer won. The story editors played up his desire to play baseball with his young son one day. "I can't show him my fastball from a wheelchair," Jack tearfully confessed to the camera. "I can't train him to work his great grandfather's farm. My boy needs all of me."

Jack, like most people, figured losing a limb was a guarantee he'd never be the same. He didn't know the full capability of modern prosthetics. However, for the purposes of the show, we never drove this point home, heightening the drama of *Jack will never be the same without the Samaritan.*

I assumed Jack's marriage wasn't in good shape because we

didn't see much of the wife during the taping and she was all but invisible in the episode, save for a few testimonial comments. But the boy was cute, and it was nice to see a boy who wasn't burned up after Patrick Debrobander's heart-wrenching ordeal in the first episode, so this one got slotted into week two even though everyone thought Farmer Jack was a colossal asshole who thought God owed him a leg. But there weren't many legless, tough-luck stories with kids out there, so Jack got his wish in the form of my right leg.

My leg's progress was a daily news bite. The anchors gave a quick update, as if my leg was a rare, just-birthed zoo animal. Then they'd go off script, sharing synonyms of the word "unbelievable" while shaking their heads.

I had a whole, functioning leg back in three weeks. The world was amazed, but I was concerned, since I was reasonably sure that if I'd lost a leg in high school, I would have had it back in half the time.

After episode two was finished taping, I had enough of a gap to take a little break. Turns out, chopping my leg off entailed a pretty straightforward recovery. Mack and I ate dinner at a trendy steakhouse, because that's where we always ate now. Sometimes I'd even get a few photographers outside, waiting for me and Mack to hit the sidewalks. Not many. Usually because I answered their questions politely and didn't mind if they took my picture. Mack hammed it up for them most of the time. We weren't difficult.

Tracy hated this. Hayes didn't mind, since I never broke his prescribed protocol, refusing to comment on the subjects he was concerned about. I said awkward things to the paparazzi. Mack was no better. On addressing the rumor that I was gay: "Only on Sundays," I said. "And Arbor Day," Mack added. "The best day to bury the old root." The quote ran. No one paid much attention. No sponsors threatened to pull their ads. I could have gone all Courtney Love batshit and no one would have budged. Really, Coca-Cola, you going to pull your support of a guy who donates organs? Of a show that saves lives?

The paparazzi get a bad rap. They're rather simple, hounds that smell fear. They feast on it. They thirst for lies. They hope for cowardice and denial. They never got it from us. So we went about our business, and Tracy scrambled to keep us away from open mikes, interviews, and cameras.

Over a steak that cost more than one of my old Wal-Mart trips, Mack asked if I was holding up okay.

"Why do you continue to worry?" I said. "If I don't hold up, you're my lone heir. How's that."

"Relax. It's just that I noticed something."

"The waitress has tippable titties?"

"Yes. And also something else. Heart transplants. You never do them."

I couldn't remember if I ever told him anything about my Internet research on my condition. He was that kind of friend—I could have a secret but be comfortable enough to tell him, and then later forget that I told him. From what I could tell, I had vascular regeneration, the same as starfish and salamanders and other creatures with similar healing abilities. The healing was heart-based, the one organ those creatures could not regenerate.

"They never approach me with them," I said.

"That's the weird thing I'm noticing. It's a pretty frequent transplant operation. People writing in, maybe half of them are begging for a heart. Yet they never even consider it."

"I wonder why," I said, but I already knew the answer.

The taping of the third episode dissolved into catastrophe, all caught on film. In any other world, it was an episode that would never air, but the coverage was so thorough on the tapings themselves, they canned and aired an episode that showed everything in the best possible light. It didn't matter. Everyone would know the details of this episode before it even aired thanks to the reliable publicity of disaster.

Marvin Randle was going to die without a bone-marrow transplant. He was forty, a country boy from Tennessee, the kind of guy who had a white fossil ring in every pair of pants from where tobacco tins ground into his pocket. He wasn't television material, with black hair that looked wet all the time, greasy stubble sprouting unevenly on his face, shirts with holes—not intentional holes, like the trendy stores have, but unintentional ones, the salt of his sweat eating through the fabric over the years, decomposition taking place at glacial speed. Yet he wasn't poor and he wasn't stupid, and he didn't want to die.

He came from a big, loving family. I met most of them during the taping. His brothers. His one sister. His cousins. His father, Carl. All of them had the welcoming slur of a Southern accent. They offered to feed me all the time. They treated me not like a savior or a celebrity, but as a family member. "I hope my boys learn something from your visit, Mr. Sampson," Carl said. "They need your heart."

I assured him that they most certainly did not need my heart, and it was lucky for them that they didn't. He scratched the bald spot on the top of his head, which was glazed with sweat, making the gray curls that surrounded it cling to his scalp at awkward angles. "One of them does," he added.

The one he was referring to was the ostracized son,

Jonathan—Marvin's brother. He was forty-five with two full-grown sons of his own. The entire family had all taken a compatibility test to see if their marrow could save Marvin's life, and of all the cousins and nephews and brothers and sisters, one lone compatible donor was found by the testing. Jonathan.

After the initial "praise Jesus" had passed, Jonathan decided he wasn't going to go through with the donation. To call it a rift is an understatement—the fractures of hurt and fear left Jonathan alone to stew in his healthy marrow. By ignoring him, the family hoped he would reconsider his position. The expulsion of Jonathan was supported by his own two sons. I spoke to both of them, and neither could contain their disgust for their father.

"Uncle Marvin taught me how to fish," one of them said. "My father isn't just killing his brother, he's killing a good person."

Killing. In America, the organ-donation system is based on altruism. Nothing can be forced. Yet here was a man being accused by his own blood of murder, not through activity, but through inactivity. I knew a little something about inactivity.

As Marvin neared death, a lawsuit followed, hoping the court would force Jonathan into donation. They didn't have a legal case, save for embarrassing Jonathan and relying on the power and pity of a judge. The ploy worked, in roundabout fashion. The judge ruled in favor of Jonathan. His body, his rights. Altruism could not be forced. Yet the judge said, "You have legal defense but no moral defense. Your family's opinion of you is justified. I find the act disgusting and you are now the very definition of a Bad Samaritan."

A beat reporter for the local paper got the quote into the

Tennessean. And that one quote turned it into a national story, because it was just so damn clever to say "Bad Samaritan" in news bites while *The Samaritan* had just come off a hot first season.

Once it hit the wires and Tracy and her gang got hold of the story, I was on a plane to Tennessee to tape an episode. The angle was for me to save Marvin's life, and with the pressure of donation out of the way thanks to my intervention, we could reunite the family as Jonathan learns the error of his ways. Or pretends that he does, at least. Tracy was saying things like "two time slots, season finale, and in the long run, we'll end up syndicated as fuck." Everyone smelled jackpot. I didn't.

Despite being classified as a "universal donor," my antigen count did not match Marvin's for bone marrow, just like the rest of his family. This was a Samaritan first that concerned our medical team. I chalked it up to my slowly fading gifts. Healing slows, antigens start fucking everyone. I figured the endgame was that something didn't grow back and I'd be stuck either dead or crippled.

Just like the rest of Marvin's family, I sat around their dinner table eating casseroles and trading anecdotes, the cameras rolling, getting their background footage for an episode that was either going to be a dud or not get made because I couldn't jump to the surgical rescue.

Tracy's idea to salvage the taping was for me and Jonathan to have a sit-down talk. In this talk, I would relay to him the gift of giving, of saving people, what it felt like, how it changed me, and it would inspire him to change his mind. My legend would grow. And it would be a cheap episode without the need for surgery.

Jonathan agreed to the sit-down. Seems that for guys, television has the same allure as unprotected sex and cold beer—hard to say no, even if it's bad for you.

We went to his home. His sons were gone. A stuffed bass was on one wall, a deer head on the other. Jonathan's wife had been dead a long time, but her pictures were on tables and on the entertainment center, which had a dinosaur of a television that sat on the floor and had an actual dial, with curved glass that offered black reflections of the crew's lighting and sound equipment and cameras. Chairs were not set up; there was just the sofa and a recliner. Just two guys having a talk, according to Tracy.

I was supposed to break the news I wasn't a match, news that Jonathan already knew, but we would cut up the footage for dramatic effect. So I was told.

I stood outside Jonathan's house, waiting for the crew to finish up their preparations. Tracy kept trying to give me talking points. "Make it real to him. Make him know that you've seen death and he doesn't want to see his brother dead. But don't badger him."

On and on and on she went. "This is quite a risk," I said, "coming from a woman who doesn't want me talking too much in public."

"No offense, Dale, but you're not warm and fuzzy, and you're not even a cool antihero. You're just awkward. But I'm hoping that you've smoothed out a little. Consider this practice for your miserable and ill-advised interview episode. Show me something. Make me less alarmed about you killing your own brand."

"When have I seen death?" I asked.

"Huh? Oh, that's just figurative. You've seen people that are going to die without your help. Death hovering over them.

That kind of crap. See what I mean? You're so literal some-times."

She had no idea how literal my thinking was.

❤

Jonathan and I shook hands. He squeezed really hard and didn't smile, a handshake of duty, fingers calloused from a life of work that required pumiced soap.

"Glad to be here," he said, because that's what people on TV said.

"This isn't *Wheel of Fortune*," I told him. The cameras weren't rolling yet. I looked at the director, Mick, a skinny, surfer type who wore hemp bracelets and never made small talk with me.

"Shoot everything," I said, my eyes darting over to Tracy, who was on her cell phone. "Don't stop, even if she begs you to stop. Just get the footage."

He looked the crew over, nodded once, and we rolled.

"So you're dead," I said. "And I can't save you. But you knew that. We wouldn't be sitting here if you didn't know that."

"He's sick, he ain't dead."

"I didn't say him. I said you. Dead. He'll get buried and get flowers and tears and you'll get jack shit."

Crew eyebrows popped up with the use of a swearword. I heard Tracy's phone clap shut, but didn't look away from Jon-athan.

"Everyone hates you. It's not about him anymore. It's about you. You're on TV. Don't you want to be loved? We'll cut all this out. Everything I've said. You just look at me and very slowly nod and say, 'I realize how much I love my brother, and I want to try to save him,' and it'll run on TV and you'll be the man who succeeded where I have failed. You may get a spot on another reality show. You'll get your own news crawl when you die one day. Do it for you, Jonathan. Fuck your brother. Right? I'm with you on that."

"That's enough," Tracy said. "Christ! What are you doing?"

"You'll get the footage," I told her. "You'll slice it up. Make it nice. You always do. Sit."

She crossed her arms and stayed silent the rest of the way.

"Where was I? . . . Oh. Yes. Fuck your brother. Are you with me on this? We on the same page?"

"I love my brother," he said softly.

"Bullshit. He did something to you, am I right? Something so bad that you can't bring yourself to save him. Even if it makes you into a true-blue hero, you just can't bring yourself to do it. You'd rather die a villain than cut yourself for him. Why? Just say it. Disarm it. Aloud, it's going to sound stupid, Jonathan. You know this. Nothing in that little head of yours, nothing he did is bigger than death. Nothing. So just say it."

He said nothing.

"This girl and I, we had this little thing when it came to talking about hard stuff," I began. "We'd say anything and if we didn't want to talk about it anymore, we'd call 'fuck it,' and it would get dropped. So just say it, say what happened and say 'fuck it,' and that'll be that."

A long silence. I looked at Mick. Thumbs-up. Still going. Jonathan fidgeted, staring at his hands. Then, he looked at the crew, at the cameras. "Does this all have to be on?"

"What happened?" I said again.

"My wife died in love with him," he said. "I don't think they ever had sex, but Marian loved him more than me."

And like that, like all good release, crying chased it right out. Good revelations always get sealed with the wet kiss of tears.

"So your wife—Marian—she loved you enough to sacrifice her love for him. You don't find that noble? She could have walked out and followed her heart. Instead, she stayed with you. Died with your ring on her finger, vows to you on her lips. You sure she didn't fuck him?"

"No," he said quickly. "Absolutely not."

"Then what the fuck is the big deal? Man, you're a shithead. Not only are you killing your brother, you're shitting on your dead wife. Let's do this scientifically: your master plan is to let your brother die so he can go into the afterlife and fuck her for all eternity? That it? Nice plan, dumbass."

"Fuck you," he said, looking poised to jump out of his chair. But I had been battle tested by then. Curb-stomped. Ribs snapped. Now I was ignored by Rae after we'd finally connected, after I finally knew the truth. I fucked Venhaus's life up, and I was stuck as the Samaritan or conscripted into the life of a guinea pig. I had been hurt and come back and pain was a reality. If nothing hurt, I'd search for something to hurt.

"Fuck me. Yes. Fuck me who has spread my innards to the four corners of the universe. You suspected your wife was in love with him, but you have a family, and kids, and you know what sleeping next to someone every night feels like. Not only do I get cut up every few weeks, I watched the contents of an innocent girl's head get blown into the blacktop of the only high school party I ever got invited to. I've screwed up every meaningful relationship in my life just because I'm full of fear and awkwardness and I'm cursed with the intelligence to know it. So fuck me. I have no right to talk. Yes or no, Jonathan. Are we doing this? Or am I packing up these cameras and crew and burning the footage and leaving you and your marrow here to rot all alone? Yes or no?"

"Yes," he said. "I'll do it." And I clapped once, stood, and shook his hand. This time, I got the limp fish. He looked down into the faded green carpet, where there were worn-down spots from walking to the recliner, his favorite spot while watching wrestling or the news or fishing shows.

"We're done," I said, and brushed by a silent Tracy on my way out the door.

Two days later, Mack broke the news. Jonathan gave himself a mouthful of shotgun and popped the trigger with his big toe.

Wouldn't you know it, he wasn't an organ donor. It wouldn't have mattered anyway, since it took two full days for anyone to find his body, which was by then attracting flies and half eaten by his own dog.

A week later, the footage spilled. The entire interview. I got all my juicy bits quote-mined out in the media, who built me into a villain who pressed the guy into killing himself. Bad Samaritan, indeed. Images of Regina popped up on newscasts. All of what I had done, stripped and frayed by a guy with enough balls to blow his own head off, killing himself and his brother in the process.

I know the feeling of putting a gun barrel in your mouth. Your muscles get awfully tired. You start finding reasons to live real quick. I could call Jonathan a lot of things, but a coward wasn't one of them.

Critics called me a sad-sack messiah who was fighting depression and internal demons. They forecast eventual tragedy for me, a slow self-destruction, inflicted by culture's thirst for sacrifice. They predicted that anyone watching the episode would be an accomplice. They proclaimed that I was naïve and being protected and used up.

Tracy begged me to issue an apology. I didn't. They were left cobbling together an episode that was so desperate for positive spin that you could smell the bullshit through the television.

Naturally, the overnight ratings for this episode made a lot of network suits crap their expensive slacks with glee, and the anticipation for my live interview episode began to take on a life of its own.

In wrestling and boxing, the main event is buffered from the rest of the card with a shitty match that precedes it. In framing up season two, that episode was the fourth one I taped, in which I donated my corneas to a lady who was mostly blind. We were going to tape the full six-episode order, but after the Randle fiasco, the pressure was too high to shut it down. Tracy slipped in the cornea surgery by saying it was already scheduled and it wasn't fair to prevent an innocent person from getting her sight back.

Takes a special kind of blindness to be cured by donated corneas. Her name was Anna, a middle-aged MILF who could still perceive light but couldn't make out any objects. Me? All I can say is that once your corneas get sliced out, it's pretty much dark. Until they start growing back. Then it's like getting born again. For a few days, the world was pretty and bright, a blur of colors, spilled paint, more light added each day, the sharpness coming slowly, two weeks of slow-motion autofocus.

The season wrapped and I went home. Mack visited regularly, letting me know how post-production was going, but I always changed the subject.

"This is it," he said. "This season is going to air and it's all over, whether you want to do a third season or not. It really does feel like fifteen minutes," he marveled.

"Maybe when it doesn't hurt," I said. "Two seasons felt like two decades to me."

He got quiet. He would bring over beers and drink most of them, the façade I'd known for so long becoming more fragile with each visit. Maybe it was guilt. Maybe it was finally realizing that there're some really sad moments between empty orgasms.

When Mack wasn't over, doctors were. The Reynolds team had Venhaus hovering in the background, the only man I trusted. They did backflips to keep up the illusion that I was still at the peak of my health and abilities.

The other medical team, led by Hayes, was far more intrusive and far more blunt.

We were past the formalities, and I knew Hayes cared more about me than Reynolds did, if only because he was more dependent upon my survival than Reynolds was my fame. I would sit down and give them my trained vein and tell them to sample away. I didn't want to fuck things up before the big show.

Rae was still gone and I needed the interview.

TWENTY-TWO

WHEN SEASON TWO PREMIERED, I DIDN'T GO TO THE party. I watched every single episode alone. I watched the fourth episode with a bag of Doritos and a tall glass of milk. Teasers galore for my live interview the following week—details of which I hadn't gotten yet, or asked for.

A rhythmic knock battered my door. No need to answer, since the knob turned instantly after the knock—Mack letting himself in.

"So here we are," he said, jumping over the couch, landing on his ass, sinking into it.

"Here we are."

"A week away."

"A week away, sure."

"And you know I carry with me the torch of Tracy's wishes."

"And probably her scent."

He looked shocked, found out, and guilty.

"Christ man, we really are brothers. You knew I was hitting that the whole time?"

"I know what a wink means," I said. "You're the blind one. You can't see that she's not above banging my handler so she can hold the leash."

"Ouch," he said. "Really, man. Fucking ouch. Handler?"

He got up and went to the fridge. "I'm going to say what's going on, and give you my advice, and then I'll leave you be. But first—"

He grabbed a beer and popped the tab, and didn't ask if I wanted one.

"Skunky beer, man. Imports for me nowadays. And this is a fuckin' dump. Are your checks bouncing or something?"

"What were you going to say?"

"Tracy quit," he said. "Quit as long as you're part of the show."

"I would think that's the same as quitting, unless you found another regenerating dude out there. I mean, there's still a show? The ship has sailed. You said it yourself."

"Not exactly. Of course your doctor friend, Venhaus, has been telling anyone who will listen that you're breaking down. Reynolds can only stiff-arm him with bullshit for so long. People are unhitching their wagons. Lots of people hate you. Have you seen what the religious fucks are doing? You were proof of God, now you're proof of deals with the devil. You know how little it takes to go from God to Satan in this town?"

"This town. Like you're a native. We're from Southern Illinois. Have you forgotten that?"

"Same as you have."

"For the record, Satan was created out of an argument. A disagreement."

"Yeah, I saw the cartoon—listen, the psych guys are moving to deem you unfit for a season three. You're on your way to being blackballed."

"Season three?" I was stunned it was even on the table after the shitshow that was the season-two tapings, but ratings were ratings. Buzz was buzz. Controversy was better than not getting buzz on Facebook.

"I came up with the perfect plan. Just go on your interview, keep it short, keep it under control, and tell them that your gifts are diminishing. Admit that you're in pain. Get some sympathy. But tell them you already agreed to one last operation. We film the footage. We present it as if you're not a match because your gifts are fading, but suddenly, I step in. I'm the match. Your best friend. I give a kidney up, inspired by you. *The Samaritan* season three is then shot with volunteer donors. Sure, it'll dry up quick with redundant donations, but we can get the juice of one more season. Cash a few more checks. And you go out with grace—"

"And you get the spotlight that you've always wanted."

"It ain't about that, it's about protecting you. You're my friend. I'm the one who told you no season two. Don't forget that shit."

"I'll handle my interview my own way."

"Fuck!" He paced the room. "I don't suppose you'd be interested in an extra fifty grand?"

"Carlton Franks?"

"Fuckin' A. He's got a different angle for you now, a different offer. This is at least an interesting one: Take the Lord Jesus as your savior, mention it during the interview, and tell the world that Franks is your spiritual adviser, that he advised you to retire and go with God, and bank the cash. Admit that you found forgiveness for what you did to the Randle family."

"Nope."

"Figured. Fuck him." He collapsed into the couch again. "You've got me a little freaked out. I don't know what else to say."

"We're in L.A.," I said. "Famous, just like you wanted. Just like you always wanted."

He took a long breath. "What's on TV?"

We stared at reruns for almost an hour, without speaking. He drank two more beers, waiting for me to talk. I didn't.

"Well," he said, clapping his hands against his thighs, the punctuation on his pending departure. "I've got to get some sleep. So when Tracy asks me 'What's Dale gonna do?' I'm going to tell her to . . ."

"Tune in," I said.

He lingered. "So that's it."

"Yep."

"This is about Raeanna, isn't it? That's what this is all about. Badger her into calling you on national television. Ruin her marriage. That about right?"

"Fuck you," I said. I hoped he would come at me, get that hate gland flexing, leave me bleeding on my living room floor. I wanted a fight, as if a fight would let him know that I really did love her. Did I love her, whatever the fuck love was?

"I know she was here," he said. All this time, I figured he knew but wasn't going to bring it up. Then, he took an envelope out of his back pocket, folded in half. I recognized Raeanna's handwriting immediately. He must have lifted the note when he came over the morning Raeanna left.

"This is some great television, right here," he said, tapping the note. "The best episode in *Samaritan* history is in this envelope."

"And you kept it from me, why? Because you're still trying to protect me?"

"Yeah, and doing a horrible job at it. Same way I let Regina suck my cock to protect you. I'm a complete failure at the protecting-Dale shit. Thanks for noticing." He threw it onto the coffee table. "No matter what happens Sunday, Dale, you're done with *The Samaritan*. I'll see to it that the show moves on without you. One way or another. And I couldn't be happier. You need to figure some shit out, and I can finally sleep at night knowing you're not getting cut on anymore."

So it was just me and the envelope and the television. I peeled back the lip of the envelope—torn and frayed, the glue worn down. Mack had opened it, of course. She left it behind after our last night together, and Mack found it. She was expecting a response from me, and she probably took my long silence as a no. I knew her cursive from the note in my locker, and as I read, the blueprint of my interview began to take shape.

When Mack was gone, I called Doc Venhaus. I didn't want to tell him my plan over the phone, so we met at the entrance to my apartment building. When he arrived, I joined him on the sidewalk. Once we were around the corner, he said, "Well, what is it then? I have to be honest, when you say you have a plan, I can't help but get a little concerned."

"It's not my plan," I said. "It's our plan. I can't do it without you, so listen."

Doc listened.

The set was ready. Two chairs. Lighting. Familiar crew. Tracy didn't talk to me. Mack wandered backstage, trying to look important.

"You read the letter, then?" he asked.

"You shouldn't have stolen it," I said.

"I don't know what you're going to say out there, but you're a big boy. You'll either survive, or you won't."

"Now, that's a best friend," I said.

He smiled. "Well, I can't say we're not going out in a blaze of complete and utter chaos," he said. "Go light up the world. And for the record, Tracy likes to fuck wearing nothing but her fake glasses." He wrapped me in an embrace so forceful I knew I'd wake up sore.

Doc Venhaus visited a few hours before live show time. "Well?" I said.

"Reconsider," he said. "The fiasco you have planned, while bold, is dangerous."

"But it can work?" I asked.

"We can try."

"Hey, turn that frown upside down. I thought things happened for a reason, right?" I said, trying to look sly.

"I guess I need to get busy, then," he said. I clapped him on the shoulder, then sought out Tracy.

"So you're mad at me?" I asked.

"I always knew this would happen. You aren't fit for the gifts you have, you know. You've always whined about your overwhelming burden, as if you hate your life of success and admiration."

"You're right," I said. "About all of it."

"I just thank God I'm not you," she said. "I'll have a career and a family and friends long after you gleefully flame out and destroy the only good things in your life."

"You don't even know what I'm going to say."

"Mack already told me. He thinks you're going to burn the entire show to the ground today."

"You got that right," I said. "For what it's worth, I think you should take your glasses off when you have sex. You have pretty eyes."

To Reynolds, who was seated in the front row, all dappered-up with his hair drenched in what looked to be 10W-30 motor oil and his teeth so white you really would want to choke the motherfucker, I said, "You're fucking fired. Jam your journal articles up your ass."

I made sure Hayes saw me. He was in plainclothes, as he usually was when his surveillance of me forced him into the public eye, sitting in the middle of the studio audience. He even looked like he was purposely slackening his posture, trying to fit in, and though I can't tell you with one hundred percent certainty, I'm pretty sure I saw the son of a bitch smiling.

The interviewer was not an esteemed journalist. Instead I got Elton Spruce, the host of the network's number-two reality show—a blond, spiky-headed, all-smiles asshole whose sole job was to console talentless contestants after they shockingly learn from a panel of judges that they have no talent. Yes, quite the juggernaut for this interview, the hook of which was that it was live, unscripted, and I would answer any and all questions. People would be posting, e-mailing, Skyping, sending them in on messenger pigeons—anything to maintain the spectacle. I fully expected the hard-hitting "Are you still a nail biter?" to lead off the interview. The juicy shit would be saved for the last segment.

But I didn't intend on doing a fourth segment.

Before we went live, I found Spruce backstage and shook his manicured, evenly tanned hand.

"Pleasure to be working with you tonight," he said.

"With me?" I said with a laugh. "Just smile and try not to look uncomfortable."

"Wow," he said. "You really are the asshole everyone says you are, huh? I've cracked tougher eggs than you on my radio show."

"If you count stoned teenage girls that can't sing worth a

shit as tough eggs, then yeah. You know what your problem is? You take this shit seriously. Really. You talk to Z-listers like they're the president."

"It's called professionalism. Maybe you wouldn't be on here begging for public forgiveness if you had a little. Any other great advice before I watch you put your foot in your mouth?"

"Yeah, Mr. Spruce. Wear Kevlar."

In the lead-in to the interview, the talking heads yapped endlessly, predicting how I would rationalize my departure, reaching for possible motivations fueling my sudden decision. What they settled on was that I was doing damage control. When the show went live, they figured I would open by apologizing for my behavior. I would gain sympathy, explaining what it's like going through what I went through for the greater good. I would apologize to Jonathan Randle's family. I would explain that I was done. Some predicted I would be handing the reins over to a new Samaritan, and assure the public that I trusted the show's team to carry on my spirit without my presence. Then I'd fade into obscurity, facing my misery and demons and emerging a new person down the road, ready for a primetime television comeback or a memoir or more interviews. Whatever I could do to make a lot of people an assload of money one more time.

Some expected me to say that Carlton Franks was my spiritual adviser, that I'd thank God and say that the Lord has shown me that my behavior must match my gift. I'd give full credit to Carlton Franks for showing me that the gifts were not mine, but tools of the Lord, and I must do his bidding humbly. I was not a messiah, just a conduit for the truth—a truth that Carlton Franks brought you every Sunday from eight a.m. until ten a.m. Pacific time. I'd say I receive the letters that people send, the ones with prayers and money, the ones that call me messiah and lord, but I would confess that only Jesus is Lord and I am just a man with a gift from the heavens, sent here to do good, and inspire people to do likewise. Despite popular belief, all major religions endorse organ donation. Sign up today. Here is a word from our sponsors. Here is when you can expect the real season finale of *The Samaritan*. Here is my body. Here is my blood. Here is me, palms open, waiting for a hug, don't think me bad, don't misunderstand me, don't cast me down into the realm of the melted down celebrity who has to say yes to *Dancing with the Stars*.

For all I know, it might have gone down just like that—if not for the letter.

Dear Dale, it began, *I wrote this letter in case I couldn't ask you to your face. I'm weak that way, but I'm getting stronger all the time. Strong enough to leave Harold.*

We went live. Elton Spruce welcomed me, and thanked me for agreeing to address America.

"With all that you have done," he asked, "do you think it's fair for people to say some of the things they have said about you?" He read some quotes. I had heard it all before. There it was on a tee. Blast it out of the park. Save your show.

I really don't know what I'm asking of you, but it's sort of your department. Harold is sick. He's dying. I took a vow, Dale. I can't leave a dying man. Even if his fists break the vows that we took, I just can't break mine. Every time I'm sure I'm walking out the door for the last time, he can say that I left him in his darkest hour, that I left him to die alone and I wouldn't be able to tell him any different.

"Shut this clown's microphone off," I said. "I don't say another word until he's gone. Get Tracy in here. My producer, Tracy. Mike her up. I'll talk to her."

Wham. Commercial. I could feel the murmur in the live studio audience.

Tracy couldn't even look at me as they miked her up. She sat down.

"I'm not ready to interview you," she said during commercial.

"Don't worry," I said. "You really think I'm going to be at a loss for words this time?"

We got cued back in.

"This is Tracy. She works with me behind the scenes of *The Samaritan*. I brought her out here because she knows me. She's for real. This is about being real, here tonight."

Tracy was a natural in front of the camera, looking interested, engaged. Inside, she must have been crackling and popping with anger—and a hint of fear.

"Do you have a question for me, Tracy?"

"Yes," she said, without missing a beat. "It's obvious you have an agenda here tonight, so my question is, why don't you just get on with it?"

I'll just be short about it. Harold has a coronary heart disease and scar tissue from a heart attack. His heart is crap. It's continued to get worse and now he's on the transplant list.

I looked at the people. All eyes on me. Not even a cough. Mack stood near the backstage entrance, watching, arms folded. Face hard, jaw with thick lines and tense muscle. No one looked away.

"I'm hurting," I said. "I'm still patching up properly, but slower. I can't remember what it's like to not heal from something. And there's more than just pain brought about by my donations. I inflicted it all on Jonathan Randle, and others. For that, I am sorry."

Deep breath. Sweat popping up everywhere, a wet patch

growing on my lower back. "But I killed no one. And I've saved no one. I've given up nothing."

"Some say that you're the greatest hero of this generation," Tracy interrupted. "Organ donations are up, lives have been—"

"This isn't a debate," I said.

She leaned back, crossing her arms, insulating herself from me.

"We're no different than our ancestors," I continued. "Kings would choose proxies to die in their place. They would assign them power. Responsibility. Fame. The people of the kingdom would kill them. Not out of hate, but out of honor, an attempt to make them immortal. And the king would sit back and smile when the knives came out. Ask me who the king is, Tracy."

She didn't.

"I'm not playing your games," she said.

"Lots of kings out there, folks, but one king is Carlton Franks. He illustrates my point exactly. Being a king is never enough. Men want to be kings, kings want to be gods. He offered me fifty grand to come on here and endorse him, to tell you that he's my spiritual adviser."

No gasp. Maybe this didn't come as a surprise from the sweating sermon-meister.

"He would have you think he's above my power, when of course in reality, he's jealous of it. You're lucky a man like Franks can't do what I do. I have no interest in kingdoms. Love your God. Or your Buddha. Or your Allah. Or your magic dragon, or your Zeus, or your cell-phone provider. I don't care. I worship nothing. But something I have learned is that sometimes, the universe is full of heavy things that drop on top of your life and stay put forever. Love is one of them. Pain is another. Sometimes they're the same thing."

A glass of water was sweating on an end table. I took a long drink.

He may get another transplant if we just wait. I say another because he got a heart already, but he rejected it. Graft-host issues. They don't think he's a good recipient. He's even lower on the list now. It's just a wait. But I'm tired of waiting. Every day, I pray for either a phone call or to find him dead in his bedroom. I can't tell you how much that chips away at your soul, the way you look at yourself, hoping to find your husband dead.

"Do you need to break?" Tracy asked. Not because she cared about me collecting myself, but because she cared about our sponsors getting their already-paid-for airtime. I shook my head.

"Before we get any further," she said, clever girl she was, diverting me from the reveal, heightening the drama. She smelled promotion, a jump out of the producer's chair into these hot lights. And why not? She was cute, cutthroat, comfortable in her role as distributor of bullshit. "Tell me—tell us—about Regina, the friend you lost in high school."

Textbook interview strategy—delay the reveal by setting up backstory, the more tragic the better. I never considered talking about Regina during the interview. But hearing her name broke that fragile forgetfulness that people like to call ignorant bliss. Like waking up happy, then remembering you have some shitty appointment and the wet and heavy blanket of disappointment wraps you tight. Yet I had forgotten her. Rae was on my mind. Maybe it was then I realized that I loved Rae and it didn't matter why. I had no business loving her. I didn't know her favorite color or what restaurants she liked and even though I'd kissed every square inch of her body in our short time together, I wasn't sure where she liked to be kissed, but I knew her handwriting, her smile, the way she could give me sweet chills when she said my name. Maybe I loved her because I needed to love her. But fuck the whys.

"A girl died, and she didn't have to. She was killed and . . ." I trailed off, finding words, breathing control back into my body. "It's one of those dark slices of life, where you assign yourself blame, even if there isn't much there. I wanted blame because it was all I had left to connect myself to her, something I did just to imagine I was more important to her than maybe I really was. And to let that go is to cut out a piece of me that doesn't grow back A little scar tissue so I can remember I was there, for once."

Hearing myself say it drew me into the role of self-observer, like when you stare into the mirror for a very long time or hear your own voice played back on a recording. Familiar but starkly foreign. This isn't me. I don't sound like this. I don't look like this, or know this, or feel this.

But the words were out, and now I had to face that even the guilt I had so carefully tended to all those years was bullshit, another smokescreen.

I'm not asking for your heart, Dale. Not in a literal sense. I just hoped that maybe, you being in that world that you're in, you or one of your doctors could make sure he got a phone call about another heart. And when he's all better, when he can't hold his death over my head, I know I can just walk away. But in his condition, with the graft-host thing going on, maybe he doesn't need just any heart. Maybe he needs the Samaritan.

"I'm making one more donation," I said, looking into the camera, but seeking Raeanna, the eye of black glass reminding me of that shiner she once hid behind a tuft of brown hair, the reason I was in the chair, putting *The Samaritan* to bed once and for all.

"After this donation, *The Samaritan* will not exist as you

now know it. My doctors and I don't expect that I will survive this final surgery."

Finally, a bit of a gasp from the crowd, but not enough to break my momentum.

And when I walk away, who knows where I'll go? Who I'll go to? I can't promise it'll be you, but when I'm honest with myself, I know it's you. I hope you don't hold this against me, this cowardly act of writing it all out. I don't know where you'll be or how we'll feel when you read this. If you read this.

"You may have noticed that I have never donated a heart on *The Samaritan*, even though it's one of the most in-demand organs out there, one of the most common transplants. It's because we have reason to believe my heart will not regenerate."

Here is my cell phone number. Let me know, one way or another. You've wanted to save me all these years, and now you can. Yours, Rae.

And underneath it, written a different color, an addendum added in red ink bled from the pen that had sat on my own countertop—*I'm yours, Dale, when I can finally be yours.* What she didn't know was the price of freeing her. She didn't know the heart does not grow back.

"There will be no cameras. No episode. No coverage. An old friend needs me to save her husband, and I'm going to do it. I'm going to give him my heart and a doctor is going to walk out and shake his head and tell everyone that I'm gone, but someone will be alive because of it. And that . . . that's a Samaritan."

Tracy cleared her throat, testing the existence of noise in the world. Satisfied it still existed, she asked a question.

"You can save a hundred more people. People might say you're being selfish."

"I can't even get bonus points for martyrdom?"

A smattering of laughter.

"It hurts, Tracy," I said. "I'm sick of it. Sick of waiting. Hoping. Caring. Not caring. Who can tell the difference, really? I almost ate the barrel of a thirty-eight before I came out here for the show. I knew I had this gift inside of me but what I really wanted was simple, unremarkable—a job, a kiss, a girl-friend."

"But there's always a chance," she said. "There's no proof that you won't recover."

"You just keep hoping and waiting, darling. After a good while, you'll know what I felt like before I went under the knife."

"We have to break, but we'll be right—"

"No, no break. No need to come back. I'm done."

I got up.

"We should really—"

"No," I said again. "There's nothing else to say. Well, maybe one more thing to say." I looked into the camera again.

"Good-bye."

TWENTY-THREE

I BRUSHED BY MACK IN THE HALLWAY. HE STARED ME down as I passed.

None of the staffers knew what to make of me. They didn't look at me as I walked by. What was there to say? Nice job, hope you don't die too painfully? Wish you all the best, thanks for ruining the show and making me search for a new job?

"Hey!" Mack chased me down. His meaty hand fell on my shoulder. "You shouldn't have said anything about Franks, man."

"Fuck him."

"He's got a lot of obsessed weirdos under his thumb. You just made some enemies."

"Good thing I won't be around to deal with them."

"I knew you'd say yes to that stupid shit. Now do you understand why I kept the note from you? Jesus. So, when's the surgery?"

"Tomorrow," I said. "The doctors are working out the particulars as we speak." He turned away. I could have sworn he was chomping the inside of his cheek, distracting from tears that were getting fat on the assembly line, ready to drop.

"All this because I wanted you to talk to a girl. All because of that stupid swing-for-the-fences shit. I don't suppose I could talk you out of this?"

"You don't want to. Trust me."

"What if I offered him my heart instead?" he said.

"Even if you were a match, he's already rejected compatible donors. I'm his only shot."

"I'm just fucking with you anyway," he said, spreading out his wolfish smile. "I'd rather eat the sideboards off a shit wagon than help that son of a bitch. Even if I could help him, I'd let him rot—and so should you."

"And that is precisely why I can't let him rot," I said, and he finally let me leave, alone.

When I got to my apartment building, I could have sworn there had been a fire or a shooting, something that would explain why the rubberneckers were out in full force. Then I saw a bearded man holding a sign that said SELFISH SAMARI-TAN! and some greasy-haired teenager waving one that said SAVE 1, OR 100? DO THE MATH! They were arguing with some pedestrians who were, from what I could tell, feebly defending my virtue—or maybe just bickering for the sake of it, as is so often the case. Either way, it became clear that my defenders were far outmatched by my critics in the realms of hostility and dedication, and they soon moved along. Funny how being in opposition to something tends to inspire tireless picketing and cleverly worded signs, while support rarely arouses that level of productivity.

I froze on the sidewalk, wondering just what would happen if I approached my door—would I catch another beating? Get pelted with eggs or spit? Or simply endure the endless, throat-ripping screams trumpeting my selfishness and cowardice?

THE HEART DOES NOT GROW BACK | 271

All because I had the audacity to die for one person instead of living to yield organs for dozens more.

"You really are dense as fuck if you thought dying was the hard part." Mack's voice again. He had followed me.

"Let's get out of here," he said.

"Where to?"

"I got a spot."

"How do I know you won't lock me up somewhere so I don't make it to the surgery? Wait till Harold dies, force me to reconsider?"

"I'm your goddamn friend, you idiot. You know the saying 'If your friend jumped off a bridge, does it mean you would too?' Well, just this once, I'll watch you jump off a bridge. No promises that I'm going to follow right away."

"Fair enough."

He hailed a cab.

"Stop where we can get a twelve-pack first, bubba," he told the cabbie. Off we went. Our last and least wild night together. The morning would be a different story.

We cracked the tops of slick and cold bottles of Budweiser or, as Mack always called it, "The Diesel."

The city unfurled below us, the metal and pavement fading from view as the sun set. Soon there was nothing but fluid lights set in darkness. We sat square-ass in the dirt, surrounded by the dry brush of the Hollywood Hills, but far from the Hollywood sign. "Too popular, too romantic. I just wanna crack a few beers with you, not make out with you," Mack said as we picked our spot.

At that moment, the movement of the world was measured by the brake lights crawling down the streets—the measurement of time was the draining of beers, as it had always been. Two bottles evaporated without a word.

"I always figured I would bring a chick up here. She would say it was just like the movies and get all moist, and I would hit it and that would be that," he said, finally, but not sounding like Mack, each word glazed with disappointment.

"I'm not unhappy, you know," he continued. "I'm lonely. But not unhappy."

"We are certainly some kind of fucked up," I said.

"I'm wired wrong, dude," he said. "I'll do anything to get a girl to like me, and by like me, I mean bang me, and by bang me, I mean just that. After the banging is achieved, then nothing. At first the conversation is normal, and the chick asks me something like, 'What do you look for in a girl?' and I tell her, 'My nine-inch dick,' and somehow I make it work. But it won't work forever."

"And you're telling me this because I'll be dead and I can't make fun of you for being a whining, sensitive bitch?"

"So you're not a virgin anymore?" he asked.

A simple "no" satisfied him just fine. I didn't want to tell him it was Raeanna, to hear him scold me for literally getting fucked into giving my heart away—a thought that had nagged me since she left.

"This is all about us getting shot up," he said. "Not about Regina, or Rae, or any of it. Like you said, we're fucked up—probably got PTSD or some shit. But I'm glad I took it in the shoulder. Built-in excuse to fail at baseball, just like you said. So I came out all right in the deal. And you? Man, what I wouldn't give to be that kind of special."

"Get to it, then," I said. "*The Samaritan* was your idea, remember. But then you tried to stop me from doing a second season. You're trying to stop me from doing this. So, one last time, tell me why I shouldn't do this."

"Fine. You're the only fucking friend I've got, the only guy who can put up with my bullshit act. What does that say about me? You cared for Regina, Raeanna, hell, even Hollie. If there's a shitshow, you're first in line for admission. I wish I had balls like that. I'm fucking serious, if you'd let me take your place in that surgery, if that was possible, I'd do it."

"I know," I said. "But fuck it. Let's finish this twelver. And then get another one. And stay in a real expensive hotel room, and charge it. Who gives a shit, right?"

"I thought you weren't supposed to drink or eat the night before a surgery?"

"Why? 'Cause it'll kill me?"

We had a good laugh, the kind that leaves the stomach muscles weak and sore, a release not just from the grim joke but from everything that had been dammed up before it.

"And we wake up," he said, "and I'll break the news to Rae and Harold that you pulled out. And we'll buy a convertible Mustang and drive all the way back to Illinois, man. Fucking Chicago, use that *Samaritan* cash to buy an apartment by Wrigley and waste the summer days holding out nets for a homer that we'll never in a million years catch. Just the wind and us, and leave all the shit behind." A warm gust tore through the hillside, rattling the bushes, teasing a slight whistle from the lips of our open bottles. "Man, that would be just the thing. I can't believe I'm saying it, but I kind of miss home."

"We're home now," I said. "We just thought we could master this place, when the best we could do was manage. But we haven't even managed."

"And here we are," Mack said, raising his can.

"Here we are," I repeated, completing the toast. I took a long drink, but Mack didn't stop until his beer was gone.

"You got my back tomorrow?"

"A guy could do worse than helping his best friend carry out his final wish," he said. Mack threw the empty can into the forage below. He immediately grimaced, favoring his shoulder.

"On the day we met, when those girls blindfolded me . . . did I ever tell you I could see the whole time?"

He laughed, which was a relief. I needed to hear him laugh. He grabbed another beer and sheepishly confessed the time he'd cried when he lost his virginity, not knowing why, just knowing that he had something and it was gone and it made him want to cry. Thirteen-year-olds get emotional like that. Sarah Odin was sixteen, he said, one year older than the last time he told me the story. I didn't mention this—one of the reasons we got along so well. He didn't need a witness, just a forum through which he could hear his own account.

He passed out the instant we got back to the hotel room. I left him there, slipping out quietly to go for a long walk, unable to sleep, wondering how the morning would go, whether or not I'd see Raeanna. I walked to the beach, where it's easy to get mesmerized by the vastness of the ocean at night, but really, it's a bunch of filthy saltwater slapping against a shore that has seen as many needles and condoms as seashells. The foam has a dirty lip and leaves rotted gunk behind to fossilize under the unrelenting sun.

Maybe in the morning Rae might actually show and ask me why I was doing this to myself. Maybe she'd say she was only hoping I could pull some strings, that she didn't want me to die. She might even kiss me and make me recall that night, ask why I was giving up on her right when we were poised to move on from the hell of our current lives, together.

I would tell her that it's because my gift is only as good as its next round under the knife, that for my life to truly begin, the damage must be permanent. My body never stopped healing, but I never gave my soul a chance to do the same. And as much as I ached for Rae, we could never truly cauterize the wounds of the past if we were together. Granting her wish was the only way to keep myself from her.

I woke up in our presidential suite to the blare of my cell phone's alarm, the haze of alcohol rusting my eyelids. Before I could even get out of bed for my morning piss, the phone sounded again—this time it was Doc Venhaus calling.

"I hope this isn't bad news," I said, picking up.

"Quite the opposite. I'm alarmed at how easily things are going," he said. "We're ready. Harold is getting prepped for surgery as we speak."

"What about Hayes?"

"As expected, he's standing sentry at the hospital. But then again, who isn't? It's a madhouse." He laughed.

I turned on the television. Three news channels were already covering the swelling crowds at many of the dozens of hospitals in L.A. County. Early that morning, word had leaked that we were going to Keck Hospital, so they had the worst of it. Signs poked out above the mass of spectators. A news reporter with one finger in his ear tried to shout an update over the mob. Sources indicated that Dale Sampson had yet to arrive—with no guarantee that he would. Police officers kept the sidewalk, entrance, and emergency-room bays clear. They were geared up with Kevlar and helmets with face shields, presumably expecting a busy day at the office. Other, unarmored officers were busy managing the crowd, trying to keep some semblance of order around the hospital's entrance.

"Jesus. We're fucking chaos personified today," Mack said. I hadn't even known he was awake. He still looked half-asleep. He ran his index finger under the kitchenette faucet and rubbed his teeth, the MacGyver way to brush.

"How in the name of fuck's potatoes are you up and moving around like a living person?" He pinched his nose and let out a groan. "I feel like a bunch of evil dwarves beat me with hammers all night. And did you shit in my mouth?"

He seemed off. Nervous, even. I was getting shoved off into the black yonder that morning, and seeing the light peek through the seams of his ego was both rare and heartening.

I still had Venhaus on the line. "Does your friend know?" he asked. "No," I said.

"Good, one less loose end to worry about. How do you intend on getting here?"

"I'll call a cab," I said, and hung up.

"I'm way ahead of you, actually," Mack said. "I booked us a chauffeur for your last ride into the sunset. Class all the way for my best bro."

Mack was dead set on seeing me to the hospital. He intended to be at my side until the moment they wheeled me away. Outside, we waited for the car with complimentary coffees from the hotel's breakfast buffet, watching the ebb and flow of traffic.

A black Lincoln with tinted windows pulled up to the curb. "There," Mack said. "All aboard."

The driver stepped out, sharply dressed, a neatly trimmed goatee. "Mr. Sampson?"

I nodded and got in.

As the outside would suggest, the interior was quiet and cool. Fine, clean leather squeaked with every move. A man was in the passenger seat. I caught a glimpse of him in the rearview mirror—brown eyes, a tuft of thin hair arranged fruitlessly on a balding scalp. Since when does a chauffeur need a partner? I thought.

"How long to get to Keck?" I asked.

"Depends on traffic," the driver said.

We drove. Classic rock on the radio—Boston. "More Than a Feeling." Curiously, no news. When we got closer to the hospital, I'd have to tell Mack the truth—that the surgery wasn't at Keck; that although Hayes and my medical team were waiting on me to get to Keck, it was all part of the ruse.

I should have considered that Mack would insist on escorting me to the hospital if given the chance. Only Venhaus knew my true intentions for the surgery's outcome, a truth that I couldn't tell Mack under any circumstances. Still, I needed to clue Mack into the surgery's true location and he'd have to digest the news real quick. Soon, it was all going to depend on him to get out of the car a couple blocks away from Keck, and sell it as if he were awaiting my arrival there. He would play the grief-stricken best friend for the crowd, and sacrifice our final good-bye to create a diversion.

The rented Lincoln sped through the city. I leaned against the window, tired and dehydrated, my dirty hair leaving a spot of oil melting on the glass. The long shadows of an early downtown morning stretched out on the pavement.

I looked over at Mack. He was staring up front into the rearview mirror. Again, I caught the passenger's eyes snapping away from me.

"So who's this guy?" I asked the driver.

"Just a helping hand," he said with a smile.

"Mack," I said, waiting until he looked at me. "Who is this guy?"

He just shook his head once, as if to say, *Don't*.

I didn't. We kept driving. Soon the shadows of downtown were behind us. Onto the freeway. I didn't know the city that well. I knew my apartment and how to get to the airport, or Tracy's office, or Hollie's place or the grocery market. That was it.

I waited for an exit. It never came. The clock said it was a quarter to eight.

"How long?" I asked.

"Not long. Fifteen minutes?" The driver didn't miss a beat. He was lying.

"Where the fuck are we?" No answer. He jerked the wheel, peeling us off the freeway and into a rundown neighborhood with tiny, fenced-in houses with brown lawns and ramshackle porches. Soon, we turned onto an access road with far less traffic, careening through the empty streets until we found ourselves puttering down a shitty two-laner, joining the rat race to get a spot on the freeway.

I tried the door. It was locked.

"Now, settle down," the passenger said. "This will be a lot easier if you just remain calm."

I looked at Mack.

"What is this?" But I didn't need to ask. I knew that Hayes was doubling down on his effort to keep me from going through with my sacrificial surgery. He didn't trust Venhaus, so he appealed to Mack. I could hear him smugly bargaining with my friend: *Are you really going to let your friend die?*

"We're just trying—" the passenger started.

"Shut the fuck up! What is this?" I repeated.

"These are the big dogs, Sampsonite. Best deal I could cut for us, man."

"All-expenses-paid trip to the Research Triangle on the East Coast?"

"Better than dying."

"That's not your call to make," I said. "You can't do this to me. You can't stick me with this bullshit forever."

I knew Hayes and the government interests he represented coveted my life, and that there was obvious value to studying my gift, but I never thought to probe for details. Who exactly benefited from their research? Government agencies, private universities, biotech startups? My death was unacceptable to the scores of researchers who jerked off over my tissue in some sterile lab somewhere, rehearsing their Nobel Prize speech.

"Turn the car around," I said.

Silence. Stares.

"Turn the fuck around!" I screamed, and started yanking at the door. I punched the glass once, but it didn't break. My finger did, though—a pop sounded in my hand, and my knuckle started to swell. A boxer's break. No matter. Not today, anyway.

I looked up into the barrel of a gun.

"Stay calm and I won't have to see if your head grows back," the passenger said.

"Fuck you," I said. "You're really going to try to kill me when you're obviously here to preserve me?"

He fired a slug into the top of my leg.

"Christ!" the driver screamed, the shot rattling him into a sudden swerve. "What the fuck you doing?"

"Relax, that shit'll be healed before we get to the airport," Passenger said, laughing. "At least he can't run now, huh?"

Blood bubbled from the wound, hot and familiar. I leaned back hard into my seat, and concentrated on my breathing. Oxygen always helped blunt the pain—that and pressing on it real good while closing my eyes so tight fluid leaked from the corners.

Mack was not pleased with this particular development. Through my agony, I heard the long-dormant sound of him flexing his hate gland, screaming at my captors, but at the time it was all just white noise. Then everything was quiet, as if the captain had flipped on a No Talking sign. I looked over at Mack.

For one of the few times in his life, he was raw. Stripped down to the wires and studs: confused, wanting desperately to keep me alive, but realizing that a life of being harvested for samples wasn't quite *living*. Too bad for us both he hadn't realized sooner.

"Well, it sounded like a good deal at the time, the way that dickhole put it," he said.

His fists were clenched. Veins protruded everywhere, dark-blue ropes snaking across the striated muscles in his neck and forearms. I saw the dent in his lower jaw where he was sucking his lip in, biting it, his eyes glossy with the threat of tears, and I knew what he was going to do.

"Swing for the fences, right?" he rasped. "You better not miss." He smiled. I followed Mack's eyes to the front seat. He nodded once, and I understood.

Passenger continued to point the gun squarely into the backseat.

"You two just need to shut the—"

Mack moved with a fast-twitch burst I hadn't seen since high school, deflecting the gun up into the roof with one hand as the other grabbed the strap of seat belt above Passenger's shoulder. With one quick jerk, Mack had the belt around the man's neck, ratcheting his throat so tight I heard a pop. Passenger fired blindly into the backseat, but missed us both—barely. My eardrums erupted with the bass of the shots. The driver didn't know what to do, but he instinctively slowed—which was exactly what I was hoping for.

I leaned back and pistoned my feet through the window glass. The whole pane broke off in one spiderwebbed piece and skidded onto the road. I reached through and opened the door from the outside, intent on jumping out on the fly. As the door swung open, another shot rang. I saw a mist of red splatter against the driver's side window as the driver's ruptured skull lolled to the side. From the corner of my eye, Mack and Passenger were struggling, four hands on the gun now, its barrel waving back and forth between them, a barometer of who was winning. Glancing back at the inert form in the driver's seat, it was clear who that round went to. The bullet had tunneled into his temple neatly on one side, leaving a soup-can-sized hole on the other.

With a carcass now behind the wheel, the car began gradually veering off the road. Glancing over to Mack, still grappling wildly with Passenger, I leapt out and rolled onto the concrete, flailing crash-dummy style, leaving behind layers of epidermis and dislocating my shoulder. I don't know if my hand got caught in the car's frame or if I landed on it, but when I came to rest in the hot and itchy grass on the other side of the roadway, I noticed three fingers were gone and all I had left was a mangled stump. I looked up right as the Lincoln eased into the drainage ditch across the road, toppling over onto its side. I listened to the crunch and squeal of metal as it gained momentum down the slope and continued flipping.

My right hand was nothing but splinters of shiny bone. I had road rash everywhere, blood slowly blooming through my shredded clothing.

I stared into the sky, a dusty blue, the clouds half dissolved by the sun's rising momentum. I could have stayed put and slept forever. But Mack was still in the ditch, in the mangled wreckage of the Lincoln, the victor of his skirmish with Passenger unknown. Assuming either of them had survived the crash in the first place. I found the strength to stand and ignored the frantic bystanders who were urging me to lie down and wait for help.

Unrelenting heat. No wind. The smell of gasoline and scorched rubber and the shavings of burned metal. Cars stopped. People were on their cell phones. Everyone telling me to sit, everyone a Samaritan.

My movements were frenzied and out-of-body. I stumbled along on my shot leg and I could see how bad I looked in the twisted faces of others. The smell of blood was in my throat and nose. Droplets hit the pavement as I staggered toward the drainage ditch, turning black when they struck stone.

Pain everywhere. Pain in my dragging leg, my sagging pieces of torn flesh. The back of my head, my right kneecap, my hand stump shorn down to the bone, white and slick, the only painless areas since the nerves had been scrubbed clean out.

The Lincoln was tucked into the ditch on its side almost neatly, as if carefully placed. The windshield was gone. The guts of the car hissed and ticked. I spotted Mack on his stomach about twenty feet from the wreckage, facedown. Not one droplet of blood, not a scratch on him, but no movement. I didn't see Passenger anywhere—most likely entombed in the remains of the car.

Mack didn't respond to my voice. "He's hurt bad, mister," a man said, crouched down beside us. If Mack had been thrown that far during the wreck, bad was an understatement. I knew I wasn't supposed to move him, but I touched his shoulder. He flopped onto his back, still limp, and I saw the stain of blood on his midsection. The wound was too long and messy to be a gunshot. He was more likely gouged and torn from the shrapnel catching him as he was tossed from the rolling car. Again, the mutter of bystanders, warnings, advice, all of which I ignored, lifting his shirt up and seeing a puncture wound, his innards pushing through the injury, purplish and glossy, hanging from his belly. His eyes were open, the pupils black and round, eclipsing his eye sockets.

I cradled his head and started sobbing, a cry that no bite could control, the kind of blazing sorrow that squeezes your lungs. It sucks away your breath, floods your head with snot and demolishes your will. I said his name and whispered, "Wake up, man. Get tough, you pussy," but I couldn't provoke him to say a word.

The sound of approaching sirens blotted out the chatter. I leaned in close, meaning to tell him good-bye, and felt the humid warmth of his breath against my forearm.

With that I started to scream "Help!" over and over and over until finally a uniformed EMT pried him away from me. They worked him, strapping him to a backboard, a pit-crew of EMTs testing and prodding and deliberating. I followed them as they shuttled him into the back of the ambulance. A thick-armed EMT held me back as they shut the doors.

I relinquished myself to my own ambulance, thinking it would get me to Mack's bedside faster. But the EMT who was now standing directly over me—Chris, by his name tag—looked at me and said, "Jesus Christ, this is Dale Sampson. The Samaritan."

According to Chris, Mack was going to White Memorial Medical Center. "Keck's a mess today, thanks to you," he said, chuckling.

I thought of letting the ambulance take me to Mack, but if I did that, what would he have swung for the fences for? What would his sacrifice have meant? Miracles start with tragedy—a person dies and his family signs a piece of paper, and their loved one's organs get harvested and sent out into the world like ashes in the wind. Meanwhile, somewhere a pager goes off and a dying man with a failing liver or kidney or heart says that he's not getting his hopes up, not yet, and as he drives to the hospital he can't help but get his hopes up.

Mack's injuries were the first domino. I would not let it fall without striking against something else.

"Take me to the UCLA Medical Center," I said. "I'm already late. And take Mack, too. I don't care if he's a mess. I can save him."

"Holy shit. Keck Hospital was a smoke screen?" Chris said. I nodded.

"You're in no shape for surgery, kid. I think we'll take you both to White Memorial. It's close."

"You're killing Mack if you don't take us both to UCLA. Him and another guy, whose chest is probably getting cracked open while we chitchat."

"I'm not so sure your superpower, or whatever it is, can help your friend. Needing an organ is one thing, massive internal bleeding is a catastrophic injury, a whole other ball game. Try prayers instead. As for the transplant, a chest can be closed. They can reschedule."

"Why do you think I'm out here? You're hardly the only one who wants me to reschedule and reconsider. If you don't get me into UCLA, that man dies."

"If I take you there," he said, "you die."

"If you don't," I said, "I will fail the one person I cannot fail, and I'll have to be the Samaritan forever."

Chris understood trauma. He had seen the inside of people laid bare, the hysterics of family members wailing over a loved one's ruined form. Here was a man without a white coat, a man in the trenches who wanted to save lives instead of being published in medical journals.

He turned to the driver. "UCLA Medical Center." He radioed the other ambulance and despite their objections, they followed suit. He was careful not to expose us, and didn't use my name. "If I had a right hand," I said, "I'd shake yours right now."

He held out his left hand, and I shook it.

TWENTY-FOUR

EN ROUTE TO THE HOSPITAL, I WAS STABLE AND THE pain had dulled to a slow throb, the lasers of hurt activating with each beat of my heart.

"You've lost some blood," Chris said. "I would normally say operating is out of the question, but if you're really going out in a blaze of glory I guess it makes no difference if you're a cadaver or not." I felt the hum of the drive with the occasional bump, the feel of turns, Chris's hand supportive on my shoulder.

"One request before we roll you in," Chris said. "Sign this?" He gave me a medical chart. My chart. I signed it, "To Chris and my rescuers . . . You are the Good Samaritans." I signed it Dale Sampson, the print barely legible, my dominant hand having been blown to bits. I stamped a thumbprint of blood underneath it.

"Turn your head to the side and keep your eyes closed." He placed some gauze on my face, disguising me. "Whatever you did to cover your ass, it worked. This joint is even less busy than usual."

"I still appreciate the discretion," I said, as he pressed another piece on my forehead. "Tell Dr. Banks I'm here." Banks was Venhaus's ace in the hole, a top-tier cardio specialist who had also been one of Venhaus's med school friends.

"You got it," he said. I rolled into the hospital, just another guy fucked up from yet another car accident. Nothing to see here. I never stopped moving, the squeak of the wheels drowning out Chris's words as we moved through the hospital. Eventually, I felt the gurney come to a stop and heard Chris's voice in the distance shouting, "Good luck, Mr. Carlson!"

Movement again, then a familiar voice. "I got you," Doc Venhaus said. "Just be still."

"Mack," I said, turning to face Venhaus, the bloody gauze falling away. "You gotta save him first. Take everything out of me, I don't give a shit."

"You have many gifts, but stabilizing a trauma victim isn't one of them. I can check in on him, but from what that EMT told me, you can't help your friend," Doc said. "He's in the hands of God and doctors, Dale."

"Bullshit. He's got fucked-up organs, so give him some organs."

"It's not as simple as just swapping organs with him, Dale. In fact, I'm calling the surgery off altogether," he said.

"Fuck that," I said.

"This isn't what you planned or wanted—scars from the road rash and your right hand gone for good. It would not be right to operate on you in this condition. And did someone *shoot* you?"

"It's too late to back out," I said. "I just can't now. Try your best, but if I die, fuck it."

"Why are you in such a hurry to die?" Venhaus said.

"I'm not," I said. "I haven't been for a while now, actually. I love a girl and I love my friend, but I never *acted*, Doc, and I can't say I could have stopped the massacre or my friend getting his shoulder blown off, but I sure as shit let her get away. Hell, I let myself get away. I have this power and what did I do? Nothing, not really. Sure, I let people take from me, a lung here, a kidney there—"

"You're giving now," Doc said.

"And I'm not going to stop," I said. "If I live through this, that is."

"The odds are not in favor of that outcome," Doc said. "Not anymore."

I reached out and took Doc's hand. He squeezed back. "You promised, Doc." I said. "This is what I want."

He got me to an operating room, but he was there as my friend now, not a doctor. There were plenty of doctors scurrying around us. All of them old, sporting neat, white beards and glasses. I was pleased to see these old men of a noble trade whose days of ambition were long behind them, men who respected Venhaus and the secrets that needed to be kept that day.

I handed my arm over for an IV and Doc never took his hand off my shoulder. He waited, along with me, for a countdown backward from ten.

No mention of Rae, which was disappointing, if only because I'd wanted to finally measure myself as a man in her eyes—maybe glimpse her looking down on me with gratitude—even love. Or maybe she'd have just seen me as a manipulative asshole anyway, parlaying her need for my heart into a chance to shackle her with memories of me forever.

❦

Harold agreed to take a huge gamble and allow his surgery to begin before I even arrived at the hospital. Doc Venhaus had taken every precaution to keep the location a secret, but with Harold's deteriorating condition, Doc had the surgical team begin Harold's surgery early. Once he was on bypass and his

heart was out, if we were discovered it would be far more difficult to shut it down and let a man die since the surgery
would already be under way.

I was home, a surgical room with cold lights, icy steel,
and unbreakable silence. Doc was only going to observe the
surgery—this was outside his realm of expertise, yet he had
screened and organized the surgical team that would be plucking out my heart and planting it in Harold. He stood over me
as final preparations were made.

"How much longer?" I asked.

"Very soon," he said.

I waited. He added nothing.

"Do you think she's coming to see me? To say good-bye?"
I said, finally.

"Surgery is imminent, Dale. I have serious doubts about
your ability to withstand an operation this serious without
complications, so please don't make me feel guilty by voicing
your regrets at the last possible second."

"Fair enough," I said, and stared at the ceiling, waiting for
the mask to fall on my face.

Doctors bustled around me as I stared at the lights.

"Any last words?" Venhaus said. "Not to scare you, Dale,
but I'd put your chances at thirty percent, and that's generous.
We'll try our best, and even if we're successful and you live,
you're not really living, so to speak. People will ask what your
last words were. So say what you will for posterity's sake."

"I guess whatever I choose will be a *Jeopardy!* question a
hundred years from now. Might be as close to immortality as
I'm ever going to get." I thought about Rae. Where would I
be if I had never seen her that day in Wal-Mart? If she had
moved to any city but Grayson?

"Fuck it," I said. "No last words. Just nothing."

Doc stood beside me. He put his hand on my forearm and I saw pain in his eyes. He was a doctor, practiced at exuding confidence and authority, but the guise fell away when he touched me, his face shaded with doubt and fear.

Doc was the one left most exposed by our little ruse, because at some point soon, he would have to answer to Hayes, whom he had double-crossed to make this happen. Venhaus was brought onto the show under the condition of being Hayes's inside man, and we'd taken advantage of that. Venhaus had whispered in Hayes's ear that I was arranging a secret surgery. He revealed the location—Keck Hospital. Then, early in the morning, he leaked the Keck location to the press, all the while setting us up at the UCLA Medical Center. I have no idea how he pulled that off with no leaks, but when it comes to miracles, sometimes you just don't ask. Sometimes you just want to believe in the magic.

"She's here," Doc said. "She wanted to see you to say good-bye, but only once you were anesthetized," he said.

"I won't say anything," I said. "I'll keep my eyes closed. I'll stay completely still."

He nodded. Another surgeon whispered something in his ear, but Doc shook his head and said, "No, it will be fine. It doesn't hurt anything."

"Hold this tube in your mouth," he said.

I pretended to be put-under, my eyes closed, my breathing slow, the tube tasting like a chewed-up plastic straw in my now-dry mouth. I waited.

I sensed her beside me. Even with the air heavy and antiseptic, I recognized the fragrance of flowery soap, remembering a time when the soapy smell mixed with the acrid and beautiful scent of sex. Not being able to open my eyes and see her was agony, but I endured and kept them gently shut. She sobbed for a few long moments, trying to bite herself back from completely losing it. I could hear Doc comforting her. Her touch was surprising and electric, popping off a jolt of tension in the muscles of my hand and arm. I wondered if that tipped her off to my consciousness, but I continued to play dead. She curled her fingers into mine and kissed the back of my hand, pressing it against her cheek and holding it there. Then, she opened my hand and kissed the center, her tears gathering in the seams of my palm.

She moved my open hand to her belly: tight, round, and swollen. The real person who drove her to pen the letter.

Nothing like finally staring down the truth until it's far too late. The possibility of ending up with Rae and settling into some normal, domestic life had once lingered deep inside of me. Once I felt her child thudding against the walls of her stomach, she was truly gone for good. Harold's child, a child she would lie for. A kid she'd fuck someone all day for. She knew Harold was scum but loved the baby so fiercely that she'd do whatever it took to give her child a father—even if it meant grinding the last happy parts of me into dust. I wondered if Harold knew about that part, if he gave her permission to seduce me into compliance. She could have told me she was pregnant and taken her chances, but what mother takes chances? She knew I loved her and wasn't about to lose that edge.

I felt her kiss upon my forehead as she placed the dry, hard remains of a flower into my hand—a withered rose that was once placed on a windowsill all those years ago, flat from being kept in some book somewhere, now completing its journey of rejection.

"I just want you to know, Harold has been good to me a long time now. I want you to know that I'm sorry. I can't say

I love you, Dale, but I can say that I could have. I might have. If things were different for all of us."

My eyes remained calm and closed, my jaw loose around the tube. I was out of my body now, visiting all those little crossroads where I might have ended up with her, but there were too many what-ifs to count. I was sick of counting them. My grip remained limp. I never felt so still. I felt like a pond on a windless morning. Another Dale might have spoken up or cried or begged for an explanation. She took my hand off of her womb.

"Good-bye, Dale."

Perhaps it was my pulse that gave me away—the final scream of my Dale Sampson factory-installed heart, but she knew.

"I'm glad he was awake," she said to Doc as she neared the door. "Now that it's over, I'm glad." And with that she was gone.

"We're going to count down from ten," the anesthetist said. "You won't make it to one."

"Maybe," I said. "I've got experience at this. Tolerance. I can make it to one." I smiled.

Doc took my hand. "So, about those last words, then?"

Goddammit—I couldn't think of anything funny or clever. I closed my eyes and took a deep breath and pictured a crowd of strangers outside with chants and signs, some with words of support and some of hate; and thought of Mack, and the burning house; and wondered when my life would flash before my eyes. But it already had, and it wasn't that I was given nothing to miss, it was that I had not created anything to miss.

"Give everything," I said, keeping my eyes closed.

"Well done, Dale," Doc said, patting my forearm. "Now, don't you go chattering and messing that one up, just in case we can't pull this off."

He was the last I heard of that world—him and the beep of machinery as the hissing mask descended upon me, driving the light away, and I counted down in my head and did not make it to one.

PART FOUR
REGENERATION

TWENTY-FIVE

THEY GATHERED UP THE PRESS IN ONE OF THE HOSPITAL'S conference rooms. Reporters huddled in a throbbing mass of mobile technology and bad fashion sense, with smartphones poked out to record whatever would be said at the haphazardly set-up lectern.

Dr. Allen Venhaus volunteered to announce the results. He said it was his responsibility, but he made everyone wait even though word had already leaked. Dale Sampson was dead.

He walked to the lectern wearing a white coat, running his hand over his stubbly scalp, perspiration shimmering in the creases of his forehead.

He approached the microphone and looked down, as if he had prepared notes, but he hadn't, and didn't even have his glasses on. He just stared at his hands, at the microphone, and all you could hear was the click of cameras. He coughed a little, clearing his throat, and then looked up into the lights, the cameras, the hungry eyes wanting to affirm what they'd already heard.

"Every surgery has complications. Risks," he said. "Dale Sampson knew them better than anyone. At eleven forty-four today, he died of complications unrelated to his heart operation.

As you may or may not know at this point, he was involved in a severe car accident this morning. His friend, Maxwell Tucker, is still in recovery and miraculously, despite severe internal injuries, his prognosis is positive. Mr. Sampson suffered similar internal injuries. Due to the tight timeline and the fact his medical team could not properly evaluate him for surgery, we suggested postponing the operation. However, Mr. Stillson, the recipient, was on bypass and awaiting a new heart. Mr. Sampson insisted on proceeding with the operation. We agreed, despite our best judgment, to allow this to continue, due mostly to Mr. Sampson's unique gifts. Gifts that failed him today."

He pinched the bridge of his nose and cinched his eyes shut. The cameras went wild as he fought tears and lost, blinking them out. He took a long, audible sigh and continued.

"Dale's last words were 'Give everything.' Words he lived by, words that cost him his life. Today I grieve as a doctor for the miracle that we lost, and I grieve as a friend for the good man who's no longer a part of my life. I don't intend on taking any questions, but Mr. Stillson did indeed get Dale's heart. But only the organ. What Dale had inside of him, the person he was, that's gone today unless we use his life as inspiration to take action. In Dale's honor, I urge you all to do something a Samaritan would be proud of."

Mack was watching from his hospital bed and tried not to let the pretty nurses see him break down.

Hollie watched, and while she didn't cry, she called Melissa over to her and hugged her for so long, the little girl asked, "What's wrong, Mommy?" Her engagement ring was gone. It was just them again, just the two of them and the struggle.

Raeanna held Harold's hand and tried not to hear, but couldn't help it. He was asleep, covered in tape and tubes, his skin crusted with the tint of iodine, and under the cover of machines beeping, she allowed herself to grieve as her baby kicked with every sob.

My new heart once belonged to a young man named Thomas, who suffered catastrophic head injuries in a car accident. He fell asleep at the wheel at the exact wrong time at the exact wrong location of the exact wrong curve. Had he missed the culvert, or worn his seat belt, or fallen asleep a moment before or after, maybe he'd have lived.

I didn't need to be there to know exactly how it went: machines breathe for him, his brain dead, a shallow pulse nourishing a vacant body. A doctor approaches his parents, bereft in the hospital, their grief held in suspension, considering the nature of God and destiny and evil and love. And he asks them, "Is your son a donor?"

But the parents don't hear a question—they hear surrender. They demand to know why he is giving up on their son. He explains clinical death but they will not listen. Not yet.

The problem with medicine is, too many people believe in miracles.

The doctor gently reminds them that time is of the essence. The parents still wait, hugging, crying, wondering, asking, wishing, hoping. The truth waits for those emotions to pass. The truth never softens. And they say yes, and Thomas's wish to be a donor is carried out. A pager goes off somewhere.

So they put his heart inside me and I lived. And I knew at once what Hollie felt when my kidney saved her, the incredible weight of responsibility and guilt. I called Thomas's family and pretended to be one of Dale Sampson's doctors. Thomas's mother spoke with pride, not only for what he had done in life, but because he had almost saved Dale Sampson from death. She talked with the wobble of a woman on the edge but never broke down, each word an act of bravery, every phrase inching her closer to reconciling herself with the loss of her son.

He was a young man of twenty-four, a hunter, a fisherman. He still dated his high school sweetheart and his family found a diamond ring in his bedroom drawer. His visitation took six hours, so well attended the funeral home could not accommodate the line. His friends rounded the block—the rowdy, twentysomething types whose lives he had touched. They did not pass by his casket quickly. They lingered.

His mother called him handsome. She called him her light. I promised her his heart did not go to waste and I meant it. I truly did.

My plan had been to kill the Samaritan, but that was useless. The Samaritan was an invention. He wasn't real. Dale Sampson was the problem. Dale Sampson had to die.

After the surgery, I woke up in a rental house Doc had rigged specially to help me recover. Understandably, Doc was out there selling my death and satisfying one final, daunting loose end—Captain Hayes. The doctor who performed the surgery, an ancient man named Jed Banks, checked in from time to time. He taught me some card games—Hearts, Pinochle. The nurse who took care of me on a daily basis was Jed's daughter, who had an easy smile and beat me at all the card games her father taught me. Doc trusted them with my secret and after getting to know them a little better, so did I.

After a few days, Doc Venhaus finally showed up. "You're recovering splendidly," he said. "If I didn't know any better,

I'd say you still had a little of that Samaritan juice running through you." I held up the gauze-wrapped remains of my hand. If I were still the Samaritan, I wouldn't have been looking at a mangled stump. After he checked my charts and vitals, he sat down next to my bed. He looked relieved. The color had returned to his face compared to his spectral complexion on the day he'd stood at the lectern.

"So, how's it looking out there?" I said.

"As with most celebrity deaths, your flaws are forgiven and your sainthood is imminent."

"And everyone believes I'm dead?"

"'Everyone' is a strong word. If you scrape the bottom of the Internet, you'll find plenty of theories about the circumstances behind your death. None of them even remotely correct. My favorite is the one in which you'll be resurrected in three days and the rapture will begin."

"It's been three days, though," I said.

"They're holding out for midnight," he said with a smile. "But, as expected, Hayes is skeptical. I was thorough and we got lucky, so I'd say skepticism versus him pulling out my fingernails with pliers is a good outcome. But you were right—his interest in you waned since the operation. It turns out that his research team had also suspected that your heart was the source of your gift."

"Whether I'm dead or alive, you still embarrassed the shit out of him with that surgical switch, so I'd keep my head on a swivel if I were you."

"He *was* embarrassed. And impressed. He offered me a job," he said.

"No shit?"

"My experience with your condition, my status as Harold's primary, my knowledge of Hayes and his research aims, my ability to pull off a covert operation . . . I guess he figures it's better to have me on the team than to have to bury me in the desert somewhere."

Harold had my heart now, and with it, the attention of Captain Hayes and the shadowy interests he represented. Even if the ability to regenerate didn't transfer to Harold with the heart, the organ was still a national treasure to Hayes. Did that mean Harold was getting his ticket punched to the Research Triangle? Frankly, if it did, I didn't give a fuck. Rae and her child would be taken care of, and I didn't imagine Harold would be getting back into the meth trade or slapping his wife around with Uncle Sam's head perpetually up his ass.

Soon after the visit, Banks and Venhaus agreed to release me, as long as I agreed to some confidential medical checkups in the coming weeks to help further monitor my recovery. The plan was for Venhaus to rent out a hotel room wherever I settled down so he could make house calls, checking to make sure my stump was healing properly, inspecting my road rash for infection, bringing me prescription meds to help get me through the always-excruciating healing process. More than that, I knew he wanted to play psychologist and make sure I was doing okay.

But it wasn't time for me to settle down. Not yet.

Dale Sampson was dead, but whatever was left behind, whatever new person would emerge, that was up to me and I wasn't going to let Dale regenerate—the Dale who would turn on the TV and wait his life away.

Instead, in the days that followed my death, when I was strong enough, I did what amounted to spreading Dale's ashes. I needed to put him to rest.

Hollie's engagement was over and she was back to working double shifts. I could never know if Dale ever crossed her mind, or if she remembered that kiss or how long her phone went without ringing. I honestly hoped not.

She was at home on a Saturday. I was in a rented Corolla, watching her house from an angle, parked along the street. The sun was out and Melissa was playing outside, her yellow dress swirling in the breeze. Hollie sat on the steps, her knees close together, hugging herself, watching her daughter at play. I should have been nervous that Hollie would spot me and recognize me, but I was just happy to see them outside. Specks of dandelion floated in the air as Mel blew on the stems. Hollie's hair was in a simple ponytail, her face devoid of heavy makeup. Just a casual day around the house. I'm pretty sure that in moments like that, she was glad she wasn't dead—even if times were hard, these were moments that softened life, making it easier to lay the bricks you had to lay to make it worth it.

I knew that Hollie was good and that she deserved two things—the truth and a fresh start of her own, a place where her darker thoughts would no longer be allowed to fester.

A UPS truck pulled up with a signature-confirmation delivery. Hollie looked appropriately puzzled as she unzipped the envelope. At first it looked empty, but she eventually fished out the cashier's check for $400,000 that now belonged to her. She collapsed onto her ass as the check fluttered through the air, her trembling hand covering her mouth. I'm pretty sure she knew it was me, that I was alive somewhere and while I wasn't so good at calling people back, I could still save someone if you gave me enough chances to get it right.

When the flowers arrived at the hospital, Rae probably thought they might've been from a friend, wishing Harold a speedy recovery, even though roses weren't exactly the flower of choice for get-well bouquets.

I sent only eleven roses. The twelfth was in the envelope tucked inside the forest of stems—the dead rose, *the* rose, the one I had left on that windowsill years ago, the one she kept, the one she gave back to me to close the loop. But the loop wasn't hers to close.

The dead rose was folded up inside of a note—one that I always kept in my wallet, allowing it to survive a fire her husband set and underneath her handwriting from all those years ago was my own sloppy shorthand: *Forgiveness makes the heart grow back. D.*

And just like that, it was her turn to wonder and wait, only this time the loop was truly closed. I believe that every time there's a knock on her door, a part of her will wonder if it's me. We all allow ourselves to think about different versions of ourselves from time to time—what would have happened if I ended up with this person, or avoided this bullet, or made this choice? She would wonder, I was sure of it. If this served as a kind of fucked-up punishment, that wasn't my priority—she simply had to know that what she did to me was forgiven, and I wasn't wondering about us. Not anymore.

Mack finished up a long recovery. When he was strong enough to convince the doctors to discharge him, for some unknown reason he took the bus, though I'm sure he had enough money to fly first class if he wanted to. Instead, I followed him to a bus station and when L.A. was in the rearview mirror, I knew he was gone for good.

I followed the bus in my rented Corolla. I wanted to know where Mack would choose to heal up and get over the death of his best friend. He went to Grayson, of all places, which was sort of touching, but kind of a bizarre choice given what we had left behind there. He checked in at the Allsop Motel and immediately went to work house-hunting. He wasn't a thorough guy—I saw him shake the Realtor's hand during his second walk-through of a brick ranch-style house in a nice subdivision near the outskirts of town.

I waited until the sale was for sure, until the Realtor showed up to take down the "for sale" sign and carry a bottle of Champagne into the house. I figured he'd leave it in the fridge with a note of congratulations or something, since Mack was about to be a first-time homeowner.

And I thought he needed a housewarming present.

He showed up in a Ford F-150 with the dealer tags still on it, and when he saw a covered car in his new house's driveway, I'm pretty sure he knew right away, even before he yanked off the sheath to reveal a brand-new, metallic green Ford Mustang. I could see the smile on his face from a block away. I didn't leave a note. I didn't know what to say. Maybe one day we'd shake hands again, finally as men. Maybe we'd head west in that Mustang just like we always said we would and make what we built in our hearts as boys into reality. We'd just drive and we wouldn't be sure of anything, but we'd be in that mythic convertible and the world would seem big again because it was a place where you could say you were going to do something someday and by God, you fucking did it.

"Sampsonite, motherfuckers!" he screamed. He walked around the car twice, then patted the hood like it was an old friend.

306 | FRED VENTURINI

My first meeting with Doc was supposed to be a week after he released me from that backwater rental hut, free to start up a new life on my own terms. He texted me directions to a Motel 6 off a California freeway and a room number, having already made a reservation.

I cared about Doc Venhaus. I trusted and respected him. I didn't want to stand him up like that, leaving him in the cold dark of some shithole motel. I never told him I wasn't going to show, that I was already long gone. I never told him I had no intention of revisiting any part of my old life for a long, long time. I imagine on the day of our meeting he called or sent a text and got an out-of-service message telling him that my phone was disconnected. He wouldn't be surprised, knowing just as well as I did that he was the final person I had to leave behind.

TWENTY-SIX

I WAS GONE FROM LOS ANGELES, AND JUST LIKE L.A., I was leaving every last piece of Dale Sampson behind.

As for the new me, after I finished with Mack, Rae, Hollie, and Doc, I ended up in a big city again. Turns out the city life was a fit—the way the streets pulsate, always on, full of attitude and opportunity. I got the highest apartment with the most glass I could possibly get. I wanted to look out into the sky-line, into the lights, into the sea of cars and people. The glass made me feel naked and barren and isolated all at the same time. My future was out there somewhere, but first I had to wait.

The healing was slow and unspectacular, but I kept telling myself it was due to the new heart. Our speculation that my healing gifts were centered, somehow, in the heart, was prov-ing to be accurate. After its removal, my power to heal was gone. From the road rash, I had thick puddles of scab tissue flaking away at the edges, with pink underneath. The scar on my chest was pink and getting smaller, but it was still a scar, not the miraculous and undetectable white line the Samaritan used to produce. I limped a little from the gunshot. All the healing was progressing at a slow, normal, human pace.

I told myself the true answer was under the stump of gauze

I had at the end of my right arm, the hand they removed during my surgery. The right hand, where it all began, and where it all might end. Soon, I'd have to take the gauze off and gaze at the stump and lament the opportunity I had lost, the gift I had wasted.

Truth was, after I got out of surgery, after the promise I made to Doc, a commitment to action, to never being the same—I wanted my road rash to vanish without a trace. I wanted to unwrap my gauze and see my hand returned, whole again. I wanted to make Thomas's mother proud of the sacrifice he had made. And it was possible—wasn't it? Maybe it was me all along, something beyond what science could explain. Maybe the gift that flowed through me could somehow accept and embrace this new heart after enough time had passed, restoring my gifts, now that I was ready for them.

I woke up each day hoping I'd feel their return. Then, and only then, I would unwrap the gauze to look at my hand.

The days brimmed with that familiar pain of healing, but I didn't waste them, not like I used to. I walked the streets at night, stopping in bookstores for coffee and bars for the occasional beer. I ate greasy meals in corner diners, I walked around shopping malls and watched teenagers hold hands. I smiled at people, almost daring them to recognize me, even though I was careful to conceal my injuries and to obscure my face with hats and hoodies. Still, they smiled back. I left big tips on small checks and put bills in the cups of beggars. Not world-changing stuff, but it felt like a start. I knew there was plenty I could do, even if my hand did not return.

Weeks after Dale Sampson's death, I fell asleep and didn't wake up for a long, long time, not until the sound of thunder shook me from my bed. I was already barely sleeping due to the unmistakable itch of healing.

I stood before my new city, the glass of my apartment's floor-to-ceiling windows wide and clear before me. The city looked as if it were melting as raindrops pattered against the glass. Lightning ripped the sky and I didn't turn on the lights. Sometimes, you don't need to see.

I unwrapped the bandages without looking down. I saw nothing but the sparkle of the skyline and the silhouette of my reflection in the darkened glass, and in that moment, it truly didn't matter if my flesh and my bone never returned; the treasures of life could still be salvaged if I was brave enough to look.

ACKNOWLEDGMENTS

When you see "Acknowledgments," a little voice tells you, *Great, I can skip this part!* I hope you don't. Yes, the names here are responsible for the book in your hands, but they are also responsible for shaping the author behind it.

I'm deeply grateful for my amazing and beautiful wife, Krissy, who always encourages me to follow my imagination, no matter where it leads. Your love continues to humble and inspire me. When you smiled at me those many years ago, you truly made my heart grow back. I'm equally grateful for Noelle, our daughter, who has brought even more magic and love into my life than I ever thought possible.

A heartfelt thank-you to everyone who supported my book when it was originally published with Blank Slate Press, which also deserves a huge thank-you for taking a chance on me when my novel was nothing but a handful of magic beans.

Thank you to Kirby Kim, Peter Horoszko, and Picador for helping me evolve this story and bring it into the world. Rachelle Mandik is the Sherlock Holmes of copy editors, and her contributions were invaluable. A simple thank-you is not enough for the patience and hard work they put into this book.

Special thanks to Dan Loflin, who spent countless hours with me exploring the dark corners of the novel's universe.

I'd like to give virtual "huggies" to Vikki Cleveland, our beloved "Miss C," who fed my writing bug until I could never imagine doing anything else. Thank you to Michael Nye, mentor, teacher, friend, writer, allegedly decent jump-shooter. I'm also grateful for perhaps my most important teacher, my grandmother, who taught me how to read and let me borrow her Stephen King books when I was far, far too young.

A round of shout-outs to my writing workshop peers who always called "bullshit" when I needed it most: Deb, Sarah, Erik.

The cold and violent small towns depicted in this book are fictional. I grew up in a small town, Patoka, and you won't find a place with more warmth, heart, and kindness.

Finally, this is a book that is in many ways about friendship, and I could never imagine listing all of my beloved friends and running the risk of omission . . . but that's just the price of doing business. Bucky—who would we be if not for each other? Spud—how the hell are we still alive? Shaun, Kevin, Preston, Podergois, Portz—you can't play defense behind the fence. Shane, Joe, and the staff at Carlyle Lake— thank you for the advice and memories. Malone—I still haven't found that poem. Selle—an expert at assembly. Ahart—my medical ace in the hole. Voss and DeBro—always prodding my imagination. Renny, Ballard, Novak, Brad, Yoder, Evans, Conant—I love you guys.

Tom Pigg, to whom this book is dedicated, was a close friend who died in 2009, the same year I started working on this novel. Tom, I speak for everyone who knew you when I say you are loved, you are missed, you are never forgotten.